RSVPS
NOT
REQUIRED

RSVPS
NOT
REQUIRED

Carina Walsh

ALSO BY CARINA WALSH

Knot Your Average Wedding Romcom Series

DEDICATION

For the reader who saw "fake fiancé" in the blurb and thought it would be all sweet pretending and slow-burn tension.

This is smut. Filthy, laugh-until-you-cry, fake-it-till-you-make-it-but-make-it-dirty smut.

There will be elaborate lies.

And car sex.

Hold onto your bouquet, buttercup.

HOW TO RUIN "NETFLIX AND CHILL" IN ONE EASY STEP

Chapter 1: Devonna

The thing about carefully constructed lives is that they're one unexpected visitor away from total collapse. Mine lasted exactly eight years, seven months, and twelve days.

"I need your mouth," I whispered to Garrett as we stumbled down the hallway to my apartment. His hands were already under my pencil skirt, fingers tracing the edge of my lace thigh-highs, sending electric currents up my spine.

"Yes, ma'am," he murmured against my neck in a way that made my knees weak.

It had been a day from hell. Three venue cancellations, one bride who changed her color scheme for the sixth time, and a mother-in-law who kept referring to me as "the help" while I single-handedly saved her daughter's wedding from her tacky suggestions. I'd spent the day managing other people's emotions while bottling up my own, and now the pressure was threatening to blow the cork across Manhattan.

Hence, Garrett. A security specialist I'd met a couple of years earlier. Built like a fortress and blessedly uninterested in anything beyond our physical connection, Garrett was perfect. No romance, no expectations, no messy feelings. Just two professionals helping each other unwind in the most satisfying way possible.

"Let me guess," he said, pressing me against my door as I fumbled with the keys. "Today's clusterfuck is sponsored by a wedding disaster?"

"Try three," I confirmed, finally getting the key into the lock. "But I don't want to talk about it. I don't want to talk at all."

I pushed the door open, already unbuttoning my blouse. Garrett kicked it closed behind us, the darkness of my apartment a welcome relief after the harsh fluorescents of the office. I didn't bother with lights. We'd done this dance enough times that we could navigate to my bedroom by muscle memory alone.

His mouth found mine again as we moved through the dark apartment, and I let myself dissolve into the kiss. This was exactly what I needed. Uncomplicated. Physical. A pressure valve release that wouldn't threaten the life I'd spent nearly nine years building.

I was already reaching for his belt when a sound registered; the distinct hum of my washing machine's spin cycle.

We both froze.

"Did you leave your laundry running?" Garrett asked, stiffening against me.

"Have you met me? I don't leave appliances running when I'm out," I said, suddenly hyperaware of every shadow in my apartment.

"Shit."

"Yeah," I muttered, peering into the darkness. "Do you have your gun?"

"What do you think?" Garrett muttered under his breath.

But before either of us could move, the lamp beside my couch clicked on, and my carefully constructed life imploded.

There, sprawled across my pristine white sofa, was a ghost. Not the transparent, floating kind. No. That would be entertaining. This was a far more dangerous kind that haunted me after I'd convinced myself I was over him.

Miles Fucking Houston. Eight years, seven months, and twelve days since I'd seen him last.

"Damn it," I hissed.

2

He looked like he'd gone three rounds with a lawn mower and lost. His left eye had swollen shut, his lip split at the corner, and a constellation of bruises bloomed across his torso. And what a torso it was, covered in ink. Some I didn't recognize; others I did, like the tattoo over his heart. A vintage skeleton key that looked exactly like the one I'd once worn on a chain around my neck for the five years I'd known him. I didn't recognize most of the tattoos, though. They were a roadmap of the years I'd missed. Geometric patterns interlaced with surprisingly delicate line-work twisted from his collarbones down his arms and disappeared beneath the waistband of the only thing he was wearing: black boxer briefs that did nothing to hide the fact that he still worked out.

He took a long swig directly from a bottle of my 25-year-old Yamazaki whisky, then winced as the movement pulled at whatever damage lurked beneath those bruises.

"Don't mind me," he said, crunching on what I now recognized as my imported black truffle potato chips. "Just waiting for the spin cycle to finish. Blood is surprisingly stubborn." He gestured vaguely toward my laundry nook with the whisky bottle. "Your detergent game has improved, Vonnie. The lavender one is my favorite."

Garrett shifted into security mode, stepping partially in front of me. "Who the hell are you, and how did you get in here?"

Miles's eyes — well, the one that wasn't swollen shut — flicked to Garrett, like a lion deciding whether a gazelle was worth the effort of a chase.

"Miles Houston," he replied, not moving from his seat on the couch. "Old... let's call it 'acquaintance.' And you must be the new distraction." His gaze returned to me, one corner of his mouth lifting in that half-smile I'd spent years trying to forget. "Been busy, honey?"

"Don't call me that," I snapped, pulling my blouse closed. The fury rising in me was almost welcome. Anger was so much safer than the other emotions threatening to surface. "What the hell are you doing here?"

"Visiting a friend?"

"Fuck no." I glared at him with every bit of anger I could muster. It was a wonder the man wasn't in flames. Stupid faulty laser vision.

3

"Ouch. That hurts, Von."

"Cry me a fucking river."

Miles raised an eyebrow, then immediately regretted it, judging by his wince. "What am I then? Old enemy? Ex-lover? The guy who ruined you for all future relationships?"

"You're an intruder," I said, reaching for my phone. "And I'm calling security."

"I *am* security," Garrett reminded me, still in a protective stance.

"More security then," I amended.

"Before you do," Miles said, setting down the whisky bottle on my glass coffee table without a coaster, because of course he did, "you might want to hear why Dimitrov's guys used my face as a punching bag."

My finger hovered over the screen. "The Peacock? What did you do this time?"

"Why does everyone assume I did something?" Miles asked the ceiling, then immediately waved off his own question. "Fine. I may have borrowed some money a while ago. And then I may have refused to marry his daughter to clear the debt."

Garrett looked between us, confusion evident. "Who's the Peacock?"

"Russian loan shark with a flair for the dramatic," I explained automatically, then silently cursed myself for engaging with Miles's chaos.

"Ix-nay on the oan-lay ark-shay," Miles whispered, drawing his hand across his neck in a signal to cut it out. "Besides, he's only *allegedly* a loan shark," Miles corrected. "Officially, Mikhail Dimitrov is a legitimate business owner with interests in various entertainment ventures and a temper problem." He shifted on my couch, revealing more tattoos crawling across his ribs; an eagle I didn't recognize and what appeared to be a series of longitude and latitude coordinates.

"And what does this have to do with breaking into my apartment?" I demanded.

"I didn't break in. I still have a key."

"From nine years ago? I've moved twice!"

"Three times," he corrected. "The Tribeca loft after we split, then that awful place in Chelsea with the suspicious mold situation, and now, here." He glanced around appreciatively. "Major upgrade, by the way. The building security is impressively inadequate, though. We should talk about that."

The casual "we" made my blood boil. "There is no 'we,' Miles. There hasn't been for nearly nine years."

"About that," he said, shifting to a slightly more upright position with a grimace. "Mikhail seems to think there is a 'we.'"

"What?"

Miles shrugged. "He thinks you and I are together again."

"Why the hell would he think that?" I ground my teeth together.

"He heard that you're my fiancée."

The words hung in the air like a piano suspended over a cartoon version of me.

"I'm your what?" I finally managed.

"Fiancée. Betrothed. Future wife. Blushing bride-to-be."

"Where did he hear that from, Miles?" I balled my hands into fists, and beside me, Garrett gave me a worried look.

"Dev, are you—"

"Who, Miles?"

"It was the only thing I could think of when he had his goons dangling me off his balcony by my ankles. 'Can't marry your daughter, already engaged, terribly sorry.'"

The metaphorical piano dropped.

"You told a loan shark with a taste for violence that we're engaged?" My voice reached a pitch I didn't know I was capable of, and I lunged for Miles.

Or rather, I *tried* to lunge for him, but Garrett caught me around the waist and held me against him.

"Don't," he whispered against me. "Legal charges don't look good on records."

"I'm going to kill him," I hissed back, struggling against his tree trunk arms. Funny, I normally enjoyed being restrained by my fuckbuddy. Not then, though. I wanted to rip Miles's face off, and Garrett was the chain holding me back.

"To be fair, I didn't expect him to check," Miles said, reaching for the chips again. "But he's thorough. Hence the welcome committee that rearranged my face when I got here."

5

"You brought dangerous men to her home?" Garrett asked in a low voice, still restraining me. "What the hell is wrong with you, man?"

"They aren't going to hurt her. At least, I don't think they are."

"Gee, that's reassuring, asshole." I stopped fighting against Garrett since there seemed to be no point. He was stronger, and he was right. I'd worked too hard putting my life in order after Miles for me to get an assault charge messing it all up. "Why did they rearrange your face?"

"Probably because they saw you with the Hulk." Miles gestured to Garrett. "No offense, man."

Garrett ignored him, releasing me and spinning me to face him. "Is he dangerous?"

"Miles?" I snorted even though I was still seeing red. "No. I could kick his ass any day. In fact, I'd like to do it today."

"Hey!"

"Shut up, the adults are talking," Garrett growled, glaring at Miles. His expression softened when he faced me. "You're sure he's safe?"

"Physically, yes." I took a deep breath.

"Again, I'm right here."

"I wish you weren't," I muttered.

Garrett, who'd been watching both of us like a tennis match, spoke. "If you're sure you'll be alright, then I think I should go."

"No!" I protested, grabbing his arm. This evening was salvageable. It had to be. "He's going. Right now."

"No, I'm not," Miles said, gesturing to the washing machine humming in the background. "My clothes will be about fifteen more minutes. Unless you want me walking through your very nice neighborhood in nothing but these." He gestured to his boxer briefs. "Though it wouldn't be the first time I've been barely clothed in public. Right, Vonnie?"

My cheeks burned. Garrett's eyes narrowed.

"I'll go check the perimeter and text you if I run into anything or anyone suspicious," he offered, already buttoning his shirt.

"You don't have to—" I started.

"It's fine, Devonna." The use of my full name was like a door closing. "Call me when... whatever this is... is resolved."

6

The polite dismissal stung more than I expected. Our arrangement might be uncomplicated, but that didn't mean it wasn't valuable. Especially on days like today when I needed the release.

"Okay, I'll text you," I whispered.

He nodded, one professional to another, and left without another word.

The door clicked shut behind him, leaving me alone with the human hurricane who'd blown back into my life without warning. I turned slowly, arms crossed over my chest, and fixed Miles with a glare that had made grown men and bridezillas alike burst into tears.

"Damn it, Miles. You have exactly sixty seconds to explain why I shouldn't call the actual police, starting now."

Miles attempted to sit up straighter, wincing as he did. I refused to feel sympathy. The tattoos across his torso shifted with the movement.

"Mikhail Dimitrov loaned me money years ago, and I've been trying to pay him back, but I don't make much at the nonprofit. That hasn't mattered because I've been...well, I've been helping Mikhail with some things on the side," he began, his usual snark giving way to something more serious. "I wanted out. He didn't like that. I offered to pay him back the full debt and interest in installments over time, but he suggested an alternative arrangement. Marry his daughter Irina, and he'd clear the debt."

"Fifty seconds," I prompted.

"Right. Well, I refused. He was insistent. His goons suspended me upside down over his balcony. Thirty-two floors up. I panicked and said I was already engaged." He spread his hands as if to say, 'What would you have done?'

"To me," I clarified. "You specifically said you were engaged to me."

Something flickered across his face too quickly to read. "You were the only name I could think of under pressure."

The admission shouldn't have affected me. It didn't affect me. "Forty seconds."

"His guys roughed me up. I needed somewhere to lie low, and..." He gestured vaguely around my apartment. "I know you hate surprises, but showing up at your fancy office seemed worse."

7

"Thirty seconds," I said, though I was beginning to get a sinking feeling about where this was heading.

"Mikhail thinks we're engaged. He's going to keep checking. If he finds out I lied..." He trailed off, letting the implication hang.

"But you said you think he already knows because his goons saw me with Garrett."

"I can explain that away. But if you don't help me with this, he might fit me for cement shoes and send me swimming in the Hudson River."

"That sounds like a you problem."

"It becomes a you problem if he decides you're involved," Miles countered. "The Peacock isn't exactly known for his measured responses or careful target selection."

A chill ran through me that had nothing to do with my partially unbuttoned blouse. "Twenty seconds."

Miles shifted, and I caught sight of another tattoo on his inner arm. A tiny, perfect rendering of a wedding cake.

"I need your help, Von—Devonna," he corrected himself. "Just until I can pay him back or figure something out. It sounded like he'd be willing to give me time to pay back the debt while we plan the wedding. It'll be a temporary engagement. On paper only."

"Ten seconds."

"You're the only person I know who's smarter than Mikhail," he breathed, the calculated charm dropping away for just a moment. "And I'm out of options."

The washing machine buzzed loudly in the silence that followed, making us both jump.

"Perfect timing," Miles said, struggling to stand. "Mind if I use your dryer?"

I stared at this man, who had crashed back into my life like a meteor, threatening to extinction-event everything I'd built. The rational part of me—the part that had created Devonna Onai, respected wedding planner and partner at Knot Your Average Wedding—knew exactly what to do. Call security. Call the police. Hell, call The Peacock himself and clear up this ridiculous misunderstanding.

But there was another part of me. A part I'd locked away eight years, seven months, and twelve days ago. A part that looked at

8

Miles—battered, bruised, and still somehow charming Miles—and remembered how it felt to be the woman who had once loved him.

That part needed to stay buried.

"No," I said finally.

"No dryer? That's cold. Literally."

"No, I'm not helping you." I reached for the front door and pulled it open. "Get your clothes and get out."

For the first time since I'd walked in, genuine surprise registered on his face. "You're kicking me out?"

"Yes."

"With Mikhail's men potentially waiting?"

"Your poor planning isn't my emergency."

Miles looked at me for a long moment, then nodded slowly. "Fair enough. I just thought..." He trailed off, then shook his head. "Never mind. I'll get my clothes."

He limped slightly as he moved toward the laundry nook, and I forced myself to ignore the pang of... something... as I watched him go. This wasn't the same charming, reckless boy I'd fallen for at nineteen. This was a man who still thought he could use me to fix his problems, just like last time.

And I wasn't the same naïve girl who would burn down her life to keep him warm.

He returned a few minutes later with damp clothes bundled under one arm, still in his boxer briefs. "Mind if I..." He gestured vaguely toward my bathroom.

"Two minutes," I said, glancing pointedly at my watch.

While he dressed, I poured myself a generous measure of the whisky he'd been drinking and fired off a text to Garrett.

DEVONNA: I'm sorry about tonight. He's leaving. Rain check?

The response came almost immediately.

GARRETT: No problem. Complicated exes happen. Didn't see anyone on my way out. Call when the dust settles.

I wasn't sure whether I was relieved or disappointed by his easy acceptance.

Miles emerged from the bathroom looking marginally more put together, though his expensive shirt was wrinkled and still spotted with what I chose to believe was wine rather than blood. The bruises on his face stood out starkly now against his pallor.

"Thanks for the use of your washing machine," he said, attempting a smile that pulled at his split lip. "And the whisky. And the chips. Quality snacks, as always."

"Don't mention it," I replied coldly. "Seriously. To anyone. Ever. Get out, Miles."

He paused at the door, the ghost of his old smile playing at the corner of his mouth. "For what it's worth, I'm sorry for dropping in unannounced."

"No, you're not."

"You're right, I'm not." The smile widened slightly, transforming his battered face into something almost familiar. "But I am sorry about interrupting your evening with Bruce Banner back there."

"His name is Garrett."

"I'm sure he's very nice," Miles said, in a tone that conveyed the opposite. "Very... stable."

"Get out, Miles," I repeated, holding the door wider.

He stepped into the hallway, then turned back. "You know, you've changed, Vonnie."

"That was the point."

Something flickered in his eyes. "Not all of it, I hope." Then he was gone, limping toward the elevator.

I closed the door and leaned against it, sliding down to sit on the floor. My perfectly planned evening ruined. My carefully constructed life momentarily shaken but still standing. And the absolute worst bit? A tiny, traitorous part of me was already wondering what would happen if The Peacock did come looking.

That part needed to be silenced immediately. Preferably with what remained of the whisky.

Because the last time I let Miles Houston into my life, I'd nearly lost everything. I'd spent the last several years rebuilding myself into someone who would never make that mistake again.

I glanced at the half-eaten chip bag on my coffee table and took another sip of whisky. Deliberately, I turned away. Whatever trouble Miles was in, it wasn't my problem. Not anymore.

The washing machine hummed in the background, completing its final rinse cycle even though there were no more clothes to clean.

Some messes, it seemed, couldn't be washed away so easily.

ROCK BOTTOM HAS A VACANCY SIGN & ACCEPTS CASH

Chapter 2: Miles

Breathe in, pain. Breathe out, more pain.

I stared at the cracked ceiling of the Starlight Inn, mapping water stains like constellations while trying to find a position that didn't feel like being stabbed. The vacuum cleaner next door attacked the carpet with the enthusiasm of a rabid badger, vibrations traveling through the paper-thin walls. I'd been awake for hours, watching morning light creep through curtains that smelled like decades of cigarettes and broken dreams.

The air conditioner rattled asthmatically, pushing around air that tasted of industrial cleaner and mildew. Ten years ago, I'd stayed at the Ritz-Carlton. Today, I was in a motel where the bedsprings had actual opinions about my life choices, and they weren't favorable.

I reached for the prescription bottle on the nightstand, rattling out two more painkillers. My fingers absently traced the skeleton key tattoo over my heart, the ink a permanent reminder of what I'd lost.

Devonna had found the original key at that little antique shop in the Hudson Valley five years ago. We'd been antiquing. Her idea, obviously. I'd complained the whole drive there, but stopped the moment I saw how her face lit up as she moved from vendor to vendor.

She'd spotted the key in a dusty display case, nestled among pocket watches and hat pins. Something about it had captivated her. Said it reminded her of the stories she used to make up as a kid; secret gardens, hidden rooms, treasures waiting to be discovered. "Some doors only open for the right person," she'd said with that smile that made her eyes crinkle at the corners.

I'd bought it for her without hesitation, though I'd played it cool, pretending it was no big deal. She'd worn it on a silver chain around her neck every day after that. Said it reminded her that there were always possibilities waiting to be unlocked.

Three years later, I'd had a replica tattooed over my heart as a surprise for our anniversary. She'd traced the fresh ink with trembling fingers, tears in her eyes. "Now you're carrying possibilities too," she'd whispered.

Three months after that, I'd locked every door between us and thrown away all the keys that mattered.

The digital clock on the nightstand read 10:37. I'd been staring at the ceiling for nearly four hours, my body cataloging new injuries with every shift of weight. Mikhail's goons had been remarkably thorough.

I winced as I finally forced myself to sit up, feeling the pull of bruised ribs and what was probably a cracked one. My reflection in the mirror across the room looked like abstract art; all purple-green splotches where my face should be, one eye swollen nearly shut.

My phone buzzed from somewhere in the tangle of cheap sheets. I patted around until I found it, squinting at the screen with my one good eye.

Alek.

I let it ring. I wasn't in the mood for his particular brand of "helpful" this morning. Alek Romano had been my friend since law school, and while he'd bailed me out of more than a few tight spots over the years, his help always came with a side of judgment wrapped in casual digs that left me feeling like something stuck to the bottom of his designer shoes.

The phone stopped, then immediately started buzzing again. Persistent bastard.

"What?" I growled after swiping to answer.

"Good morning to you too, sunshine." Alek's voice was irritatingly chipper. "You sound like hell. Rough night with the Russian?"

"How do you even know about that?" I shifted, biting back a groan as my body registered complaints from various battered regions.

"Because you drunk-texted me at 2 AM saying, and I quote, 'The Peacock wants me dead, tell my goldfish I love her.' You don't have a goldfish, Miles."

"It was metaphorical."

"It was pathetic. Where are you?"

I glanced around the dismal motel room. The peeling wallpaper and suspicious stains on the carpet completed the aesthetic of rock bottom.

"The Starlight Motel Inn on Lexington."

"Jesus, Miles." His voice dripped with that familiar blend of concern and condescension, like I was a particularly disappointing child. "That place is one health code violation away from being condemned."

"Yeah, well, it's cash only, and they don't ask questions about guests who look like they've been hit by a truck." I struggled to stand, the sheets clinging to me like they'd been shellacked to my skin with cheap whiskey and regret. "The truck being Mikhail's gorillas."

"What did you do to piss him off this time?"

I hobbled to the bathroom, each step a negotiation between dignity and pain. The mirror revealed the full damage: split lip crusted with dried blood, black eye swollen nearly shut, a rainbow of bruises blooming across my torso. The tattoos that covered most of my upper body provided a colorful backdrop for the fresh injuries. The skeleton key over my heart seemed especially vivid against the bruising.

"I...I told him I wanted out."

"Shit, man, what's wrong with you? Do you have a death wish?"

"Apparently."

"How do you plan to pay him back? You still owe him, what, a quarter of a million at this point with interest?"

I splashed cold water on my face, hissing as it hit the cut on my lip. "I've been negotiating."

"Clearly, it went well." His sarcasm was thick enough to spread on toast. "You know, for someone so smart, you make remarkably stupid decisions."

14

I gripped the edge of the chipped porcelain sink. "Thanks for the pep talk, Coach. Really feeling the support."

"Support isn't what you need, Miles. You need a reality check."

I caught my own gaze in the mirror; the one eye I could still open staring back at me with a mixture of self-loathing and defiance. Alek wasn't wrong, which only made it worse.

"He wanted me to marry his daughter to clear the debt," I said, changing the subject.

Alek's laugh was sharp and humorless. "Of course he did. Irina, right? The one with the collection of vintage weapons? And you said...?"

"I told him I was already engaged."

"To whom?" There was genuine curiosity in his voice now.

I hesitated, my fingers unconsciously tracing the outline of the key tattoo. "Devonna."

There was a long silence at the other end of the line. Then, "Devonna? As in your ex-fiancée Devonna? The woman who told you that if she ever saw you again, she'd perform an amateur vasectomy with her stiletto heel? That Devonna?"

"Yes, that Devonna." I limped back toward the bed, moving like an arthritic ninety-year-old. "It was the first name that came to mind when I was hanging upside down over his balcony."

"I'm sure she'll appreciate that."

"She didn't."

"Shit man. You've already spoken to her?"

I hesitated, and then sighed, running a hand through my hair, only to find more bruises on the side of my head. "Yeah." I explained how my evening had gone and waited for Alek's inevitable critiques.

"Of course you went to her place. Damn, Miles. Dumb move."

"I needed to tell her before she heard it from one of Mikhail's guys. I didn't know his men were following me, let alone Vonnie and her fuckbuddy."

"Shit. Think they told Mikhail?"

"Yeah. But I can still make this work."

"Really? And how is this all working out for you?"

I closed my eyes, the scene from last night replaying in vivid detail. Devonna, her blouse half-unbuttoned, with that familiar flush on her

15

cheeks that used to be for me. The tree trunk of a man behind her, his hands possessively on her hips. The look of shock on her face when she saw me.

"About as well as you'd expect. I didn't expect her to have male company."

"Oh?" The single syllable dripped with morbid interest. "You expected her to be a reborn virgin like you after all these years? Have you seen her? That woman could have any man she wanted on his knees begging like a fucking dog. And I bet she has. Who was the flavor of the night?"

"Fuck, Alek. I've already been punched in the nuts. I don't need you being an ass too."

"Who was he?"

"Some security specialist. Built like a CrossFit instructor had a baby with a brick wall. They were in the middle of... you know."

"Ah." Alek sounded almost pleased, which irritated me to no end. "So she *has* moved on. Good for her."

There was something in his tone I didn't like, a satisfaction that felt personal. Alek had always thought Devonna was too good for me. He'd made a point of reminding me every chance he got, especially after things ended. He wasn't wrong, but he didn't have to be so smug about it.

"She kicked me out," I continued, ignoring his comment. "Told me to handle my own problems."

"Smart woman."

My phone vibrated with an incoming text. I pulled it away from my ear to check.

My stomach dropped.

DIMITROV: *One week to produce your fiancée for dinner, or the debt doubles. No more extensions. Remember Karasov? Don't make me repeat that unpleasantness. - M.D.*

Karasov. The club owner who'd asked for an extension from the Peacock. They'd found pieces of him washing up along the Jersey Shore for weeks.

"Shit."

"What now?" Alek asked.

16

"Mikhail. He's giving me one week to bring Devonna to dinner or the debt doubles." I swallowed hard. "And he mentioned Karasov."

"Fuck." For once, Alek sounded genuinely concerned. "That's not good, Miles."

"Really? I thought a reference to a guy who was turned into shark chow was a positive development." Fear made my sarcasm sharper, meaner.

"You have two options," Alek said, his tone shifting to business mode. "Pay the debt or produce a fiancée."

"Brilliant analysis. Why didn't I think of that?" I rubbed my temples, feeling a headache building behind my eyes to complement the symphony of pain elsewhere.

"The money problem is easier to solve than you think, depending on your timeline."

I snorted. "I'm listening."

"Well, if you're short on time, I know a guy who needs some consulting work. Off the books, good pay."

"What kind of consulting?" I asked, though I already knew the answer. This was Alek's world; the gray area between legitimate business and outright criminal activity. The space I'd been trying to crawl out of since I'd left Devonna.

"The kind that would clear your debt in one job."

I closed my eyes. "And the catch?"

"It's in Dubai. You'd need to leave within the week."

I thought about it for all of five seconds. "I can't leave the country right now. Not with Mikhail breathing down my neck."

"Then your only option is to produce a fiancée and hope that you can buy enough time to pay back the debt before Dimitrov collects."

"I can't exactly hire an actress. Mikhail knows Devonna. He's seen her before, back when we were together." A memory surfaced; Devonna in a midnight blue dress, laughing at something Mikhail had said at a charity gala years ago. Before it all went to hell. "He fucking loved her."

"So get her to play along."

I laughed, then winced as my ribs protested. "She'd rather let me drown."

"Then you're fucked, my friend." There was almost a note of pity in Alek's voice. Almost. "Though, you know, this wouldn't have happened if you'd stuck with the hedge fund job I got you after law school."

And there it was. The reminder that any success in my life came through Alek's connections, and any failure was my own stupid fault.

"Thanks for the retrospective career advice. Very helpful in my current situation."

"Just saying. That job paid six figures, had full benefits, and didn't involve Russian loan sharks."

"It also involved selling my soul to help billionaires avoid taxes."

"As opposed to your current soulless state of working for a firm that pays pennies. You're being beaten up weekly, and staying in a fleabag motel. Yeah, that's much better."

I reached for the remote and flicked on the ancient TV, needing background noise to drown out both Alek and the growing panic in my chest. The local morning news filled the screen—traffic, weather, a society segment about some high-profile wedding.

"—planner to Manhattan's elite, Devonna Onai of Knot Your Average Wedding, shared these exclusive photos of the Katz-Beam ceremony, which insiders are calling the event of the season—"

I froze, my finger hovering over the volume button. There she was; Devonna, looking professional and polished in a navy dress that hugged every curve I still remembered too well. She was standing next to a beaming couple, smiling that perfect customer service smile that never quite reached her eyes. The smile she'd perfected after us, when she'd rebuilt herself into someone who didn't let people like me anywhere near her heart.

"Miles? You still there?" Alek's voice seemed distant.

I'd been keeping tabs on her, of course. Not in a stalker way; just occasional checks of her company's social media, celebratory whiskeys when she landed a major client. Pride from a distance. I knew she'd become a partner at Knot Your Average Wedding, transforming from assistant to industry star in just a few years.

I also knew that she'd gone through one of the hardest years of her life after I left her. Knew that not six months after I'd left, her mother had gotten cancer. It'd happened so fast that they'd lost her within four months. I'd drunk myself into a stupor knowing I'd forfeited the right to comfort Devonna during that time.

No wonder she'd turned me away last night. I deserved it. And more, if I was being honest. She owed me nothing.

But seeing her on screen now, composed and successful while I sat in a motel room that charged by the hour, made something twist painfully in my chest that had nothing to do with my bruised ribs.

"I gotta go," I told Alek, cutting off whatever he was saying.

"Miles—"

I ended the call and tossed the phone aside, transfixed by Devonna's image on the screen. She was answering questions about the wedding, professional and poised, not a hint of the fiery woman I'd known.

I grabbed the complimentary newspaper from the nightstand and flipped to the society pages. Sure enough, there was a feature on the Katz-Beam wedding, complete with gushing praise for the planner who had pulled off the "magical event."

At least she was doing well at her wedding planning business.

It likely kept her busy with all the consultations and appointments. Very busy. She likely had to jump from meeting to meeting.

An idea formed in my mind.

I ran a hand through my hair, wincing as my fingers caught on dried blood. This was manipulative. It was desperate. It was probably the worst idea I'd ever had, which was saying something considering my track record.

But it might work. And as I'd told her the night before, I really did need her. Just until I figured out a more permanent solution of how to pay off my debt.

My phone buzzed with another text from Mikhail:

DIMITROV: *Dinner at La Grenouille. Friday, 6 PM. Bring your lovely fiancée. Looking forward to celebrating your engagement. I've sent a little something to ensure her attendance. - M.D.*

Before I could wonder what that meant, a second text came through, this one with an attachment. I opened it and the blood drained from my face.

It was a photo of Devonna, taken that morning judging by her outfit, walking into her office building. The message was clear: the Peacock knew exactly where to find her.

The pain in my body seemed distant now, replaced by a cold, sharp fear that had nothing to do with my own safety. I'd dragged her into this mess by saying her name. If anything happened to her because of me...

I grabbed my wallet and what remained of my dignity. I needed coffee, painkillers, and to cement out my plan. Not necessarily in that order.

One week to get the woman who hated me more than anyone on earth to pretend we were engaged.

One week before the meeting with the Peacock.

One week to save us both.

I looked at the skeleton key tattoo in the mirror one last time before pulling on a shirt.

EIGHTY-SEVEN WAYS TO KILL YOUR FAKE FIANCÉ

Chapter 3: Devonna

"No, Mrs. Carpenter, doves won't poop on your daughter's veil," I explained for the third time that hour, pinching the bridge of my nose. "But if you're concerned, we can position the release point away from the ceremony area."

The Carpenter-Shea wedding was turning into my own personal Everest—if Everest could constantly shift locations, change its mind about the weather, and demand fifteen different cake tastings.

"But my sister-in-law's wedding had a dove incident," Mrs. Carpenter's voice crackled through my phone's speaker. "Poor Jennie looked like she'd been caught in a very localized hailstorm."

I caught Caroline's eye across the office as she silently mouthed, "Again?" while twirling her finger next to her temple.

"That's... unfortunate," I replied, scribbling "NO BIRDS," in capital letters on my tablet. "Perhaps we could consider alternatives; butterflies, bubbles, sparklers—"

"But the doves symbolize their eternal love taking flight!"

I doodled a small dove with a red X through it. "Of course. Let me research dove-handlers with proven anti-pooping techniques and get back to you."

After reassuring Mrs. Carpenter that her daughter's wedding would, in fact, be the most unique celebration Manhattan had ever witnessed (a promise I'd made to approximately 147 mothers-of-brides), I ended the call and dropped my head to my desk with a thud.

"Twenty bucks says she calls back within the hour to ask about trained hawks instead," Caroline said, setting a fresh coffee beside my collapsed form.

"No bet." I straightened up, accepting the caffeine offering. "That's exactly where her mind went last week before circling back to doves."

Caroline perched on the edge of my desk, her red curls catching the afternoon light. "Three more weeks and it's over. Then you can sleep again."

"Sleep? What's that?" I took a sip of coffee, savoring the vanilla notes. Caroline had perfected my order within days of starting. "Did the Baxters confirm their final guest count?"

"Yes, and they've only added sixteen people since yesterday."

"Only sixteen? They're showing remarkable restraint."

My phone vibrated with an incoming text. I glanced down to see Garrett's name and felt a small flutter in my chest.

GARRETT: *Conference session on advanced security protocols. Would rather be getting a root canal. Without anesthesia. While listening to my mother's Kenny G collection.*

I smiled despite my exhaustion.

DEVONNA: *My morning featured a detailed discussion of dove excretory habits. I think I win.*

The reply came almost instantly.

GARRETT: *Dove shit > Kenny G. You win. Drinks when I'm back to make up for all this suffering?*

Before I could reply, Caroline cleared her throat.

"Earth to Devonna? Your delivery from the stationer arrived."

I looked up, suddenly aware I'd been grinning at my phone like a teenager. "Thanks. Can you check if they got the monogram right this time? Last sample looked like a drunk spider dipped in ink."

As Caroline went to retrieve the package, I quickly texted back:

DEVONNA: *Thursday? I'll require at least two martinis to recover from wedding planning trauma.*

GARRETT: *It's a date. Might need to make it three after this conference.*

I was about to respond when Caroline reappeared, placing a stack of envelopes on my desk. "Perfect monogram this time. Also, you got a call while you were with the florist. A Mr. Smith? He wants to meet tonight about his daughter's wedding."

"Mr. Smith?"

"Yeah. He said to meet him at La Grenouille at 6. He made a reservation." Caroline tilted her head.

"Alright." I glanced at my calendar, though I knew perfectly well it was clear. Mari and Anica were in Chicago for the week, leaving me to handle the New York office while trying not to think about Miles and his unexpected reappearance in my life.

Five days. It had been five days since he'd shown up in his underwear on my couch, battered and bruised, and eating my favorite chips. Five days since my carefully rebuilt life had threatened to tilt off its axis.

I'd spent those five days burying myself in work, refusing to think about how, for a split second before anger took over, I'd felt something dangerously close to relief at seeing his face again.

"Devonna? You okay?" Caroline's voice pulled me back to the present.

"Fine. Just mentally rearranging my evening. I had plans to rewatch season four of *How I Met Your Mother* while downing some pho." I straightened the already aligned stack of papers on my desk. "Is Mr. Smith a new client? Did he mention how he heard about us?"

"He just said he was impressed by your work and wanted to discuss options for his daughter's special day." Caroline checked her notes. "Oh, and he said it was very important that you come alone, as this is a delicate family matter."

A prickle of unease started and soon became a full-body shiver. "Did he now."

"Is that weird? It sounded weird when he said it, but I didn't want to be rude."

"It's unusual to have to specify it." I checked my watch. Almost 4:30. If I was going to make a 6:00 meeting at La Grenouille, I'd need to leave soon. "Did he leave a number to confirm?"

"No. He just said he'd see you there."

I drummed my fingers on the desk, debating. My instincts said to decline a mysterious meeting with a man who didn't provide a callback number and requested I come alone. But curiosity—and the possibility of a high-end client—won out.

"Alright. Hold down the fort while I'm gone. If Mrs. Carpenter calls about the doves—"

"Tell her we're researching anti-pooping technology. Got it."

THE HOSTESS AT La Grenouille led me through the dining room. I'd arrived fifteen minutes early, dressed in a dark purple sheath dress that I'd originally bought for a client meeting with a Broadway producer who'd mentioned his fiancée wanted "classic with an edge."

I scanned the restaurant, looking for anyone who might be my mysterious Mr. Smith, when I spotted him—unmistakable even after eight years, with his flashy diamond cufflinks and signature peacock-blue pocket square.

Mikhail Dimitrov. The Peacock.

My stomach dropped to my Jimmy Choos.

The Russian loan shark whose men had used my ex's face as a punching bag grinned at me from across the room.

Damn it, Miles.

Now I understood the cryptic meeting request. The damn menace had clearly arranged this, though I wasn't sure why.

I had approximately three seconds to decide whether to approach or flee. Professional pride won out over self-preservation, but just barely. I smoothed my dress, straightened my spine, and approached his table.

"Mr. Dimitrov," I said, my voice remarkably steady considering the circus acrobatics my internal organs were performing. "What a surprise."

The Peacock rose as I approached, his smile all teeth and no warmth. "Miss Onai. You remember me."

"You make quite an impression." I offered my hand, which he took with excessive gallantry.

"As do you. Please, sit." He gestured to the chair across from him. "These are my associates, Shane and Erik."

I glanced at the two men standing behind Dimitrov's chair. Security detail, clearly, though they were trying to look like regular dinner companions who just happened to prefer standing to sitting. Yeah, completely normal. Shane was tall with dark hair and surprisingly kind eyes. Erik was shorter, with a scar through one eyebrow that made him look perpetually skeptical. I wondered if they were the ones who'd banged up Miles, or if Dimitrov had even more men to do his bidding.

"Gentlemen," I nodded. "I must admit, Mr. Dimitrov, I'm surprised to see you here."

Dimitrov smiled as a waiter appeared with a bottle of champagne. "So this dinner is a surprise to you, then? How interesting. Well, I'm glad you could make it, nonetheless. I'd like to celebrate your engagement, but where is your fiancé? We can't very well start without him."

My blood turned to ice water. "My..."

"Your engagement to Miles Houston." He studied my face. "My dear friend who is so desperately in love with you that he could not possibly marry my Irina."

The champagne cork popped like a gunshot, making me flinch.

"I think there's been a misunderstanding," I began, my mind racing to formulate a response that wouldn't get Miles—or me—killed.

"Has there?" Dimitrov's smile remained fixed, but his eyes hardened. "That would be... disappointing. Miles was quite clear about your reconciliation and engagement."

The waiter filled three champagne flutes. I noticed neither Shane nor Erik received glasses. Apparently, goons didn't get to celebrate.

"Mr. Dimitrov—"

"Please, call me Mikhail. We are practically family now."

"I didn't realize you and Miles had gotten so close."

"Like a son to me, that one."

"A son you had roughed up?" I raised an eyebrow. "Very fatherly." I reached for the champagne flute, needing something to do with my hands before they betrayed my anxiety. There was no telling how far I could push him. I hadn't spoken to the man in over eight years.

"Sometimes children need to be taught important lessons. But it all worked out. And now I know about your engagement."

"About that—"

"Sorry I'm late."

The familiar voice sent a jolt through me. I turned to find Miles sliding into the chair beside me, looking far better than he had any right to given the beating he'd taken less than a week ago. The swelling around his eye had subsided, though traces of bruising remained visible beneath what I suspected was concealer.

He was wearing a charcoal gray suit that fit his broad shoulders perfectly, his blonde curls styled in that deliberately tousled way that had always made my fingers itch to either smooth them or mess them up further.

Before I could react, he leaned in and pressed a kiss to my cheek, his hand coming to rest on my shoulder in a gesture that would look affectionate to anyone watching.

"Don't scream, don't slap me, and please don't tell him we're not engaged," he whispered against my ear, his breath warm against my skin, carrying a hint of the mint gum he'd always chewed before important meetings. "I'll explain everything later."

He pulled back, giving Dimitrov a smile that didn't reach his eyes. "Mikhail! Thank you for arranging this. I've been telling Vonnie how much I wanted you two to reconnect."

The nickname used to make my heart flutter and now made me want to stab him with my appetizer fork.

"Of course," Dimitrov nodded, raising his glass. "To the happy couple. May your reunion be... permanent."

The threat beneath the toast was about as subtle as a sledgehammer. I took a small sip of champagne, buying time to recalibrate. Miles's hand found mine under the table, squeezing in what I assumed was meant to be reassurance but felt more like a restraint to keep me from bolting.

"Miss Onai was just explaining how surprised she was to see me," Dimitrov continued, his gaze moving between us. "Almost as if she wasn't expecting this meeting."

Miles laughed. The sound was natural but his fingers tightened around mine. "I wanted it to be a surprise. She's been so busy with the other people's weddings, we've barely had time to celebrate our engagement properly."

"How... romantic." Dimitrov's smile didn't reach his eyes. "Though I'm curious. Why keep such joyous news private? I see no ring on your finger, no announcement in the papers. Nothing on social media either."

Miles tensed beside me, ready to jump in with another fabrication, but suddenly, irrationally, I was annoyed that he thought I couldn't handle this myself.

"Actually, we're keeping things quiet because of the company I work for. I didn't want word getting out and having clients be concerned," I said, giving Miles's hand a warning squeeze when he opened his mouth. "In my business, perception is everything. If clients think I'm distracted by my own wedding plans, they lose confidence."

"Very professional," Dimitrov nodded. "And the ring?"

I traced the empty spot on my finger. "Being sized. It seems only one in ten of my clients guess correctly, and half of them cheat and spill the secret before the proposal."

"Wouldn't want to spill the secret," Miles said, smirking. "I guessed the size wrong, but boy, you should've seen her face when it all happened."

Though I kept a smile on my lips, under the table, I dug my sharp nails into Miles's hand. He didn't flinch, but he did clear his throat.

"Yes, it was certainly a surprise," I ground out with an obnoxious chipper smile.

"How lovely." Dimitrov signaled the waiter. "Now, shall we order? The duck here is exceptional."

As Dimitrov consulted with the sommelier, Miles leaned close.

"Nice save with the ring," he murmured, his lips brushing my ear. "Maybe hold back on the maiming, though."

"I'm going to kill you, you know." I said, faking a giggle behind my hand. "And they'll never find all the pieces of you."

"God, I forgot how terrifying you are."

"Damn right," I whispered, my cheeks starting to hurt from the forced smile I kept holding on my face. "If you don't explain yourself later, I'll feed you to a carnivorous dove flock. They're always ravenous before weddings."

His answering smile was a flash of the old Miles—the one who'd always appreciated my dry humor, who'd made me laugh even when

I was furious with him. I squashed the warmth it stirred in my chest like a juicy worm after a rain storm.

The dinner proceeded with Dimitrov dominating the conversation, regaling us with stories about his various business ventures while I focused on not choking on my perfectly seared duck. Miles kept up a steady stream of charming responses, his hand occasionally touching my shoulder in a falsified display of affection.

I noticed Shane watching me with an odd expression whenever Dimitrov was focused elsewhere. Not threatening, exactly, but... assessing. When our eyes met once, he gave an almost imperceptible nod before returning to his stoic surveillance.

As dessert was served — a delicate chocolate soufflé I was too tense to enjoy — Dimitrov leaned forward, his voice dropping.

"I must say, I'm relieved to see you two have reconciled. When I heard about your separation, I worried. Miles was... shall we say, adrift without you."

Miles coughed into his napkin beside me.

Dimitrov dabbed his lips with his napkin. "Now you can move forward together. And I'll oversee the wedding preparations, of course. We wouldn't want to put too much on your plate, Miss Onai."

"That's very kind," I managed, trying to remember where I put my passport so I could flee the country as soon as the meal was over. "But I do work for a wedding planning company. And as I mentioned, we're taking things slowly."

"Of course, but I do insist." Dimitrov's smile didn't reach his eyes. "I do love a good wedding."

I smiled, all the while plotting eighty-seven different ways to kill the blonde man sitting next to me.

PAY UP OR PLAY ALONG

Chapter 4: Miles

Devonna's fingernails carved a map of my bad decisions into my thigh while Mikhail asked about our wedding, and I knew she was going to murder me. Not metaphorically. Literally. Probably with the steak knife she kept glancing at between fake smiles.

"More wine?" Mikhail asked, already pouring before we could answer. The Barolo glugged into Devonna's glass. She'd downed half of it before he'd finished refilling mine.

"Thank you," Devonna said, her voice honey-smooth. Under the table, her heel ground into my foot and I clenched my jaw to keep from making any noise. God, she was vicious. I managed to transform my wince into what I hoped looked like adoration.

"So tell me," Mikhail continued, settling back in his chair like a well-fed python, "When will your happily-ever-after take place?"

"Oh, not for a while," I said, draping my arm across the back of Devonna's chair. "Maybe next year."

"We don't have a date yet. We've only just recently gotten engaged. Wouldn't want to race through the early excitement. Too many couples do," Devonna clarified.

My chest tightened. After the way she'd sent me away the other night, I was in wonder over the fact that she hadn't thrown me to the blood-thirsty Peacock. I needed to send her flowers. And chocolates. And I definitely needed to replace those chips I'd eaten that night. Knowing her, though, she'd probably donate everything to the hospital down the street from her office.

"Next year?" Mikhail's eyebrows rose. "No, that won't do."

"It's what we both want," Devonna said, and though she continued that godforsaken fake smile, her tone had hardened. "We're still getting used to being together again."

"No."

"No?" Devonna's voice went up an octave. "What do you mean, no?"

Mikhail's smile turned predatory, and Shane shifted position behind Dimitrov's chair, moving closer to our table. My body responded before my brain caught up, angling to put myself between Devonna and potential danger. Her fingers found my thigh under the table—not attacking this time, just... there. A warning or a thank you, I couldn't tell.

"You two are getting married in six months."

Shit.

"And I'm going to arrange everything."

Double shit.

Devonna's fingers tightened on my leg.

"And if you have a problem with that, Miss Onai, I'm sure your fiancé can remind you that I have ways of making things happen unlike anyone else." Mikhail studied her.

I cleared my throat, drawing his attention to me. Unfortunately, I hadn't thought far enough ahead to come up with something clever to say. I just wanted him to stop looking at Devonna the way he looked at me before I "accidentally" took a spill down a flight of stairs a few months ago.

"Yes, Miles?" Mikhail raised an eyebrow. "you had something to add?"

"I... um..." I bit my cheek, glancing sidelong at Devonna. Behind Mikhail, Erik scowled at me and cracked his tatted knuckles. God, I hated that guy. "I think... I think six months sounds perfect."

Devonna's heel found my ankle bone. I kept my expression neutral through what I was pretty sure was permanent nerve damage.

"Perfect," she echoed. "Though as a wedding planner myself, I have to ask—what exactly do you mean by 'arrange everything'?"

"My wife, Florence, has already started planning. She's quite excited. Says it will be a wedding to remember."

"And, remind me, how long have the two of you been married?" Devonna asked. She was buying time, processing.

"Twenty-seven years next month," Mikhail confirmed. "She has exquisite taste. You'll love what she has in mind. The venues she's chosen alone—"

"We couldn't possibly impose," Devonna interrupted smoothly. "Planning a wedding in six months is—"

"Not an imposition when I insist," Mikhail's tone suggested the discussion was over. "Consider it my engagement gift. After all, I have a vested interest in Miles's happiness." His gaze slid to me. "Happy men make better business partners. Wouldn't you agree?"

Pay up or play along. Those were my options.

"Absolutely," I said, squeezing Devonna's shoulder in what I hoped looked like affection rather than desperation. "We're incredibly grateful for your generosity."

"Good."

"Great," I said, trying not to grimace.

Erik snorted from his position by the wall. Even the hired muscle thought I was pathetic.

"Oh, and Florence and I will stop by your office this week, Miss Onai, to discuss some of the details of your wedding. She'll want to see it. She has quite the eye for the finer things. And speaking of Florence, she'd want me to ask about your wedding party. Bridesmaids, groomsmen, guests, that sort of thing."

"We're planning on keeping it small," Devonna said. "Intimate."

"Nonsense. A proper wedding needs proper attendance. I'll provide the guest list."

Devonna's spoon clattered against her plate. "You'll... what?"

"Three hundred of our closest friends and associates," Mikhail continued, either oblivious to or enjoying her distress. "Don't worry about the cost. I insist on covering everything."

31

"Mr. Dimitrov," Devonna started, her composure finally cracking. "That's incredibly generous, but—"

"No buts. A wedding is a celebration of new beginnings. And new beginnings should be memorable." His smile turned sharp. "Especially when they involve correcting past mistakes."

"We're honored," I said, because what else could I say? 'No thanks, I'd rather you break my legs than plan my fake wedding'?

"Excellent." Mikhail signaled for the check. "This has been illuminating. I'll be seeing you two this week."

Shane and Erik flanked Dimitrov as he stood, but not before he took Devonna's hand and lifted it to his lips in an old-world gesture that made my jaw clench.

"Radiant," he murmured. "Miles is a fortunate man."

"Yes, he is," Devonna replied.

The moment they were gone, her mask shattered.

"Six months?" She turned on me, eyes blazing. "We're getting married in six months?"

"I didn't know he'd—"

"With three hundred of his closest criminal associates?" She whispered, smacking me on the arm over and over again until I caught her wrists in mine.

"We can figure this out—"

"And his wife is planning everything? His wife who probably considers cement shoes a fashion statement for the less fortunate? Isn't she the daughter of a mobster?"

"Alleged mob—ow!"

Devonna pinched my thigh under the table with her free hand, twisting her nails into my leg way too close to my dick for comfort. "You fucking asshole," she seethed.

"Devonna—"

"Outside. Now."

She squirmed out of my grasp and stood abruptly. I scrambled to follow, but she wasn't heading for the door. She moved straight for me, and the look in her eyes suggested I should probably run.

I didn't move fast enough.

Her hand shot up and grabbed my ear twisting until I cringed.

"Ow—Vonnie—people are staring—" I protested, hunched over to relieve the pressure as she marched me through the restaurant.

"Good," she hissed. "Maybe they'll learn what happens when you drag someone into a fake engagement."

Diners watched our progress with expressions ranging from amusement to secondhand embarrassment. Our waiter pressed himself against the wall to let us pass, clearly deciding this was above his pay grade.

She didn't release me until we were on the sidewalk, then immediately grabbed my arm and dragged me into an alley beside a dumpster that smelled like seafood that had given up on life three weeks ago.

"Six months, Miles!" She shoved me against the brick wall. "We're getting fake married in six months!"

"Technically, we just have to plan it in six months. We could always fake our own deaths before the actual ceremony."

"This isn't funny!"

"I'm not laughing!" I rubbed my throbbing ear. "Trust me, the last thing I wanted was Mikhail's wife planning our wedding. She probably registers at weapons dealers."

"He's choosing our guest list. Our venue. Everything!" Devonna paced the narrow alley like a caged animal in designer heels. "Do you have any idea what this means?"

"That we're comprehensively fucked?"

"That we have to actually plan a wedding! A real wedding that real criminals will attend!" She whirled on me. "What happens when we don't go through with it? When Dimitrov realizes this was all fake?"

The question I'd been avoiding. Great.

"I'll have the money by then," I said with confidence I didn't feel. "I'll pay him off before—"

"How?" Her laugh was borderline hysterical. "What are you planning to do, rob a bank?"

"I have leads—"

"You have nothing!" She pressed her palms against her eyes. "God, what am I doing? I plan weddings for normal people. Doctors and lawyers and hedge fund managers who only commit white-collar crimes. Not... this!"

"Vonnie—"

"Don't call me that." But the heat had gone out of her voice, replaced by exhaustion.

"Devonna," I corrected. "I'm going to fix this. I promise."

"Like you fixed things eight years ago when you fucking left?"

"That was different—"

"Was it?" She looked at me then, really looked at me, and I saw something I hadn't expected—disappointment. "Because from where I'm standing, it looks exactly the same. You making promises you can't keep and I'm being stupid enough to believe them."

"You're not stupid."

"I'm pretending to marry you. That's the definition of stupid."

"No," I said, stepping closer. "Stupid would be actually marrying me. This is just... strategically questionable."

"You're impossible."

"Part of my charm."

"You don't have charm. You have audacity masquerading as charm."

"That counts, right?"

She shook her head. "We need rules, Miles. Real ones. In writing."

"A contract for our fake engagement that's now becoming a fake wedding?"

"Yes."

"Should we include a section about the mob-planned reception?"

"Miles!"

"I know." I sobered, meeting her eyes. "I know. And I know I've put you in an impossible position. But I swear to you, I'll keep you safe."

"I don't need you to keep me safe," she said. "I need you to have a plan that doesn't end with both of us in witness protection."

"I'm working on it."

"Work faster." She pulled out her phone. "God, this is a nightmare."

"Vonnie—Devonna," I caught her hand before she could walk away. "Thank you. For tonight. For not throwing me under the bus when you had every reason to."

She looked down at where our hands touched, and for a moment, neither of us moved.

"I didn't do it for you. I did it because I don't want to end up as an unsolved disappearance. Besides, I'm not going to throw you under a bus. I'm going to gag and bind you to a train track and laugh maniacally as you're shredded into fish food."

"Shit, Von." I let go of her and shoved my hands into my pockets. "Still. Thank you."

She studied me for a long moment. "You really stepped in it, didn't you?"

"Yeah."

"God, you're the worst."

"Noted. Anything else?"

"Yes." She stepped closer, and for one insane moment, I thought she might kiss me. Or slap me. Instead, she straightened my tie—the one with the elephants she'd bought me years ago. I flinched. "If you ever trick me into a dinner again, I'll tell Dimitrov you're actually gay and having an affair with Erik."

"That's... specific."

"I've had the entire dinner to plan your destruction." She patted my chest. "Sleep tight, Miles."

She walked away, her heels clicking against the pavement in a rhythm that sounded like a countdown. Six months until a wedding that couldn't happen. And approximately zero ideas for how to fix any of it.

My phone buzzed with a message from Dimitrov.

DIMITROV: I CAN SEE WHY YOU'D RISK EVERYTHING. DON'T DISAPPOINT ME. - MD

Attached was a photo from tonight—the moment she'd fixed my tie just a second ago, looking every inch the concerned fiancée.

Okay, I was definitely doomed.

But at least I'd be doomed wearing my lucky tie.

35

OH SUGAR, THIS IS GOING DOWNHILL FAST

Chapter 5: Devonna

I was in the middle of a meeting when the door to my office flew open so hard it bounced off the wall, and there stood Miles looking like he'd sprinted here from a crime scene. His perfect hair was disheveled, his tie askew, and his expression suggested we were all about to die.

"We have a problem," he announced, then noticed Anica and Mari staring at him like he'd materialized from another dimension. "Oh. Hi. Sorry. You. Me. We need to talk. Now."

I froze mid-sip of my coffee, which was unfortunate because I then choked on it and spent the next ten seconds coughing while everyone watched.

"Who," Mari said slowly, her voice dropping to that dangerous purr, "is this absolute snack of a man, Dev?"

"No one," I managed between coughs.

"Her boyfriend," Miles said at the same time.

The silence that followed could have been measured in centuries. Entire civilizations rose and fell. The universe experienced heat death and was reborn.

"I'm sorry," Anica said finally, removing her glasses to clean them as if that might change what she'd heard, "did you just say boyfriend?"

"Ex," I corrected quickly, shooting Miles a look that promised dismemberment. "Ex-boyfriend. Who's... back. In my life. Temporarily. Very, very temporarily. Like a rash. How the hell did you get past Caroline?"

"You mean the red head?" Miles shrugged. "I winked at her. I think she'll wake up soon." He crossed the room in three strides, ignoring my murder-eyes. "Mikhail is on his way here. Right now. Florence is with him. They're probably five minutes out."

My stomach relocated to somewhere near my shoes. "What? How do you — they're coming here now and — shit, damn it — "

"Who's Mikhail?" Mari interrupted, but her eyes were still doing a full-body scan of Miles that was about as subtle as a foghorn. "Actually, wait, more importantly — Dev, you dated him?"

"Mari, you're in a committed relationship. Remember? Hudson? And shouldn't you be heading to the airport?" I cut her off desperately. "Chicago? Your very important flight?"

"My flight's not for four hours." She turned to Miles like a shark scenting blood. "Devonna never talks about her relationships, past or present. I bet you have a lot of stories."

"Oh, do I." Miles's smug look gave me a minor conniption.

"Can we please focus?" I continued, my voice climbing toward hysteria.

"But — " Miles argued, but I cut him off with a lethal glare.

"I'm supposed to have lunch with Callan's grandmother," Anica said, checking her watch. "But I can cancel if — "

"No!" I practically shouted. The last thing I needed was witnesses to whatever madness was about to unfold. "Don't cancel. Mari, you should go too."

"But I don't need to leave for — "

"Yes you do. You should always be at least two hours early for your flight."

They must have heard the barely contained panic in my voice because they started gathering their things like people evacuating before a natural disaster.

"Wait," Mari said, pausing at the door. "Is this why you've been wearing your crisis cardigan all week?"

I looked down at the gray cashmere cardigan that had seen me through every disaster of the past eight years. "This is just a regular cardigan."

"You only wear it during emergencies. Remember the butterfly plague in that wedding a few months ago?"

"That was different. Those butterflies were weaponized."

"And that time the mother of the bride tried to perform an exorcism on the groom during the vows?"

"Anyone would need comfort cashmere after that."

The elevator dinged in the hallway.

"Go!" I hissed. "Now!"

They fled, but not before Mari whispered, "He's hot, Von. You better tap that," and Anica added, "We're discussing this later. In detail. With wine."

The door had barely closed behind them when it opened again, and in walked a woman I didn't remember until that moment.

Florence Dimitrov was tiny—maybe five feet in heels—with perfectly coiffed blonde hair, a pink Chanel suit with a bedazzled collar, and a smile that could sweeten tea or plan an execution, depending on her mood.

"Devonna, sugar!" She sailed toward me with her arms outstretched, enveloping me in a cloud of expensive perfume. "Oh, don't you just look pretty as a peach today! Bless your heart for trying so hard with this little outfit."

Behind her, Mikhail filled the doorframe like a well-dressed mountain. However, the way he watched his wife suggested he knew exactly who the real danger in the room was.

"Mrs. Dimitrov," I managed, extracting myself from her grip. "What a... surprise."

"Oh sugar, call me Florence! We're practically family now!" She grabbed my left hand, her smile flickering for just a moment at my bare ring finger. "Still no ring? Oh, that's just heartbreaking. Mikhail, doesn't that just break your heart?"

"Yes, dear," Mikhail said automatically.

"The resize is taking longer than expected," Miles said smoothly, appearing at my side with his hand settling on my lower back. The warmth of his palm through my dress made me want to simultaneously lean into him and elbow him in the ribs. "Three different jewelers, actually. Devonna has very specific requirements."

38

"Well of course she does!" Florence patted my cheek like I was a slow child. "When you've been waiting nearly nine years for your man to come to his senses, you deserve perfection. Isn't that right, pudding?"

She directed this at Mikhail, who nodded obediently. "Whatever you say, dear."

"Your office is just adorable!" Florence continued, looking around my small office. "So... cozy. Like a little dollhouse where you play wedding planner! And that darling IKEA desk? How precious. You know, I always say it's not about what you have, it's about what you do with it. And you've done so much with so little!"

I felt Miles's hand tighten on my waist, probably sensing I was about to commit murder.

"I'm still settling in," I said, trying to keep my voice level. "Just got promoted to a partner a little while ago. Coffee or tea?"

"Oh sweetness, I'm alright at the moment." She waved a dismissive hand that sparkled with enough diamonds to fund a small country. "Now, let me show you what I've planned for your wedding!"

She pulled out an iPad with a custom pink leather case and started swiping through photos that made my blood pressure spike with each image.

"First, the venue. I've narrowed it down to three itty-bitty options." She showed us a literal castle. "This one's in the Valley. They were booked full, but there was an emergency and now they have an opening in five and a half weeks."

"What kind of emergency?" I asked, though I immediately regretted it.

Florence's smile made my blood turn to a slushie from 7/11. "Oh honey, the kind where they realized they desperately needed to visit their grandmother in Switzerland. For a year. Starting immediately. Isn't it funny how these things just work out? The good Lord works in mysterious ways."

"Mysterious," I echoed weakly.

"And violent," Mikhail added under his breath, earning a sharp look from his wife.

"What was that, Mikkie?"

"I said 'how provident,' dear."

"That's what I thought." She patted his arm like he was a particularly well-trained pit bull. "Now, we'll tour all three venues on Saturday."

"I'm overseeing a wedding Saturday," I interjected. Next to me, Miles choked on air as Florence turned a withering look in my direction. "I apologize, Florence, but I have a job."

"Right, well, I'll see if we can move the tours to Sunday."

I opened my mouth to point out that I was supposed to help Anica with a different wedding on Sunday, but Miles pinched my side. He must've forgotten that I was ticklish, because I squeaked and pulled away from him like he'd shocked me.

For a second, the room fell silent as both loan shark and terrifying wife stared at me.

Miles let out a low chuckle and yanked me back against his side. "Sunday works perfectly," he said in a smooth voice. "Right, Vonnie?"

"Right," I forced out.

Florence's smile had all the warmth of a frozen lake. "Sunday it is, then. We wouldn't want this dream wedding delayed by pesky work, now would we?"

"Of course not," I replied, forcing a smile that felt more like a grimace.

"Now, for flowers, I'm thinking white orchids flown in from Thailand. Sixty dozen should do for the ceremony, don't you think?"

"Sixty dozen?" I squeaked.

"You're right, sugar, that's thinking too small. Let's make it a hundred. Go big or go home, as they say!" She laughed, a tinkling sound that made my teeth hurt. "Oh, and I've arranged meetings with vendors. The best of the best! Well, the best who were available once I explained how important it was to make time for us."

"Explained," Miles repeated carefully.

"Oh, you know how it is. Sometimes people just need a little encouragement to rearrange their schedules. Mikhail's associates are so helpful with that sort of thing. Aren't they, dumpling?"

"Very helpful," Mikhail confirmed. "Very encouraging. Miles knows firsthand, don't you?"

Miles nodded. "Very encouraging."

"And for your dress!" She pulled up a photo of something that looked like a meringue had exploded. "Isn't this just to die for?"

Poor choice of words, considering.

"It's... very white," I managed.

"Eight hundred thousand seed pearls, hand-sewn by blind nuns in Italy. They lost their sight doing the detail work, but what a way to go, right? Creating beauty like this? Perfect for a virgin on her wedding day."

Miles made a choking sound beside me that he tried to cover with a cough.

"Are you alright, sweet pea?" Florence asked him, her tone suggesting the correct answer was yes.

"Perfect," he wheezed. "Just overwhelmed by your... generosity."

"Oh, this is nothing! Wait until you see what I have planned for the reception. Did you know you can rent trained swans? They do a whole routine to Tchaikovsky. Of course, we'll need insurance. I heard that the last time someone tried it, one of the swans attacked the mother of the groom. Went straight for the jugular. But don't you worry—I know a man who specializes in swan training. He's a former KGB operative. Very thorough."

"Swans," I repeated, wondering if this was what a stroke felt like.

"Unless you prefer doves? Though between you and me"—she leaned in conspiratorially—"doves are overdone. Plus they have terrible aim when they do their business, if you know what I mean. But I'm sure you already know that."

Miles's hand was now gripping my waist hard enough to leave marks, though whether he was holding me up or holding himself up was unclear.

"This all sounds... elaborate," I ventured.

"Oh sweetness, nothing's too good for family!" Florence beamed. "And Miles here is family. Aren't you, sugar?"

"Of course, he is," Mikhail echoed, and there was something in his tone that made the temperature drop ten degrees.

"Oh, there's so much to plan. It's going to be a magical day, even if that day is happening in less than six months because some people can't wait to make things official."

She shot a meaningful look at Mikhail, who suddenly found the ceiling fascinating.

"Six months is very fast," I said weakly.

41

"Oh honey, when you know, you know! Why, Mikhail and I got married three weeks after we met. Of course, that was because my daddy had a shotgun and a very specific opinion about what should happen to boys who compromised his daughter's virtue, but look at us now! Twenty-seven years of wedded bliss."

"Bliss," Mikhail repeated in a tone that suggested he'd learned agreement was the key to survival.

"Perfect! Oh, Devonna, sugar, I'm so happy for you." Florence's voice turned syrup-sweet. She air-kissed both my cheeks again, leaving me in a cloud of perfume and barely suppressed rage.

"Come along, pudding," she said to Mikhail. "We have that thing with the Colombians."

"The coffee import meeting?" Mikhail asked.

"Sure, sweetheart, let's call it that." She patted his chest. "Two o'clock Sunday, Devonna. A car will pick you up."

"Can't wait," I managed through gritted teeth.

The moment they were gone, Miles dropped into my desk chair, propping his feet up on my carefully organized workspace and scattering my sticky notes.

"Well," he said, picking up my favorite pen—the one I'd stolen from a fancy hotel in Prague—and twirling it between his fingers, "that went better than expected."

"Get. Your. Feet. Off. My. Fucking. Desk."

"Come on, Vonnie. We survived Florence Dimitrov. That calls for celebration. Or at least alcohol. Lots of alcohol."

"It calls for murder. Specifically yours." I shoved his feet off my desk hard enough that he almost tipped backward. "Did you hear her? She's already got this whole thing planned!"

"Saves you the hassle."

I snatched my pen back. "Damn it, Miles! Trained swans!"

"Former KGB swan trainer. That's actually kind of impressive."

"I'm going to kill you. Then I'm going to bring you back to life just so I can kill you again."

He grinned, and damn him, it was the same crooked smile that had made me agree to a first date all those years ago. "You're beautiful when you're homicidal."

42

"Don't."

"I mean it. That little vein in your forehead is throbbing and everything."

"Miles."

"And the way you didn't stab Florence with your letter opener shows real growth—"

"We were engaged before," I blurted out, then immediately wanted to stuff the words back in my mouth.

His smile faltered. "Devonna—"

"Eight years ago. We were engaged. We had a venue, a date, everything planned. And then you left. Two days before the wedding. With nothing but a note saying 'I'm sorry' and a fucking cactus."

"The cactus was symbolic."

"The cactus died."

"Oh." He had the decency to look ashamed. "That's... less symbolic than I intended."

"You know what the really pathetic part is?" I laughed, but it came out bitter. "I kept waiting for two years. Two fucking years, Miles. Like you might just pop back up and explain everything."

"I wanted to—"

"But you didn't. And now here we are, fake engaged, real mob involvement, and I have to pretend to be happy about swan choreography while Florence plans my wedding."

"Our wedding." He stood up, and suddenly the office felt too small, like all the oxygen disappeared through a black hole.

"Fuck. If we are going to be around them, we need to practice," I said, turning away from him.

"Practice?"

"Our story. Tonight. Seven o'clock. My apartment."

"Devonna—"

"Bring Chinese food from that place on forty-second. The one with the soup dumplings."

"The ones that explode?"

"Those are the ones."

"Vonnie, I—"

"Don't." But my voice lacked conviction. "Just... bring the dumplings. And maybe some of that garlic green bean thing."

"The one that made you cry because it was so spicy?"

"I have a higher tolerance now."

"Noted." He headed for the door, then paused. "I wanted to come back."

"Well, you didn't."

"I did. I was just eight years late."

I wrapped my arms around myself. "Too fucking late."

"Hope is a hell of a drug." He left before I could respond, which was good because I had no idea what to say to that. Eight years of carefully constructed walls, and he could still knock them down with a single admission.

A text from an unknown number came in on my phone.

UNKNOWN: *Sugar pie! I forgot to mention, wear white Sunday. All the brides in the family wear white to venue tours. It's tradition! Also, I've made you a hair appointment at 10 AM. My hairdresser will fix those split ends right up! Kisses! - F*

I stared at the text. Then I did the only reasonable thing.

I stomped down the hall to Mari's office and opened her desk drawer, pulled out her emergency vodka, and took a shot straight from the bottle.

Six months until a wedding that couldn't happen. A handful of hours until I had to practice being in love with the man who broke my heart. And approximately zero chance of surviving this with my sanity intact.

But at least I'd have exploding soup dumplings.

44

SPIDER-WOMAN AND HER EX

Chapter 6: Miles

"Yes, I promise I'll be there Mar, I just have one little thing to do first." Devonna arrived at the venue, phone pressed to her ear, exasperation written all over her face. It quickly switched to contempt when her gaze found me.

I seemed to have that effect.

"I promise, Mari, your party is my priority," Devonna insisted. She sidestepped a waiter, nodding politely to him while continuing her conversation. "Yes, I'm know your wedding planning app is the next best thing since sliced bread. No, I absolutely won't be late."

I watched her as she made her way towards me, amused by the flush of irritation that made her cheeks pink. Leaning against a pillar, I winked at her and flashed a grin. Her sharp glance told me I didn't look nearly as disheveled as she would have preferred. Instead of letting the wind perfectly tousle my hair in the kind of "just-woke-up-perfect" way, she probably wished I had that "just-hit-by-a-double-decker-bus" look instead.

"I'm hanging up now. Yes, I have to go," she said in an affectionate yet firm tone. "Yes, now. Yes, okay. No. Bye, Mar."

She pocketed her phone, shaking off her coworker's lingering chatter as she strode toward me. Her expression shifted as soon as she was clear of her best friend's clutches. "How long did you stand in front of a mirror this morning?"

"Only two minutes. Impressed?" I asked, shrugging lazily. "You know what they say about the blessed ones."

"And yet, never blessed with an off switch."

"You wound me, Vonnie," I said, pushing away from the pillar and clutching a hand to my heart. "What else do you have going on today?" I gestured towards her phone.

"I don't remember the part where that was any of your business." She tucked her phone away in her purse. "Where is Florence? She was supposed to meet us here, right?"

Before I could answer, Florence appeared. "There you are, darlings!" She linked her arm through Devonna's and mine, dragging us forward. "You have to come meet Enzo Lombardi. He owns this delightful venue."

Florence led us through the grand foyer. "Enzo is an old friend of Mikhail's," she whispered. "A very dear friend, if you understand my meaning. He has connections," Florence continued, though neither of us had asked. "The kind that can make problems... disappear." She wiggled her fingers in a way that suggested something sinister. Or magic. Could've been either.

We turned a corner and entered a reception area where a short, impeccably dressed man was instructing staff this way and that. His voice held the faintest trace of an Italian accent.

"Enzo, darling!" Florence called out, immediately drawing his attention.

Enzo Lombardi turned to us, his face lighting up. He was shorter than I'd expected, barely reaching Devonna's shoulder, but he carried himself with the confidence of someone who owned not just the room, but the entire building, which, I supposed, he did.

"Florence, my treasure!" He air-kissed both her cheeks. "Always a vision. Always, always."

His gaze traveled over Devonna with appreciative interest before settling on me. His eyes narrowed as they caught on the edge of my tattoo peeking out from beneath my collar. Of course, I took offense. I spent a lot of money on the stylized phoenix, whose wing curled up toward my neck.

Enzo's smile tightened. "And this must be the happy couple!" He clasped his hands together, the numerous gold rings on his fingers catching the light. "Mikhail told me so much about you, specifically you, Mr. Houston."

"All terrible, I'm sure," I said with a grin, extending my hand.

Enzo's handshake was quick and dismissive. "Mikhail mentioned your... charm," he said in a tone that suggested Mikhail had described it as more of an affliction than an asset.

He turned to Devonna, his demeanor transforming instantly. "But you!" He grabbed Devonna's hand and kissed it like someone who'd learned romance from telenovelas. "When Mikhail told me about you, I was starstruck. I've heard of your company, but have not had the pleasure of working with Knot Your Average Wedding yet. I didn't realize you were such a vision. We'll have to work together in the future."

"I'll speak with my partners and see if we can't get you on the venue list. My friend, Mari, is actually launching her wedding planning app tonight. That's what we've been using to track our associates in this crazy business," Devonna said with a smile. It was strange, watching her slip into a persona I'd only just started to see when we broke up years ago. She did it effortlessly, and it was no surprise that the co-founders of Knot Your Average Wedding asked her to become a partner.

"She's wonderful, isn't she?" I agreed, sliding my arm around her waist. Devonna stiffened for exactly one second before melting into my side, her hip fitting against mine like it had been designed for that specific purpose. God, I loved those hips.

Enzo's smile hardened when he glanced at me. The ass. "And how did you end up with someone so..." He drew out the word while simultaneously looking at me like I was some disgusting undead thing that crawled out of a crypt.

"Unique?" Devonna suggested.

"Sure," Enzo said, clearly unconvinced. "Let's go with that."

"I'm basically a charity case she took pity on," I said, shrugging.

Florence clutched Devonna's other arm, her pink nails digging in just enough to leave marks. "Oh sugar, tell Enzo your love story! I've so wanted to hear it."

"Which version would you like?" Devonna asked, and something in her tone made my stomach flip. "The short one or the one where Miles humiliates himself repeatedly?"

"Humiliation, obviously," Enzo said, settling back against a gold-leafed pillar like he was about to watch a show.

"Well." Devonna's fingers found mine, and she interlaced them together. For some reason, that made my chest tightened. "We met about a little while ago. Well, re-met. We'd known each other years ago, but Miles had... left."

"Left?" Florence's eyebrows rose above her sunglasses—yes, she was wearing sunglasses indoors.

"Disappeared, actually," Devonna continued, her thumb stroking across my knuckles in a way that would have been soothing if it didn't feel like she was planning where to break them. "Right before our wedding. With nothing but a note and a cactus."

Enzo whistled low. "Harsh."

"The cactus was symbolic," I offered.

"The cactus died," Devonna informed them. "Which was probably also symbolic."

Florence pressed a hand to her chest. "But you took him back? After such betrayal?"

"Oh, I didn't take him back." Devonna's smile turned sharp. "He had to earn it. Tell them what happened next, honey."

This was payback. This was absolutely payback for every single thing I'd done wrong in the last eight years, being served cold with a side of public humiliation. But there was a reason we'd practiced our story over dumplings.

"I sent flowers," I said carefully.

"He sent flowers," Devonna agreed. "Every day. For six weeks. To my office. Do you know how many flowers that is?"

"Sugar, that must have been—" Florence started.

"Forty-two arrangements. I donated them to hospitals, nursing homes, anyone who would take them. The funeral home down the street started asking if someone important had died."

Enzo was trying not to laugh. Florence looked delighted. I was reconsidering my life choices.

48

"Then came the coffee," Devonna continued, clearly enjoying herself. "Every morning, he'd leave my exact order on my desk before I arrived. Oat milk cortado with half a pump of vanilla and exactly four ice cubes."

Enzo looked me up and down, his nose scrunched. "No pastries?"

"Oh, there were pastries. I could've sworn he was trying to make me fat, because there were chocolates and desserts too."

"My Vonnie has a sweet tooth." I grinned, pulling her towards me to kiss her on the cheek. I fully expected her to become a stiff board again, but she surprised me by giggling. God, she should've been an actress.

"So he stalked you?" Enzo asked, still frowning at me.

He didn't know how right he was. Maybe it hadn't been flowers and coffee and sugar overloads, but I'd kept Devonna in my peripheral vision for years, managing to stay just out of hers.

"It was definitely stalking," Devonna agreed. "But romantic stalking, which is apparently different. Then there was the mariachi band."

Well that was off script.

Had she taken improv classes since we broke up?

Maybe I didn't stalk her enough.

Apparently, Devonna was enjoying the chance to embarrass me a little too much. But the audience was gobbling up the crap she was spewing.

"No," Florence breathed, her eyes sparkling.

"Oh yes. Full mariachi band. In the middle of the grocery store. They followed me down every aisle." Devonna's fingers tightened on mine. "They played 'Sorry' by Justin Bieber. In Spanish. While wearing matching purple velvet suits."

"Purple is your favorite color," I defended.

"It is." She looked at me with fond exasperation that seemed almost real. "I had to explain to the cashier why six men were serenading us while he scanned my box of tampons."

"But it worked?" Florence asked eagerly.

"It absolutely did not work. What worked was when he showed up at my apartment in the middle of a thunderstorm, soaking wet, holding a new cactus, and said—" She paused, and for a moment, something flickered across her face. "Tell them what you said, Miles."

I knew what she wanted. The grand romantic gesture story. The perfect movie moment. But looking at her, remembering that night last week when I'd actually shown up at her door (minus the thunderstorm and cactus), what came out was: "I said I'd spent eight years becoming someone who might deserve her. And I probably still didn't. But I wanted to try anyway."

The silence stretched. Devonna stared at me, her expression blank in the most infuriating way. I wanted a reaction. Some indication that she heard me. But no. Her face was an empty wall.

"Well," Enzo cleared his throat, clearly uncomfortable. "Let's see the venue, shall we?"

He led us through room after elegant room, each more excessive than the last. Every surface that could be gold-leafed was. Every chandelier looked like it could kill someone if it fell. Florence kept up a running commentary.

"The main ballroom holds five hundred," Enzo announced, pushing open doors that belonged in a cathedral. "Though we've fit seven hundred before. Had to get creative with the seating."

Devonna had switched into full wedding planner mode, asking about catering kitchens and backup generators, her fingers occasionally tapping against her thigh. I started cataloging all her tells again, like I was desperately trying to learn the language of Devonna Onai.

"And this," Enzo said, stopping at a set of French doors, "is the crown jewel."

He pushed them opened with a flourish, revealing a stunning balcony. The view was admittedly spectacular—the world stretched out below, the city skyline catching the afternoon light.

"Oh, it's perfect!" Florence squealed, dragging Devonna to the railing. "Can't you just picture it? The ceremony right here as the sun sets? We'll release doves at the exact moment you say 'I do'!"

"Doves tend to defecate when startled," Devonna said automatically. "The acoustic trauma of applause triggers their bowels."

"Speaking from experience?" Enzo asked.

"Fifty doves. One very unfortunate grandmother. Three ruined Vera Wangs." Devonna shuttered.

I watched her as she talked, the sun turning her dark skin to gold, her hands gesturing as she explained the biomechanics of dove disasters. She was magnificent. She'd always been

50

magnificent, but somehow I'd forgotten the specific way she lit up when talking about her passions.

"Enzo, sugar," Florence said suddenly, touching his arm. "We should go talk pricing."

"Of course." Enzo nodded.

They headed inside, Florence calling over her shoulder, "You two enjoy the view! Take your time! Really... explore the space!"

The French doors closed with a decisive click. As soon as it did, the smile dropped off Devonna's face and her posture dropped to something more natural.

"God, this is awful. I could be at work being productive, or better yet, at home catching up on reality TV. But no. I have to tour a venue with a mob wife, a kiss-up venue director, and my ex. I hate you. I hope you know that."

I put my hands in my pockets and leaned back against the balcony railing. Even as frustrated as she clearly was, she was beautiful. I took a moment to appreciate her before shrugging and responding.

"You're doing wonderfully, though. They're eating up everything you say."

"We should've gone with them," Devonna muttered, walking over to try the handle on the door. It didn't budge. She tried again, harder. "You've got to be kidding me."

"What?"

"We're locked out."

"No we're not," I said, joining her at the door. "You're probably just doing it wrong. Here, let me try."

"Be my fucking guest," Devonna growled, stepping to the side and gesturing towards the door.

I jiggled the handle. Nothing. I tried harder. Still nothing. I shook the whole door as I pulled.

"Maybe you're not trying hard enough," Devonna mocked. She stood next to the railing, her arms crossed over her chest. "Or, maybe I was right, and it's locked."

"Maybe it's just stuck?" I kept trying to no avail.

"Or maybe your mob friends just locked us on a balcony." She pulled out her phone, then groaned. "No signal. Of course there's no signal. This is how people die, Miles. This is literally how people end up as cautionary tales."

"We're not going to die on a balcony."

"We're going to die of starvation on a balcony, and they'll find our bodies in three weeks, and the headline will be 'Couple Dies at Own Wedding Venue.'"

"Okay, first of all, that's a terrible headline. Second—" I looked around, spotting another balcony about six feet to our left. "We can jump to that one."

"Jump?" Her voice went up an octave. Are you serious? You can't be serious. This is a joke."

"Would you rather stay here?"

"No." She looked at the gap between balconies. "This is insane."

"Well, if you'd rather wait for Florence, by all means," I quipped, glancing at the adjacent balcony. The gap wasn't impossible, but Devonna eyed it like it led directly into a chasm.

"We can't stay here. Mari's party is in"—she looked at her phone—"oh shit, it's starting in an hour and it's all the way across the city."

"So? What's your choice?"

Devonna groaned, her attention flicking back to the balcony across from us. "You know this is textbook stupidity, right?" she asked, leaning over the railing. Her voice, usually so fierce, trembled. "Just waiting to become one of those 'Florida Man' stories."

A laugh rumbled through me. "I think we've got better odds of making it than the average Florida man."

I climbed onto the railing and wobbled as I tried to catch my balance. The concrete below seemed to shrink and stretch, and a thrill danced up my spine.

Devonna rolled her eyes but took a step closer, likely against her better judgment. "Just be careful, asshole."

"Aw, do you care about me Vonnie?"

"I will push you."

"Step one, get my balance," I remarked, wiggling my toes over the abyss. "Step two, don't fall to my death. Or yours." I winked to assure her. The sun warmed my back. "Watch and learn." I turned my focus to the other balcony, rooted my feet. "Catch you on the other side."

I launched myself, heart momentarily following Earth's gravitational pull. The landing was less graceful than I'd hoped. My knee connected with the balcony floor hard enough to tear my pants, but I was alive.

"Damn, and here I thought you might break something." Her voice floated over.

"I'm insulted!" I protested, stumbling up and brushing concrete dust from my pants. "Now, channel your inner Spider-Woman."

"This is such a bad idea." But she was already kicking off her heels, muttering something that sounded like "I should have let Mikhail kill him when I had the chance." Then, after tossing over her shoes, which I caught and put on the ground, she said louder. "I'll haunt your ass if I don't make it," she warned. Devonna climbed onto the railing with significantly more grace than I had, her dress riding up enough to scramble my higher brain functions.

Focus, Houston.

"On three?" she asked.

"On three."

"One... two..."

She jumped on two and a half. I caught her, but her momentum sent us both tumbling onto the balcony floor. We landed with her on top of me, her hands braced on my chest, her face inches from mine.

Time did that thing where it pretended to stop, giving me a perfect snapshot of Devonna above me—eyes wide, lips parted, a coil of dark hair falling across her cheek. My hand had landed on the curve of her waist, thumb brushing the underside of her ribs, and I could feel her heartbeat racing. Or maybe that was mine.

"Hi," I said, because apparently near-death experiences made me eloquent.

"Hi," she breathed back.

"Miles?"

"Yeah?"

"Your hand is on my ass."

I became very aware that my other hand had, indeed, landed on her ass. "But at least I caught you."

"Get your hand off my ass, Miles."

"It's a nice ass."

"Miles."

"Right. Hand off ass." I resisted the urge to give her a good slap on said ass before lowering my hand.

She scrambled off me, smoothing down her dress while I tried to remember how breathing worked.

"The door?" She asked, nodding towards it.

Thankfully, the door to this balcony was mercifully unlocked. We crept through what appeared to be a storage room full of wedding supplies—Devonna's eyes went wide at a wall of vintage champagne flutes—and made our way through the venue's back hallways.

"There," she whispered, pointing to a side door marked 'Emergency Exit.'

We'd made it three feet from freedom when Enzo's voice echoed behind us.

"Leaving already?"

We spun around, guilty as teenagers caught sneaking out.

"We were just—" I started.

"Looking for you and Florence." Devonna finished.

Enzo looked between us—Devonna's hair mussed, my pants torn at the knee—and burst out laughing. "Florence said you two couldn't keep your hands off each other. She'd hoped you two would take advantage of the balcony. I love it!"

Meanwhile, I was highly insulted he assumed I'd be that fast. However, it did serve as a good out.

"That's... exactly what happened," I agreed, pulling Devonna against me. "Can't help ourselves."

"Young love!" Enzo, who seemed to miraculously gotten over his dislike of me, clapped me on the shoulder hard enough to dislocate something. "But don't disappear on Florence. She'll send out a search party. With actual bloodhounds. She bought them specifically for finding people."

"I'm aware," I muttered.

"Noted," Devonna said weakly.

We endured another twenty minutes of Florence showing us some of the preparation rooms, including the bridal suite, that looked like they'd been designed by someone experiencing a fever dream.

54

Finally, mercifully, Florence had to take a "business call" that definitely wasn't about having someone's kneecaps adjusted. We said goodbye to Enzo, waved to Florence, and made our escape.

The second we were in the parking lot, Devonna whipped out her phone and checked the time, her eyes widening. "Crap, it's already five-thirty. Mari's party starts at six."

"Well, you're in luck." I fished my keys from my pocket and dangled them. "I have a car."

She eyed my vintage Mustang across the lot with skepticism. "You mean that death trap you call transportation?"

"It's a classic."

"It's a lawsuit waiting to happen. Last time I was in that thing, the seatbelt came undone when you took a turn."

"I've made improvements since then."

"Like what? Adding actual brakes?"

"Among other things." I grinned and opened the creaky passenger door with a flourish. "Your carriage awaits, m'lady. Unless you want to try to hail a taxi out here."

She looked at her phone, then the road, clearly calculating her odds of finding a taxi on the outskirts of Manhattan. Even an Uber would take too long to get here. After a heavy sigh, she slid into the passenger seat.

"If I die in this car, I'm haunting you for eternity," she said as I slipped behind the wheel. "And not in a cute Casper way. Full-on vengeful spirit. Throwing plates. Slamming doors. Writing 'Miles sucks' on fogged mirrors."

"That's twice in one day you've threatened to haunt me," I quipped, starting the engine. It roared to life with a satisfying rumble. "Does that mean you like spending time together?"

"No," she muttered, buckling her seatbelt and then tugging on it twice to make sure it was secure.

She gave me the address, and I navigated through traffic while Devonna checked her makeup in the visor mirror. Even in the harsh overhead light, she looked stunning. I'd forgotten how her profile could catch me off guard—the perfect slope of her nose, the fullness of her lips, the determined set of her jaw.

"Shit."

"What?"

"We need to stop somewhere," she said suddenly. "I can't show up to Mari's party in this. It's a formal event."

"What's wrong with what you're wearing?" I asked, genuinely confused. She looked incredible in her sleek, professional dress.

"This is business formal. I need evening formal. Mari will kill me if I show up underdressed to her big night." She scrolled through her phone. "There's a boutique on 82nd. They know me there."

"Isn't that in the opposite direction?"

"Then find somewhere closer! I'm not showing up looking like I came from a board meeting."

I made a quick left turn, earning a yelp from Devonna as she grabbed the dashboard.

"Sorry," I said, not feeling sorry at all. "I know a place. Friend of mine owns it. She'll hook us up."

"Us?" Devonna raised an eyebrow. "You're not coming."

"I'm your fiancé."

"Fake fiancé."

"Well, in that case," I said, pulling the car over to the side of the room and slowing to a stop. "You can walk."

"What the hell, Miles?"

"I want to come to the party." Yes. I did sound like a petulant child. I also didn't care.

"Why do you even want to come? You've met Mari once."

"I like free food and alcohol. I'm a simple man, Von."

"That's for sure," she growled. And after a second, where she banged her head back against the headrest multiple times, she hissed out air through her teeth. "Fine. You can come. And your suit is fine."

"It has a tear in the knee, thanks to our balcony adventure."

"Whatever, just go!"

Ten minutes later, we pulled up outside a small boutique tucked between a coffee shop and a record store. The sign read "STITCH" in elegant gold lettering.

"Wait here," I instructed, getting out of the car.

"If you think I'm letting you pick out my dress, you've lost your tiny mind," Devonna said, already unbuckling her seatbelt.

The bell chimed as we entered, and a tall woman with silver-streaked black hair looked up from behind the counter. Her face split into a wide smile when she saw me.

"Miles Houston! Where have you been hiding?"

I ignored Devonna's muttered, "in the gutter," comment as I grinned at the woman. "Hey, Whitney. Been busy. Listen, we have an emergency." I gestured to Devonna beside me. "This is Devonna. We need something formal. Party starts in—"

"Less than twenty minutes," Devonna supplied, checking her phone.

Whitney's eyes lit up at the challenge. She circled Devonna once, assessing her. "Gorgeous. We'll need something to complement that beautiful skin tone. And you, Miles?"

"Something that doesn't have a hole in the knee."

Whitney disappeared into the back room, returning moments later with an armful of dresses for Devonna and a garment bag for me. She shooed us into separate dressing rooms, and I heard Devonna gasp as the door closed behind her.

"These are couture!" she hissed through the wall. "I can't afford these."

"Don't worry about it," I called back, shrugging off my torn suit. "Whitney owes me a favor."

"What kind of favor equals thousands of dollars of designer clothing?"

"I helped her son beat a possession charge a few years back for free."

"Of course you did," she muttered, but I could hear the rustle of fabric as she tried on the dresses.

I emerged in a tuxedo that fit surprisingly well off the rack. Whitney made a few quick adjustments, pinning here and theres.

"So," Whitney said casually as she worked, "is this the famous Devonna? The one who—"

"Yes," I cut her off quickly. "That's her."

Whitney smirked, pins between her lips. "Interesting."

Before she could say more, Devonna's dressing room door opened, and I nearly swallowed my tongue.

She stood there in a deep purple gown that hugged every curve before flowing to the floor in a waterfall of silk. The neckline dipped just low enough to be interesting without crossing into inappropriate, and the back featured an intricate lattice of straps that showcased her shoulders. God, those pilates classes she'd taken had paid off.

"Well?" she asked, turning slowly.

"I—" For once in my life, words failed me.

"Perfect," Whitney declared, saving me from my sudden inability to form sentences. "Like it was made for you."

Twenty minutes later, we were back in the car, Devonna in her stunning gown and me in my new tux, Whitney's promise to return our other clothes to her dry cleaner ringing in our ears.

"I can't believe you just did that," Devonna said as we pulled away from the curb. "That dress costs more than my monthly rent."

"Consider it an engagement present."

"We're not actually engaged, Miles."

"Details." I winked at her, earning an eye roll that was almost fond. Almost.

We hit every green light on the way to the party venue, which felt like the universe finally cutting me a break. As we pulled up to the valet, Devonna turned to me, her expression serious.

"Listen to me very carefully," she said, her voice low. "Mari and Hudson don't know this is fake. No one can know this is fake."

"Got it."

"I mean it, Miles. No slipping up. No stupid jokes. No elaborate fake backstories or whatever ridiculous scenarios your brain concocts in the moment."

"I don't know why you think I'd—"

"Because I know you." She glared at me. "We stick to the simple story we agreed on. We reconnected. You apologized. I forgave you. We're taking things slow but realized life's too short. End of story."

"So no mariachi band playing Justin Bieber in Spanish?"

"I will murder you and no jury would convict me."

"Your eyes do that thing when you're making death threats," I observed. "That little flash. It's cute."

She took a deep breath, closing her eyes briefly. "Let's just go in."

The party was in full swing on the rooftop when we arrived, the venue transformed into a glittering wonderland of Edison bulbs and exposed brick.

"Remember," Devonna whispered as we made our way inside, "we're madly in love."

"That part's easy," I murmured, and she shot me a warning look that I pretended not to see.

We'd barely made it ten feet into the event when Devonna spotted Mari. Devonna's eyes lit up, and she called out excitedly, her voice cutting through the ambient party noise.

"There's my absolute queen!"

Next to Mari stood a tall, dark-haired man who had to be Hudson, her business partner and apparently soon-to-be something more, judging by his nervous energy and what Devonna had told me in the car.

"Devonna!" Mari exclaimed, accepting Devonna's enthusiastic hug.

"You made it!" Mari continued, pulling back to look at us. "And you brought..."

I watched Devonna's face, noting the slight shift in her expression as she prepared to say the words we'd rehearsed.

"Miles," she supplied, pulling me forward. "Miles Houston. My... fiancé."

I caught the nearly imperceptible hesitation before "fiancé" and wondered if anyone else noticed. Mari's eyebrows shot up immediately, so apparently she had.

"Fiancé?" she repeated, eyes wide. "That's... new. And fast."

Time to play my part. I slipped into the charming persona that had gotten me out of countless tight spots over the years.

"When you know, you know," I said smoothly, extending my hand to Hudson. As I reached out, I felt the sleeve of my jacket ride up, exposing the edge of my tattoo sleeve. Hudson's eyes flickered to it briefly before returning to my face. "Miles Houston. I've heard a lot about you, man. The app looks amazing."

I'd only heard about the app today. God, I was good, judging by the smile that popped up on Hudson's face.

"Hudson Jones," he replied, shaking my hand. His grip was firm, professional. "Nice to meet you. And congratulations on your engagement."

"Thanks." I glanced at Devonna, deciding to push her buttons just a little. The script called for affection, after all. "Don't know what I'd do without my little lady."

I felt Devonna stiffen beside me as I put my arm around her shoulder. The daggers in her eyes could have sliced through steel, but she buried them when she glanced back at Mari.

"Right," she said tightly. "Anyway, lovely party. Good to see you both."

Mari was watching us with narrowed eyes. I could practically see the wheels turning in her head, her suspicion meter cranked to maximum.

"Uh-huh," she said slowly, studying her friend, who responded with her most innocent smile. "Well, we'll definitely need to get together soon to hear all about this whirlwind romance."

"Absolutely," I agreed, unable to resist taking the opportunity to mess with Devonna a little more. I flashed what I knew was my most insincere grin. "It's quite a story. Involves a case of a jilted daughter, a minor debt, and a very angry peacock."

Hudson blinked, clearly caught off guard. "A peacock?"

"He's joking," Devonna said quickly, elbowing me in the ribs with more force than was strictly necessary. God, I'd forgotten how sharp her elbows were. "Isn't he hilarious? Always making up wild stories. Anyway, we should circulate. Congratulations again on the app launch!"

As we moved, I caught her leaning in close to Mari's ear to whisper something I couldn't hear. Whatever it was, it looked serious. Devonna dragged me away by the arm, her grip tight enough to leave marks.

"What did I just say about peacock stories?" she hissed once we were out of earshot.

"Technically you said no elaborate fake backstories. That was just a teaser."

"God, I hate you."

"So you've said." I signaled the bartender. "Champagne?"

"Fuck yes."

I ordered two glasses, then turned to face her, leaning against the bar. "You know what's funny? They actually believe we're engaged."

"That's the point, Miles."

"No, I mean they really believe it. Mari, Hudson—they see us together and think, 'Yeah, that makes sense.'"

Devonna took a long sip of her champagne. "What's your point?"

"Maybe we're more convincing than we thought."

"Or maybe they're just distracted by their own lives," she countered, nodding toward Mari and Hudson, who were now across the room, deep in conversation.

"Or maybe," I said, moving closer, "there's still something here."

Her eyes met mine, guarded but not cold. "Don't."

"Don't what?"

"Don't make this into something it's not. This is business, Miles. A transaction that we still need an out for."

"Right. Just business." I nodded, stepping back. "My mistake."

The bartender returned with our champagne, and I handed Devonna her glass. She took it without meeting my eyes.

"I should go find Anica," she said. "Stay here and try not to start any rumors about exotic birds."

"No promises."

She walked away, and I watched her go, admiring the way her dress caught the light with each step. Yeah, I missed her ass. Eight years ago, I'd walked away from her, convinced I was wrong for her.

Maybe that'd been a mistake.

WEDDING DRESS SHOPPING WITH A MOBSTER'S DAUGHTER (AND FRIENDS)

Chapter 7: Devonna

"I need the garden roses in blush, not pink. Blush. B-L-U-S-H." I enunciated each letter while simultaneously finalizing seating arrangements for a different wedding on my tablet. "If I receive one more hot pink centerpiece, I will personally come to your greenhouse and explain the color wheel with hedge clippers."

My office door cracked open, and Anica poked her head in, eyebrows raised in silent question. I held up one finger, signaling her to wait.

"Perfect. Thank you. Our assistant will confirm tomorrow." I ended the call and looked up. "What fresh disaster awaits me now?"

"No disaster," Anica said, setting a latte on my desk. "Just checking if you've seen your phone in the last twenty minutes."

I glanced at my phone, which I'd silenced during my florist battle. The screen lit up with fourteen text messages—all from Florence Dimitrov—and one particularly ominous voicemail from Mikhail.

"Shit." I grabbed the phone, scanning Florence's increasingly caps-locked messages.

The final one made my stomach drop:

FLORENCE: Dinner tonight. 7 PM. Our home. Mikhail insists. Bring your handsome fiancé. NO EXCUSES.

The last two words were followed by a string of knife emojis that seemed less like decoration and more like a forensic preview.

"What did I do to deserve this? Was I a serial killer in a previous life?" I muttered, dropping my phone like it had suddenly grown teeth.

"That bad?" Anica perched on the edge of my desk, sipping her own coffee.

"Florence and Mikhail Dimitrov are summoning Miles and me to dinner tonight." I tapped the screen. "And by 'summoning,' I mean Florence has threatened bodily harm via emoji if we don't show."

"Which ones?"

"Six knives."

"Yikes." Anica winced. "She must really want you there."

I took a desperate gulp of coffee, willing the caffeine to solve my problems. The past week had been a professional nightmare — three last-minute vendor cancellations, a bride with sixteen dress alterations, and Garrett texting to see if I was still willing to meet up. I'd had to cancel on him, and I'd felt horrible afterwards. But the last thing I needed was Dimitrov catching wind that I was still hooking up with my fuckbuddy. Add to all of that my elaborate charade with Miles, which had been limited to carefully orchestrated public appearances and terse text exchanges about our "relationship timeline," and I was one crisis away from fleeing to Tahiti.

"I can't keep living like this, Ani," I confessed, rubbing my temples where a headache was taking up permanent residence. "Planning this wedding is going to be the death of me. And if not that, Miles will be."

"Remind me why you're marrying him so quickly?" Anica asked, examining her manicure with sudden interest.

I choked on my coffee, splattering droplets across the seating chart on my desk. "I—We—He—" I sputtered, grabbing tissues to blot the damage. "We're making up for lost time and—"

"Oh, please." Anica rolled her eyes with such force I worried she'd strain something. "I've known you for seven years, Devonna. You never jump into something this important this quickly."

"I'm not jumping," I muttered, feeling my face heat. Despite Anica and Mari being my closest friends, I still had yet to tell them about the ruse.

"My point is," Anica continued, ignoring my brilliant defense, "You're moving quickly with a man who, according to what little I know, Sharpied all over your heart, and it's messing with your head."

"I just thought I'd moved on from that part of my life. Moved on from him," I said, straightening the stack of papers on my desk. "I got over him, under someone else, sideways with another someone, and upside-down with—"

"I get the picture," Anica cut in, raising a hand. "But getting over someone and moving on aren't the same thing. You must've been carrying him around like emotional baggage with a designer label—too expensive to throw away, too painful to use. And now he's back and pulling all those bags into the front of your mind."

I hated when she was right, which was approximately 97% of the time. It was her most annoying quality, right after her ability to eat an entire pizza without gaining an ounce and her perfect hair-flipping technique that made her look like a shampoo commercial instead of a drowned rat when it rained.

"It doesn't matter," I said finally. "He's back, and now we're getting married."

"And what if that's not what you want?"

Before I could formulate a suitably cutting response, my phone buzzed. It was Miles.

MILES: *Just got summoned to dinner at the Dimitrovs'. Should I wear a bulletproof vest or will a regular tie suffice? Also, how many knife emojis did YOU get? I got eight. I feel special.*

Despite everything, I smiled. Then immediately forced my face back into neutrality when I caught Anica watching me with the smug expression of someone who's just proven a point without saying a word.

"I need to get ready for tonight," I said, standing.

"Are you going to need me to call you with an emergency halfway through?" Anica asked, not moving from her perch on my desk.

"Quite possibly," I said, grabbing my purse.

"Good luck."

"Thanks, Ani." I gave her my best reassuring smile, the one I used on nervous brides and vendors who'd just been informed they needed to provide 300 champagne flutes in the next four hours.

A MOTEL ROOM. My so-called fiancé was living out of a fucking motel room.

God, how did my life come to this.

I arrived at Miles's room at 6:30 PM, having spent the afternoon selecting an outfit that said "respectable future-honorary-daughter-in-law" rather than "woman being blackmailed into fake engagement to a man who once abandoned her with only a point houseplant as a parting gift."

He opened the door before I could knock, as if he'd been waiting by the peephole. He probably had. "You're early."

"And you're not ready," I observed, taking in his half-buttoned shirt and bare feet. Damn his stupid muscles and sexy tattoos. I didn't need the reminder that beneath his infuriating exterior was an attractive man. Damn it. Damn it. Damn it.

"We need to leave in fifteen minutes to make it on time. Being late to a Dimitrov dinner is like asking to be the 'before' photo in a cement shoe demonstration."

"Relax, Vonnie. I'm almost done." He stepped back to let me in, and I tried not to notice how good he smelled — like sandalwood and citrus and memories I'd spent years suppressing. The feeling of his hands running up my legs, beneath my skirts, on my skin.

God fucking damn it. Why did I have to be ovulating?

His motel room was nothing special. I'd imagined a bachelor pad with mismatched furniture and empty beer bottles, maybe a neon beer sign and a refrigerator containing nothing but condiments and questionable leftovers. Instead, the space was surprisingly neat. Modern furniture in muddy muted tones, floor-to-ceiling bookshelves that were mostly empty, and — most shocking of all — a rather large king size bed that was actually made.

"This place is..." I struggled to find a word that would fit.

"Not a total disaster?" he supplied, disappearing into what I assumed was the bathroom. His voice floated back to me. "Try not to sound so surprised. I've evolved beyond pizza boxes as coffee tables."

"You're in a motel room, Miles."

"Temporary setback."

"Did you pick this stuff out yourself, or does your parole officer have excellent taste?" I called, examining a particularly interesting sculpture on the coffee table.

"Funny," he replied, reappearing in the doorway, now fully dressed in that charcoal suit that fit him perfectly. Damn him. "No parole officer. Most of it belongs to the motel."

"We should go," I said, looking at my watch to keep from checking him out. "Florence seems like the kind of woman to follow through with her threats."

Miles grabbed his keys and wallet. "Yeah. She does.'"

"Scary woman," I muttered.

The drive to the Dimitrovs' was surprisingly comfortable, filled with Miles briefing me on Florence and Mikhail's daughter, Irina, who would apparently be joining us for dinner.

"She graduated from Harvard Business School, currently running the legitimate side of Daddy's empire," Miles explained as he navigated through traffic. "From what I can gather, she has zero interest in the family's more colorful business ventures."

"And you didn't want to marry her why?"

Miles frowned for a moment, and then his charming mask slid back into place. "I have my reasons."

A wise little voice in my head told me not to push the issue because I had a feeling I wouldn't enjoy the answers.

"And does she hate you for refusing to marry her?"

"Not at all."

"I doubt that."

Miles shrugged. "I don't think she had any interest in marrying me either. It was mutual, but Mikhail wouldn't listen until—"

"Until you decided to drag me down with you."

"Exactly."

We pulled up to a gated mansion in the most exclusive part of town, where the houses were so far apart they had their own zip codes. A security guard checked our names against a list, then waved us through with a nod that felt vaguely threatening.

The massive front door swung open, revealing Florence in a flowing kaftan covered in what appeared to be hand-painted peacocks. The garment swirled around her as she moved, creating the impression that she was constantly surrounded by a flock of judgmental birds.

"My darlings!" she exclaimed, air-kissing both our cheeks in a cloud of perfume so expensive it probably contained actual gold flakes. "You're right on time. Mikkie appreciates punctuality almost as much as he appreciates loyalty."

"We wouldn't miss it," I said warmly, slipping into professional mode. "Thank you for inviting us."

"Oh, it wasn't my idea," Florence said, leading us through a foyer larger than my entire apartment. Her kaftan birds seemed to watch us as we walked. "My husband was quite insistent. He wants to get to know his future daughter-in-law better."

Miles shot me a nervous glance that I pretended not to see.

"Miles is practically our son," Florence explained, her hand fluttering to her heart. "Mikkie has always thought of him that way."

"Uh huh," I said, rolling my eyes when she turned away for a second. Because it was completely normal to threaten bodily harm to family members and actually intend to follow through with it.

We entered a living room the size of a small country, where Dimitrov stood at a bar cart mixing drinks. His massive frame seemed to take up half the room, his tailored suit doing little to disguise the fact that he was built like a refrigerator with arms. The kind of refrigerator that might contain bodies.

"Miss Onai!" he boomed, setting down a crystal decanter with hands that looked capable of crushing it between two fingers. "Beautiful as always. And Miles. Still alive, I see."

"Against the odds you keep throwing at me," Miles replied with a smug grin.

"Bourbon for you?"

"Neat," Miles said with a nod. "Hold the poison."

Dimitrov nodded approvingly, reaching for a bottle. The tension in the room relaxed slightly as Dimitrov handed Miles a generous pour of amber liquid. He turned to me next. "And for you, Miss Onai?"

"White wine, please," I said.

"Mama, are you terrifying Miles's fiancé already?" A voice called from the doorway.

I turned to see a lovely young woman, Irina Dimitrov I assumed, entering the room, elegant in a simple black dress and minimal jewelry. Her dark hair was pulled back in a sleek ponytail, emphasizing sharp cheekbones. She looked exactly like what she was—the Harvard-educated daughter of a billionaire with questionable business practices. Her eyes, however, held the same calculating intensity as her father's, as if she were constantly assessing threats and opportunities.

"Just making drinks," Florence replied, gliding over to kiss her daughter's cheek. "This is Miles's fiancée, Miss Devonna Onai."

Irina's gaze flicked over me with undisguised curiosity. "So you're the one he left at the altar."

"Yes," I said with a small smile.

"Right," she said slowly. "And now you're engaged again. How... romantic."

"Love works in mysterious ways," Miles said smoothly, extending his hand. "It's nice to see you again, Irina. Congratulations on the expansion into sustainable energy. Bold move. This is my fiancée, Devonna." He pushed me towards her by the small of my back.

Irina's expression shifted from skepticism to surprise as she shook my hand. "It's nice to meet you, Devonna. I've heard... interesting things."

"All good, I hope," I said, though I sincerely doubted it.

"Mostly that you were foolish enough to take this one back," she said, jerking her head toward Miles. There was something in her tone; not jealousy exactly, but perhaps relief?

Miles shifted his weight, accidentally knocking into an end table. A small crystal figurine—what appeared to be a delicate bird—wobbled precariously. He lunged to catch it, but in the process knocked over his bourbon. The amber liquid splashed across the pristine white carpet, forming a Rorschach blot that looked distressingly like a crime scene.

"I am so sorry," Miles stammered, still clutching the crystal bird. "I'll pay for the cleaning, or replacement, or—"

To my horror, Dimitrov's face darkened, his massive frame seeming to expand with displeasure. "That carpet is imported. From Belarus."

I had no idea why that made it worse, but apparently it did.

Before Dimitrov could advance on Miles, I jumped in.

"What a shame to waste such excellent bourbon," I said smoothly, stepping between Miles and potential dismemberment. "This reminds me of a wedding I worked on last month. A jealous ex-lover of the groom spilled wine on the wedding dress. I have an excellent cleaner I can call. They deal with imported fabrics all the time."

The tension dissipated slightly as Florence launched into a story about a different miraculous carpet cleaner and the increasingly concerning "accidents" it had remedied. Miles shot me a grateful look, which I pretended not to see.

"Darling," Florence announced once I'd sent a quick text to my favorite cleaner, "dinner is ready. Shall we move to the dining room?"

We followed her into a dining room dominated by a table that could have seated twenty comfortably. A chandelier that looked like it was constructed from actual diamonds hung overhead, and the walls featured what I was pretty sure were original Monets.

"We're a small group tonight," Florence explained, noting my wide-eyed stare. "Usually we have at least ten for dinner, but Mikhail wanted this to be more... personal."

The word "personal" coming from Florence while her husband stared at Miles like he was calculating how many concrete blocks would be needed to sink his body in the river made me finish the rest of my wine.

Dinner began with a soup course that looked too beautiful to eat. As the conversation circled around safe topics like weather and traffic, I noticed Miles growing increasingly nervous, especially when the two goons from the restaurant—Shane and Erik—showed up and stood near the doors. Miles kept glancing at Dimitrov, who maintained a stoic expression that revealed nothing.

"So, Devonna," Irina said as the main course arrived, "How long have you been a wedding planner."

"I started out as an assistant and just recently got promoted to partner," I replied, relieved to have something comfortable to talk about. "Anica Burkhardt and Mari Landry started Knot Your Average Wedding, and I have loved working with them, even if it can be stressful."

"Impressive firm," Florence nodded approvingly. "You've certainly done well these last eight years. Made a name for yourself and all that."

"Yes, well—"

"It's a wonder you've chosen to take Miles back, given your history." Dimitrov cut me off, his narrowed gaze on me. "Typically people prefer to leave their past in the past."

"Yes," I said honestly. "Well, I'm not the same naive girl I was eight years ago. I know what I want now, and what I don't."

"And what you want is Miles?" Florence asked, her tone making it clear she found this questionable at best.

I looked at Miles, finding his gaze already on me. Something about it froze me in place, and the words I was going to say got lodged in my throat. To my horror, something closer to the truth spilled from my lips instead.

"What I want is someone who chooses me," I said softly. "Every day."

Something flickered in Miles's expression. I chose to ignore it.

The conversation shifted to safer topics after that, but I could feel Miles's attention on me all too often.

By the time dessert was finished, the earlier tension had dissipated somewhat. Miles had managed to avoid any further catastrophes, and Mikhail seemed slightly less murderous.

"So," Irina said as coffee was served. "Have you found a dress yet?"

"Not yet," I admitted. "I haven't had time to look since this has happened all so quickly."

Florence gasped as if I'd confessed to a capital crime. "Oh no, sugar. That's just unacceptable! Tomorrow, we go shopping."

"Oh, that's not necessary—"

"I insist!" Florence declared, slamming her delicate coffee cup down with enough force to make me wonder if it was reinforced. "I'm sure you know all the best boutiques, but I know a few too. We'll make a day of it. You, me, perhaps your coworkers—what are their names again?"

"Mari and Anica," I supplied weakly.

"Yes! Perfect. And didn't your Mari just get engaged too?"

70

"How did you—"

"I like to keep track of people."

God, that sounded threatening. I shifted uncomfortably in my chair as Florence continued.

"Mari can look for her dress too. A double shopping expedition!" She clapped her hands in delight. "Mikkie, darling, call Andreas and tell him we need the entire boutique to ourselves tomorrow afternoon."

Dimitrov nodded, as if commandeering an exclusive bridal salon was a perfectly reasonable request.

"I have appointments tomorrow," I protested feebly.

"Cancel them," Florence said with a wave of her hand. "This is more important."

"I—Thank you," I said, surrendering to the inevitable. "That's very thoughtful."

Under the table, Miles squeezed my hand. In return, I dug my pointed nails into him. It was the asshole's fault. As long as I remembered that, I could at least ground myself in reality.

"*I STILL CAN'T BELIEVE YOU AGREED TO THIS,*" Mari whispered as we waited in the plush reception area of Andreas's Bridal Boutique.

"I didn't agree so much as surrender to superior firepower," I muttered, eyeing Florence as she examined a display of veils way too far out of my budget for my entirely fake wedding.

"Well, I think it's wonderful," Anica said, scrolling through her phone. "Cal sends his regards, by the way. He wants to know if you and Miles had good make up sex."

I rolled my eyes. "Tell your husband to mind his own business."

"I would, but he gives the best orgasms in exchange for gossip, so..." Anica shrugged, unrepentant.

I said wrinkled my nose at the same time Mari squealed and begged for more information.

The boutique was as cute as I'd come to expect from most bridal shops. It had soft lighting, plush seating, and champagne on ice. The air smelled of expensive perfume and even more expensive fabric, with just a hint of desperation from brides who had discovered that their "dream dress" cost more than a semester of college.

Andreas himself, a tall man with dramatic hand gestures and even more dramatic eyebrows, fluttered around Florence like an anxious butterfly.

"Ladies!" he announced, clapping his hands. "We begin with the brides-to-be!"

Mari bounced to her feet, nearly spilling her champagne in excitement. "That's me! I'm the bride! Well, one of the brides. She's the other one." Mari pointed at me and tried to drag me over. I dug in my heels.

"It's nice to meet you, Andreas," I said, holding out my hand for him to shake. His palms were sweaty.

"Oh my god, that one is so pretty," Mari said, pointing to a dress nearby. "And did you see the one on display at the front window? Ani, do you think Cal would buy my wedding dress as a present to me?"

"No."

"Come on, I promise I'll stop asking how many times a day he rails you if you would just—"

"Mari," I chided. "Go try on dresses before you give Andreas an aneurysm."

"Right!" She beamed, following Andreas to a dressing room.

Florence settled beside me on the ivory sofa, patting my knee. "You'll have your turn soon, darling. Though I must say, I'm surprised you don't seem more excited."

"I'm just tired," I lied, forcing a smile. "Work has been busy. Yesterday a bride called me fourteen times because she couldn't decide if their signature cocktail should be called 'Mint To Be' or 'Love You Berry Much.'"

"What did you tell her?" Anica asked.

"That if she called me a fifteenth time, it would be called 'Restraining Order On The Rocks.'"

Florence burst into peals of laughter. "Ah, work." She waved dismissively. "Always with the work. Life is about more than bridezillas and vendor contracts, my dear. It's about love and family and occasionally

72

having someone killed for wearing white to your wedding." She patted my knee affectionately. "I'm only joking, of course."

Before I could process that casual reference to murder, Mari emerged in the first dress—a princess ballgown with so many crystals she practically blinded us.

"Well?" she demanded, twirling. "Is it me?"

"It's certainly... sparkly," Anica offered diplomatically.

"You look like a disco ball with a train," I said, then immediately regretted my honesty. But instead of her face falling, Mari giggled.

"I do, don't I? Hudson would hate it."

"Considering how your relationship started, I wouldn't be surprised if you wore it out of spite." I gave her another once over. "I think you enjoy giving the poor man heart palpitations."

"It's my favorite hobby," Mari said with a mischievous grin, spinning around to catch the light on the crystals.

"I think what she means," Florence interjected, "is that while you look absolutely stunning, this dress perhaps doesn't capture your vibrant, sophisticated personality. It's wearing you, rather than the other way around."

Mari brightened even more, if that was possible. "You think I'm sophisticated? Fuck yeah! In your face, Ani!"

"Right." Florence cleared her throat. "Andreas, something more streamlined for our fashion-forward bride."

Andreas whisked Mari away, and Florence turned to me with a wink. "Spot on with the disco ball, sugar."

I couldn't help grinning. "Her fiancé would hate it."

"He really would," Anica agreed next to me.

"Well, if he's the right man, you could wear a garbage bag, and he'd still cry at the end of the aisle," Florence said, refilling our champagne. "And if he doesn't cry, kick him in the balls, walk back down that aisle, and try again. There will be tears."

Laughter bubbled out of me, and I clinked my glass against Florence's. "Amen to that."

Mari's appeared again, and this time she wore a sleek sheath dress that hugged her curves perfectly, with delicate beading that caught the light with every movement.

"Now that," I said sincerely, "is stunning."

"Really?" Mari turned to the mirror. She wrinkled her nose, frowning. "I don't think it fits my personality."

"Then we try again," Andreas said, gesturing for Mari to go with him. She tried on at least six more dresses before she finally chose one with a deep V-cut and intentional sections of see-through lace. The off the shoulder billowing sleeves were by far my favorite part. She looked like she belonged in a fantasy story book.

Her expression was soft with wonder. "It feels right."

"Because it is right," Florence declared. "It shows off your figure without overwhelming it."

"You look stunning," I agreed, snapping a picture on her phone for her to drool over later. "I love it."

"Absolutely beautiful." Anica beamed at Mari, and I handed both of them a tissue before the water works truly started.

"I can't believe I found it so quickly," she sniffled as Andreas made notes about alterations. "When I pictured this moment, I thought it would take weeks of searching."

"When it's right, it's right," Florence said wisely. "Just like with people."

She gave me a pointed look that I pretended not to notice.

"Your turn, Miss Onai," Andreas announced once Mari was back in her regular clothes, clutching the receipt for her dream dress.

"It's getting late. Maybe we should—" I began, but Florence was already pulling me to my feet.

"No excuses, sugar," she said firmly. "Every bride deserves her moment, even if it's her second time around."

Yeah, fuck. That's what I was avoiding. I'd already gone through this. I'd tried on the pretty dresses. I'd played princess. I'd teared up while staring at myself in the perfect dress. And I'd never gotten the chance to walk down that aisle. Worse yet, my mom wasn't here this time. She'd never get to see me wear another wedding dress.

God, grief was the worst. As the years had gone by, the moments of overwhelm and depression had lessened, but every once in a while, like right now, it would strike me. I missed my mom. I was the woman I was today because my strong, single mother had raised me. In that moment, I would've traded everything to see her again. To have her there with me. To laugh as I tried on dresses. To cry when I found the one.

The last thing I wanted to do was go through that again, especially knowing it was all fake. But Florence refused to let me leave, and I valued my kneecaps too much to refuse her.

In the dressing room, Andreas presented me with a selection of gowns he'd pre-chosen based on Florence's guidance. I stared at them, feeling suddenly overwhelmed. The fabrics were exquisite—French lace, Italian silk, delicate beading that must have taken hundreds of hours of handwork.

"Perhaps this one to start?" Andreas suggested, holding up a sophisticated A-line with a sweetheart neckline and subtle beading along the bodice.

I nodded numbly, allowing him to help me into the dress. The heavy fabric settled around me. When I looked in the mirror, my breath caught.

It was beautiful. Classic yet modern, elegant yet simple. It was exactly what I would have chosen for myself. The ivory color complemented my skin tone perfectly, and the cut accentuated the curves I was so proud of.

As Andreas fussed around me, the dress transported me back eight years, to another fitting room, another dress. My mother had been with me then, crying happy tears as I twirled in what should have been my wedding gown. We'd spent months finding it; visiting twelve boutiques before discovering "the one" at a tiny shop in Brooklyn.

I'd kept that dress for two years after Miles left, unable to bear parting with it but equally unable to look at it. It had hung in the back of my closet.

"Shall we show your friends?" Andreas asked, his voice gentle, as if sensing my emotion.

I nodded again, not trusting myself to speak.

The expressions on my friends' faces when I emerged told me everything I needed to know. Mari's hands flew to her mouth, Anica's eyes widened, and Florence looked smugly satisfied.

"Dev," Mari breathed. "You look incredible."

"Turn around," Anica instructed, making a circular motion with her finger.

I complied, the dress swishing softly around my ankles. When I completed the turn, Florence was dabbing at her eyes with a monogrammed handkerchief.

"It's perfect," she declared. "Absolutely perfect."

I looked at myself in the three-way mirror, and for a moment, I allowed myself to imagine that this was real. That I was actually planning my wedding to Miles. That he would actually be waiting for me at the end of the aisle, his eyes lighting up when he saw me in this dress. That maybe it would happen this time.

The fantasy was so vivid, so achingly desirable, that tears pricked at the corners of my eyes.

"I need a minute," I managed, gathering the skirt of the dress and retreating to the dressing room.

Once alone, I sank onto the velvet ottoman, the tears flowing freely now. This was ridiculous. I was crying over a man who had abandoned me, a dress I would never wear, and a wedding that would never happen. I was supposed to be over this. Over him.

But sitting there in a wedding dress I loved for the second time in my life, both times connected to the same man, I had to face the truth I'd been running from: I wasn't over Miles. I had never been over Miles. And pretending to be engaged to him was slowly breaking down every defense I'd built since he'd walked away eight years ago.

"Dev?" Mari's voice came through the door, followed by a soft knock. "Can we come in?"

Before I could answer, the door opened, and Mari and Anica slipped inside, closing it behind them.

"Oh, babe," Mari said, sitting beside me and wrapping an arm around my shoulders.

"I'm fine," I insisted, wiping at my tears, smearing mascara across my cheeks. "Just a momentary lapse in judgment. Probably low blood sugar. Or an allergic reaction to tulle. Or—"

"It's okay not to be fine," Anica said gently, kneeling in front of me. "But sweetheart, what's got you so upset?"

I looked at my friends, their faces full of concern, and something inside me broke. God, I needed to tell them, even if I was dreading it.

76

"The last time I tried on wedding dresses was eight years ago," I whispered. "My mom was there."

"You were engaged?" Mari asked, eyes widening.

I nodded.

"To who?" Anica asked.

"Miles."

"What the actual fuck? How did we not know this?" Mari glanced at Anica, who shook her head.

"Because I didn't tell you. I—I haven't told anyone really. I left it all behind. But then he showed up in my apartment and—" The truth spilled out of me. I explained about Miles's debt and his refusal to marry Dimitrov's daughter, and using me as his scapegoat. I explained that Florence and Dimitrov didn't know it was fake. That Miles was trying to find a way to pay back the debt for we were supposed to be married.

"I think I was just pulled back in time. With my mother. We found the perfect dress. I was so sure, so certain that Miles was the one. And then he left. With a note and a fucking cactus."

Mari's arm tightened around me. "That asshole."

"And now I'm pretending to marry him," I continued, a hollow laugh escaping me. "Trying on dresses for a wedding that will never—can never—happen. It's like the universe is playing some cosmic joke on me."

"You could call it off," Anica suggested. "Tell Mr. Dimitrov the truth. He seems to like you."

I shook my head. "I can't. Miles would be in trouble with Dimitrov."

"So?" Mari countered. "He left you. Why do you care what happens to him?"

It was the question I'd been avoiding.

"Because despite everything," Anica said softly, understanding dawning in her eyes, "you still care about him."

I didn't deny it. I couldn't.

"Oh, Dev," Mari sighed, resting her head against mine. "What are we going to do with you?"

"Help me get out of this dress," I said, attempting a smile. "And then buy me enough alcohol to forget this ever happened."

"Deal," Anica agreed, standing to undo the back of the gown. "But just so you know, if he hurts you again, Callan also has ways of making people disappear, and most of them are legal."

"And Hudson knows a guy who knows a guy," Mari added helpfully. "He's very connected for someone so adorably straight-laced."

I laughed through my tears, grateful for these women who would apparently arrange a hit on my ex if necessary. "I love you both."

"We know," they said in unison.

As I stepped out of the wedding dress, I made a silent promise to myself. I would see this fake engagement through to its conclusion. I would help Miles, because despite everything, I did still care about him more than I wanted to admit. But I would guard my heart more carefully this time.

Because falling for Miles Houston once had nearly destroyed me. Falling for him a second time, knowing it wasn't real? That would finish the job.

TAX WRITE-OFFS & OTHER TERRIBLE LIES

Chapter 8: Miles

"**S**o you're telling me," Alek said, gesturing with his whiskey glass, "that she agreed to pretend to be engaged. The incredible woman whose life you ruined. She was a fucking mess, man."

When he put it like that, it sounded like the plot of a bad movie. Or my actual life, which apparently wasn't much different.

"I know, but I don't have much of a choice," I mumbled, staring into my own drink.

"Right, right." Alek waved dismissively. "Except you could've taken the job in Dubai. Then you wouldn't be ruining her life a second time. But, no. Now it's too late, and the job is filled. Poor Devonna."

We were sitting in his sleek corner office at the law firm he worked for. Alek had made partner two years ago; the youngest in the firm's history, as he reminded anyone within earshot at least three times per conversation.

"At least it's just temporary," I said, "She's helping buy me time. Just until I can pay off the Peacock."

"And how's that going?" Alek raised an eyebrow, leaning back in his leather chair. "The paying him off part."

I sighed, rubbing my temples. "Slow. I've picked up some extra consulting work, but at this rate, I'll be free around the time the sun burns out, and Devonna will either be stuck with me and plotting my early demise, or she'll have revealed the truth to Mikhail because the idea of marrying me disgusts her and Mikhail will be plotting my early demise. Either way, I'm dead."

"You know," Alek said, swirling his whiskey like he was auditioning for a scotch commercial, "I suppose you could come work here. Christoff's been asking about you."

I nearly choked on my drink. "Christoff? As in Billy Christoff? The same William Christoff who called me, and I quote, 'a bleeding-heart waste of a Harvard education' when I turned down his offer years ago?"

"People change." Alek shrugged, his custom suit shifting perfectly with the movement. "And we just lost someone to that environmental firm in Portland. Christoff needs someone with corporate experience who can start immediately."

"I have a job," I reminded him.

"You have illegal work for a mob boss and you have a glorified clerkship at a firm that specializes in nonprofit work and lost causes," Alek corrected. "When was the last time you took a vacation? Or bought a new suit that wasn't off the rack?"

I looked down at my suit, which was perfectly acceptable despite being last season's style and showing minor wear at the cuffs. "Some of us have different priorities."

"Like fake engagements to ex-fiancées?" Alek smirked. "I still can't believe she agreed to it. What's in it for her?"

"She's doing me a favor."

"Devonna Onai doesn't strike me as the favor-doing type. Not without something in return." He leaned forward. "What the hell would she get from you? You have nothing to offer her, man."

He wasn't wrong, and it was one of the reasons I'd left her eight years ago, not that I'd told her that.

"It doesn't matter because it's not going to happen. I'll find a way to pay back the debt to get Mikhail off my ass, and Vonnie can go back to her life before I set it on fire." I rubbed the back of my neck, glancing out at the large windows.

"Aw shit. You're not falling for her again, are you?"

"Of course not," I lied, avoiding his gaze. "It's strictly business."

"Good. Because you remember what happened last time."

As if I could forget. The cactus. The note. The three months of sleeping on Alek's couch while trying to piece my life back together. The constant reminders that I'd helped her dodge a bullet, that she was better off without me, that I'd made the right call even if it felt like carving out my own heart with a rusty spoon to give her up.

"Yeah, I remember. And I know what I'm doing."

Alek gave me his patented "poor misguided Miles" look—the one that made me feel simultaneously judged and pitied. "You always think you know what you're doing. That's your problem."

Before I could respond, my phone buzzed with an incoming text from Devonna.

DEVONNA: *Need to talk. Dimitrov and Florence are suspicious for some reason. Call me.*

My stomach dropped. "I have to go."

"Let me guess," Alek drawled. "The ball and chain beckons?"

"Don't call her that," I said, more sharply than I intended.

Alek raised his hands in mock surrender. "Touchy, touchy. Just remember my offer. Christoff will want an answer by Friday."

"I'll think about it," I promised, already heading for the door.

"That's what you always say," Alek called after me. "And then you make the wrong choice."

THE STORAGE FACILITY smelled like dust and for the life of me, I could not stop sneezing. I punched in the access code, trying to ignore the way my heart hammered against my ribs. Unit 333. Third floor, end of the hall.

I hadn't been here in years, though I'd faithfully paid the monthly fee, unable to part with the contents even when I'd been down to my last twenty bucks and eating ramen for the fifth night in a row.

The key stuck in the lock for a moment before turning with a rusty screech. The metal door groaned open, revealing a small unit containing three cardboard boxes, a guitar case, and a small fireproof safe.

I knelt beside the safe, my fingers hesitating over the combination dial. The numbers came back to me easily. Devonna's birthday. I'd never bothered to change it, even after everything fell apart.

The lock clicked, and I lifted the lid. Inside lay a stack of important documents—birth certificate, passport, the deed to my grandfather's cabin in Vermont that I'd never had the heart to sell. And beneath them, a small velvet box that represented both the best and worst decision of my life.

I opened it slowly, my breath catching at the sight of the ring. It was still beautiful, a large amethyst surrounded by brilliant round cut diamonds, set in white gold. I'd had it specially made by a custom jeweler. I knew it was meant for Devonna. It wasn't traditional, wasn't what most women would want, but Devonna had never been most women.

She'd cried when I proposed. Happy tears, she'd said. She'd worn the ring for ten glorious months before I left.

She'd thrown it into the lake at Central Park the week after I left. What she didn't know was that I'd hired a guy to find it; paid him an obscene amount of money to wade through that disgusting water until he recovered it. I'd kept it all these years, initially thinking I might sell it when things got really tight, but never quite able to go through with it.

And now here it was again, about to go back on her finger for all the wrong reasons.

God, Alek was right. I couldn't put her through this. She couldn't be stuck with me. I'd only ruin her life further.

My phone buzzed. Devonna, again.

DEVONNA: *Where are you? This is important.*

I tucked the ring box into my pocket and closed the storage unit, my decision made. If Mikhail was suspicious, we needed to make our engagement look as real as possible. And nothing said "real" like the actual ring I'd originally proposed with.

I just hoped I could handle seeing it on her finger again without completely losing my mind.

And after that, I'd call Alek and tell him I'd accept Christoff's offer.

"HE WHAT?" I asked, certain I'd misheard.

Devonna paced the length of her living room, her bare feet silent against the hardwood floor. She was wearing leggings and an oversized sweater that slipped off one shoulder, her hair wrapped in a silk scarf on top of her head. She looked soft, comfortable. Nothing like the polished professional she presented to the world. This was the private Devonna, the one I'd once had exclusive rights to.

"Dimitrov hired a private investigator to watch us," she repeated, rubbing her temples. "Florence let it slip at the dress fitting yesterday. Apparently, he's still suspicious."

"So he knows we're faking it?"

"I don't think so. Not yet." She stopped pacing to face me. "But he knows something's off. Florence said he's been asking questions."

I sank onto her couch, trying to process this new complication. "This is bad."

"No shit, Sherlock." She resumed pacing. "If he finds out we're lying, you're screwed. And by extension, so am I, since I'm now complicit in this ridiculous scheme."

"I'm sorry," I said, meaning it. "I never meant to drag you into this." Running a hand through my hair, I slumped against the wall. "I didn't mean to mess up the life you've made for yourself."

She stopped again, her expression softening. "I know. But here we are anyway, so we need a plan."

"I have one," I said, reaching into my pocket. "Or at least the beginning of one."

Devonna's eyes widened as I pulled out the velvet box. "Is that—"

"Yeah," I confirmed, my mouth suddenly dry. "I thought it might help make things more convincing. If you don't want to wear it, I understand, but—"

"How the hell did you find it?" She asked, her brows scrunching together in a way that made my stomach flip. "I threw it away."

"I'm aware."

"Did you—"

"Pay someone to get it out of the lake? Yes."

"And you kept it?" she asked, her voice barely above a whisper. "All this time?"

I nodded, not trusting myself to speak.

Confusion clouded her features. "I was so angry... I stood on that bridge and chucked it as far as I could."

"I know." I twisted the box in my hands, avoiding her gaze. "I was watching."

"You... you what?"

"I saw you throw it. And then I hired a guy. His name was Dave, and he specialized in underwater recovery. Cost me two grand and probably gave him at least three different infections, but he found it."

Devonna stared at me like I'd grown a second head. "Why would you do that?"

Because I couldn't bear to lose that last piece of you. Because even though I left, I couldn't let go completely. Because I'm an idiot who ruins the best things in his life and then tries to hold on to the pieces.

"Tax write-off," I said instead, aiming for levity. "Plus, it seemed wasteful to let a perfectly good ring live at the bottom of a lake."

She didn't laugh. Instead, she sat on the couch and patted the seat beside her. "Sit."

"Woof," I said, smirking at her. But I moved closer. Close enough that I could smell her shampoo.

"Can I see it?" she asked in a soft voice.

I handed her the box, our fingers brushing in the exchange. She opened it slowly, and the small gasp she made was a well-deserved punch to my gut.

"It's exactly how I remember it," she murmured, staring at the amethyst. "I used to catch myself just staring at it, especially when the light hit it just right."

"You said it was like wearing a tiny piece of magic," I recalled, the memory surfacing.

Her gaze snapped to mine, surprise evident in her expression. "You remember that?"

"I remember everything, Vonnie," I admitted.

Watching her examine the ring, I felt that old, familiar ache in my chest. Her delicate fingers traced the band, catching the light just right, turning it into something magical. Every detail of her seemed heightened in this moment—the curve of her cheek, the soft slope of her shoulders beneath the sweater, her lashes casting shadows on her skin.

"Well," she said, closing the box. Within a second, she'd slipped effortlessly back into her composed demeanor. Her gaze met mine, a knowing smile on her lips, the wall between us back in place. "This will certainly be convincing. Dimitrov will be impressed by the authenticity."

"So you'll wear it?"

She hesitated, then nodded. "For the sake of the charade."

I took the box and removed the ring, holding it between my fingers. "May I?"

Another hesitation, longer this time, before she extended her left hand. Ignoring Alek's voice in the back of my mind, I lowered myself to the ground, propping up one knee. Images from the past danced across my mind. God, she'd been so excited when I proposed the first time. She'd had beautiful tears in her eyes.

Now she stared at me like I'd lost my goddamn mind. Maybe I had.

Taking her soft hand in mine, I slid the ring onto her finger, trying to ignore how perfectly it still fit, how right it looked against her skin.

"There," I said, my voice rougher than I intended. "Just like old times."

Her gaze met mine, and for a moment, everything else faded away—the years apart, the pain, the circumstances that had brought us back together. There was just Devonna, with my ring on her finger, looking at me like she used to. Her hand in mine. Me, kneeling before her wishing to worship her like the queen she knew damn well she was.

I didn't decide to lean towards her. My body moved of its own accord, drawn to her by some irresistible force I couldn't resist. Her breath hitched, her lips parted, and I knew with absolute certainty that if I kissed her right now, she wouldn't push me away.

Her phone rang, shattering the moment.

Devonna jerked back as if burned, fumbling for her phone on the coffee table. "It's Florence," she said, not meeting my eyes. "I should take this."

I nodded, trying to regulate my breathing as she answered the call and walked toward the kitchen, her voice deliberately casual as she greeted Mikhail's wife.

I stared at my hands, wondering what the hell I was doing. Falling for Devonna again would be the definition of insanity. And Alek was right. She deserved someone better. We were doomed the first time, and we'd be doomed now.

As I pushed myself up from the floor to sit on her couch, my phone beeped with a text from Alek.

ALEK: *Christoff wants an answer tomorrow. Don't fuck this up, Houston.*

Working with Alek and making the same amount of money he made would solve all my problems. I could pay off Dimitrov, end this charade with Devonna, and let her walk away and get back to her regularly scheduled life. She'd had everything she needed before I'd shown up. A good job, great friends, and a giant named Garrett to fuck. I'd messed things up, but I could fix things. I could pay off the debt and get Mikhail off her scent.

It was the smart choice. The responsible choice.

And it was the last thing I wanted to do because goddamnit, I wanted to marry her again.

Devonna returned from the kitchen, her expression carefully neutral. "Florence asked me to help plan the rest of the details Irina's birthday party next week."

"And?"

"Well I can't tell her no. She'll kill me."

"Don't be ridiculous." I leaned back on the couch and tried not to focus on the ring on her finger. I was like a crow, drawn to the damn sparkles. "She'd hire someone else to kill you."

"Ha. Ha. You have to go to the party too."

86

"Sounds fun," I said, though "fun" was definitely not the word I'd use for an evening of pretending to be happily engaged while actually wanting what I couldn't have.

"You're messed up."

"Well aware," I said, shrugging. "We need to keep up appearances, especially now that we know Dimitrov is suspicious."

She nodded, her gaze also dropping to the ring on her finger. She twisted it absently.

"I should probably head out," I said, standing before I did something stupid like actually ask her to marry me for real. "Early meeting tomorrow."

"Right." She walked me to the door, keeping a careful distance between us. "Thank you for the ring. It's... it helps make this more convincing."

"Anytime," I said, as if I made a habit of giving engagement rings to ex-fiancées for fake engagements every day.

At the door, I turned to face her. "Vonnie, about what almost happened —"

"Nothing almost happened," she interrupted, her tone firm despite the uncertainty in her eyes. "We got caught up in the moment. That's all."

"Right," I agreed, ignoring the hollow feeling in my chest. "Just playing our parts convincingly."

"Exactly."

We stood there awkwardly for a moment, neither quite ready to say goodbye.

"Goodnight," she finally said, her hand resting on the doorframe, the violet color catching the light just so.

"Goodnight, Vonnie."

THIRTY DAYS TO FINANCIAL RUIN OR MATRIMONIAL DISASTER

Chapter 9: Devonna

The ring weighed a ton. Objectively, I knew this was impossible. The amethyst was substantial but not ridiculous, the white gold band delicate but sturdy. Yet somehow, in the days since Miles had slipped it back onto my finger, it had gained the gravitational pull of a small planet.

I stared at it constantly. During client meetings, while brushing my teeth, as I lay in bed trying to sleep. My thumb kept finding it, spinning it in absent circles. I was annoying myself.

And now here I was, checking the centerpieces for Irina Dimitrov's birthday party, wearing the same ring Miles had originally proposed with, and fighting the simultaneous urges to throw it in another lake or never take it off again.

"Those look beautiful, sugar," Florence said, appearing at my elbow with two champagne flutes. She handed me one, her eyes immediately dropping to my left hand. "And so does that ring. I don't think I've properly admired it yet."

"Thank you," I said, accepting the champagne and willing my pulse to steady. "Miles surprised me with it. It's the ring he originally proposed with."

"Is it now?" She took my hand, examining the ring more closely. "Quite unusual. Most men would have bought something new."

"Miles isn't most men."

"No, he certainly isn't. A man who retrieves a ring from a lake is either a romantic fool or dangerously obsessed. Sometimes both."

I nearly choked on my champagne. "He told you about that?"

"No. Mikkie has ways of discovering things," she said with a delicate shrug. "And I have ways of discovering things from Mikhail."

My stomach dropped. "So you know—"

"That you threw it away in a fit of righteous anger? Of course." She patted my hand. "And that Miles paid a small fortune to recover it? Absolutely charming. Men so rarely understand the value of grand gestures these days."

Relief washed over me, though it was short-lived. If Dimitrov knew about the ring, what else had his investigation uncovered? And how did he hear about the ring? We'd spoken about it privately in my apartment. A chill traveled through me.

"The party looks wonderful," I said, eager to change the subject. "You and Irina must be thrilled."

"Irina is never thrilled about anything," Florence sighed dramatically. "Twenty-seven years old and still in her rebellious phase. Did you see what she's wearing? Black. At her own birthday celebration. Like she's attending a funeral instead of a party with two hundred of her closest friends."

I glanced across the ballroom at Irina, who did indeed look like she was plotting an assassination rather than celebrating. She stood against the far wall, elegant in a fitted black dress, nursing what appeared to be straight vodka while glaring at the guests.

"She seems... pensive," I offered.

"She's impossible," Florence countered, though her tone held more affection than annoyance. "Just like her father. Speaking of impossible men, where is your fiancé?"

"Running late," I replied, checking my phone. "Work emergency."

In reality, Miles had texted an hour ago saying he was going to be late because of something important. I'd told him to jump off a cliff while he was at it, and that I could handle the party setup solo. A large, petty part of me resented having to face the Dimitrovs alone.

"Well, he'd better arrive soon," Florence warned. "Mikhail has an announcement to make, and he expects both of you to be present."

"An announcement?" I asked, my anxiety spiking. "What kind of announcement?"

"No clue, sugar. Now, I'm going to go speak to a couple guests who are in the negative."

She drifted away, leaving me with my champagne and a growing sense of dread. What was Dimitrov planning? And why did it involve Miles and me?

I scanned the room. Crystal chandeliers dripped from the ceiling, ice sculptures glistened on marble pedestals, and enough flowers to fill a small botanical garden adorned every surface. The guests were equally impressive. Men in custom suits, women draped in jewels and designer gowns, all speaking in that particular cadence of the obscenely rich.

I felt distinctly out of place, despite my carefully selected navy cocktail dress and the little fortune sparkling on my finger.

"You look like you'd rather be anywhere else," a voice said beside me.

I turned to find Irina, who had apparently abandoned her wall to join me in my isolated corner.

"Just admiring the party. Everything turned out beautifully."

"It's grotesque," she replied, knocking back the rest of her vodka. "But that's how my parents show love; excessive displays of wealth and at least three kinds of caviar."

I laughed despite myself. "To be fair, the caviar is excellent."

"Everything my mother touches is excellent," Irina agreed. "Terrifying, but excellent." She studied me for a moment, her dark eyes calculating. "You're good at this, you know."

"At what?"

"Pretending. Looking like you belong here when we both know you'd rather be working on one of your weddings or home watching reality TV in sweatpants."

"I do love sweatpants," I said, sipping from my champagne glass.

Irina smiled, and it brightened her entire demeanor. "You seem more... genuine than most people in my parents' circle. It's refreshing."

"Thank you, I think."

She glanced at my ring, then back at my face. "You really love him, don't you?"

The question caught me off guard, and I had to remind myself of the charade. "Miles? Of course."

"Interesting," she mused.

"Oh? How so?"

"Because you two seem like such opposites. You're very clearly put together. You know who you are. You're respectable and seem like an incredible person. And Miles... Well, Miles—"

"Don't." I tensed, not sure what was about to come from my mouth before the words were already spilling out. "He's my fiancé. He's passionate and sentimental. He's funny and charming. He's respectful of women and the man is damn sexy." I lifted my chin. "He has his flaws, but we all do. And most people have hidden depths."

"They certainly do." She signaled a passing waiter for another drink. "I'm sorry. I didn't mean to insult either of you. It's just, you're not what I expected."

"What did you expect?"

"Someone vapid. Someone desperate. The kind of woman who would take back a man who abandoned her before her wedding." She accepted a fresh vodka from the waiter. "But you're nothing like that."

"That's good, I suppose. What about you?" I asked, eager to shift the focus. "Anyone special in your life?"

"No." Irina's gaze scanned the room, and she bit her bottom lip before returning her gaze to mine. "No one my father would approve of."

"That's not what I asked."

"No, it isn't." She leaned closer. "Can you keep a secret?"

"Better than most," I replied, intrigued by her shift in demeanor.

"Good. I need some air. Join me outside?"

I nodded, following her through the French doors onto a spacious terrace overlooking the city. The night air was cool, and I shivered. Irina moved to the railing. After checking over her shoulder, she turned to me.

"I never wanted to marry Miles."

I blinked, processing her words. "And? Miles already told me you weren't keen on the idea."

"Well, my father has been pressuring me to marry for years. Wants grandchildren to continue the Dimitrov legacy." She rolled her eyes. "When he pushed the last time, I saw an opportunity."

"An opportunity for what?"

"To buy time." She took a sip of her vodka, her gaze drifting to a figure standing by the entrance to the terrace. I recognized him as one of the two thugs who always followed Dimitrov around. I couldn't remember if he was Erik or Shane. He wasn't conventionally handsome, but there was something compelling about his quiet intensity. "That's Shane. One of my father's security team."

"You and he are..."

"For two years now," Irina confirmed. "My father would never approve. Shane doesn't come from money or connections. He's just a regular guy with a regular job."

"And he works for your father," I pointed out.

"Details," she said with a dismissive wave. "The point is, I knew Miles would never agree to marry me, even with the debt. He's too... squirrelly. So I convinced my father it was a good match, knowing Miles would refuse."

"You used him as a decoy," I said, annoyance flaring on Miles's behalf.

"I used the situation to my advantage," she corrected. "Miles wasn't harmed."

"He was held over the edge of a balcony by his ankles by your boyfriend until he mentioned our engagement. Not to mention the fact that he showed up in my apartment with a swollen black eye and more bruises than a professional MMA fighter."

"And yet here you are, wearing his ring." Irina raised an eyebrow. "Perhaps I did you both a favor."

I opened my mouth to argue, then closed it. What could I say? That she'd complicated my life? That I'd been perfectly fine before Miles crashed back into my existence? That I'd spent eight years building walls that were now crumbling because she'd decided to use him as a pawn in her romantic chess game?

"Does your father know?" I asked instead.

"About Shane? No. But he's growing suspicious." She drained her glass.

"I never meant for things to get this complicated. I thought Miles would pay his debt and disappear, or I'd convince my father to forgive it entirely. I didn't expect him to drag you into this."

"Well, he did."

"I know, and I'm sorry."

The apology caught me off guard. Before I could formulate a response, a commotion from inside drew our attention. Through the glass doors, I could see Miles had finally arrived, looking unfairly handsome in a tailored suit. He was scanning the room, obviously searching for me.

"Your prince has arrived," Irina observed. "Better go to him before my father does."

I nodded, moving toward the doors, but Irina caught my arm.

"Devonna," she said, her expression earnest. "I'm sorry. Truly."

"It's fine. Good luck with Shane."

"Thanks," she said releasing me.

I made my way back inside, navigating through the crowd toward Miles. He spotted me and his face lit up with a smile that made my treacherous heart skip a beat.

"Sorry I'm late," he said when I reached him, bending to kiss my cheek.

"It's fine," I assured him, though it wasn't, not really. "You're here now."

His gaze dropped to my hand, where the ring glittered under the chandelier light. "Have they seen it?"

"Florence has. Irina too."

"Good." He glanced around the room. "Quite a party. You outdid yourself."

"Florence planned most of it earlier. I just helped with some of the details," I reminded him.

"I'm sure your contributions were the best parts."

As if she'd been summoned by me saying her name, Florence appeared beside us. "Ah, there you are! Miles, sugar, so glad you could join us. Mikhail was beginning to think you'd forgotten about our little celebration."

"Wouldn't dream of it," Miles replied smoothly, slipping his arm around my waist. The casual touch sent a wave of warmth through me that I desperately tried to ignore. "Just catching up with something."

"Well, you're here now, and that's what matters." Florence beamed at us. "And look at you two, so perfectly matched. That ring is simply divine on Devonna's hand."

"Thank you," Miles said, his fingers tightening at my waist. "It belongs there."

The simple statement, delivered with such quiet conviction, made my chest ache. This was the problem with Miles. He could say things like that and sound like he meant them. Like this wasn't all an elaborate performance to save his skin.

"Mikkie is ready to make his announcement," Florence continued, oblivious to my internal turmoil. "Come, come, you need to be front and center."

She ushered us through the crowd to where Dimitrov stood by the main staircase.

"Everyone is here now," he said to Florence, his accent thicker than usual. "Let's begin."

Florence clapped her hands, and the room gradually fell silent. A waiter appeared with champagne flutes for Dimitrov and his wife, while another handed fresh glasses to Miles and me.

"Esteemed friends and family," Dimitrov began, his voice carrying easily across the room. "We gather tonight to celebrate my daughter Irina's twenty-seventh birthday. A momentous occasion that reminds me how quickly time passes, and how important it is to secure our legacies."

He raised his glass toward Irina, who had reappeared by the bar, looking distinctly uncomfortable with the attention.

"But tonight, we also celebrate another joyous occasion," Dimitrov continued. "The engagement of Miles Houston and Devonna Onai."

A murmur rippled through the crowd as heads turned in our direction. I forced a smile, leaning into Miles's side as if I couldn't bear to be separated from him.

"What the hell is this?" I whispered into Miles's ear with a wide grin on my lips.

"I don't know," he replied with the same pained smile. He pecked my cheek, and I ground my molars together.

"When Miles first told me he could not marry my Irina because his heart belonged to another, I was... intrigued." Dimitrov's smile did nothing to soften the menace in his eyes. "But seeing them together, seeing the love they share, I understand now. Some things are meant to be."

Miles's arm tightened around me.

"As you all know, I am a man who values family above all else," Dimitrov went on. "And soon, Miles and Devonna will join our extended family. But I believe in expediting happiness. Why wait when love is so clearly present?"

My stomach knotted with dread as Dimitrov raised his glass higher.

"That is why I am delighted to announce that Miles and Devonna will be married within the month!"

The room erupted in applause while I stood frozen in shock. A month? We were supposed to have at least five more months of this charade before finding a way to gracefully end it.

"Unless, of course," Dimitrov added in a quieter voice as he stepped down to embrace us both in a hug at the same time, "you choose to settle your debt in full before then. But I suspect a wedding will be more... economical."

The threat was clear. Pay up or get married for real.

Dimitrov raised his glass one final time as he stepped back. "To Miles and Devonna, and to new beginnings!"

The crowd echoed the toast, and I mechanically raised my glass, my mind racing. We were trapped. Either Miles had to produce an impossible sum of money in thirty days, or we had to get legally married. There was no third option that didn't involve one or both of us disappearing permanently.

As the guests resumed their conversations, buzzing with excitement over the unexpected announcement, Miles leaned down to whisper in my ear.

"I'll fix this," he promised, his breath warm against my skin. "I'm so sorry, Vonnie."

I turned to look at him, taking in the genuine distress in his eyes, the tension in his jaw, the way his hand trembled slightly against my waist. He hadn't planned this. He was as blindsided as I was.

"We need to talk," I said under my breath. "Privately."

He nodded, and we made our excuses to Florence before slipping away from the celebration. We found an empty sitting room down the hall, closing the door behind us.

"What the hell just happened?" I demanded once we were alone.

"Dimitrov just backed us into a corner," Miles said, loosening his tie with a frustrated tug. "He's calling our bluff."

"Because of Irina and Shane," I muttered.

Miles's head snapped up. "What?"

I quickly explained what Irina had told me on the terrace — how she'd manipulated her father into pushing Miles toward an arranged marriage, knowing he would refuse.

"That conniving little—"

"Miles, focus." I snapped before he could finish. "We need a way out of this."

"I know. And I was working on something, but it's going to take longer than a month. Goddamnit!" Miles ran a hand through his hair, disheveling it in a way that was unfairly attractive given the circumstances.

"What are we going to do?" I asked, pacing the length of the sitting room. "What were you working on?"

Miles hesitated, and something in his expression made me stop pacing.

"What?" I demanded. "What aren't you telling me?"

"I got a job offer," he admitted. "You remember Alek?"

Wrinkling my nose, I nodded. I didn't particularly like his friend, but now wasn't the time to bring that up. "Yes."

"The job offer is from Alek's firm. The pay would be enough to clear my debt to Dimitrov in a about six months, but—"

"But that's not fast enough," I finished for him. "We need the money in thirty days."

"There might be a signing bonus," he said, though he didn't sound convinced. "And I could get an advance against future earnings."

"Would that be enough?"

"Maybe. I don't know." He sank into an armchair, looking more defeated than I'd ever seen him. "I'm so sorry I got you into this mess, Vonnie."

"Stop apologizing," I said, more harshly than I intended. "It doesn't help."

"What would help?" he asked, looking up at me with those damn eyes that still made my stomach flip. "Tell me what to do, and I'll do it."

I stared the man who'd broken my heart and now held my future in his hands. The man whose ring I was wearing for the second time in my life. The man I was apparently going to have to marry in thirty days unless a financial miracle occurred.

"I need some air," I said, turning toward the door. "I can't think straight right now."

"Vonnie, wait—"

But I was already gone, hurrying down the hallway and out a side door onto a smaller, more secluded terrace than the one where I'd spoken with Irina. The cool night air hit my face, and I gulped it down, trying to steady my racing heart.

This wasn't happening. This couldn't be happening.

Here I was, facing the very future I'd once desperately wanted, and all I felt was panic. Because this wasn't real. It wasn't a choice we were making out of love.

The door behind me opened, and I knew without turning that it was Miles.

"I meant what I said," he said quietly, coming to stand beside me at the railing. "I'll fix this. You won't have to marry me."

"And if you can't fix it?" I asked, still not looking at him. "If you can't come up with the money in time?"

"Then I'll take the fall," he said simply. "I won't drag you down with me. I'll tell Dimitrov the truth. That I lied about us being engaged. That I forced you into this against your will. He likes you; he'll spare you."

"That's your plan?" I turned to face him, incredulous. "Martyrdom?"

"It's better than making you marry me," he said with a humorless laugh. "I'm pretty sure that falls under 'cruel and unusual punishment.'"

"Don't do that," I said, anger flaring. "Don't make jokes when we're talking about Dimitrov potentially having you killed."

"He won't kill me. Probably. I'm his favorite."

"Miles!"

"Would you prefer I panic? Because I'm doing that internally, trust me."

"I'd prefer...I...I don't know." I leaned my head back and closed my eyes. When I finally opened my eyes again, he was watching me.

The concern in his expression was so genuine it made my chest ache. The Miles I remembered from eight years ago would have been pacing, running his hands through his hair, making elaborate plans that were equal parts brilliant and absurd. This Miles was calmer, steadier, his focus entirely on me rather than the chaos surrounding us.

"You're shivering," he said quietly.

"What?"

"Vonnie, you're shivering."

I hadn't even noticed, but he was right. The night air had turned chilly, and my sleeveless cocktail dress offered little protection.

Before I could respond, Miles shrugged out of his suit jacket and draped it over my shoulders. The warmth of him still lingered in the fabric. It smelled woodsy and fresh like him.

"Better?" he asked.

I nodded, pulling the jacket tighter around me despite myself. "Thanks."

"It's the least I can do, considering I've completely derailed your life." He turned to look out at the city lights, his profile sharp against the night sky. "Again."

I followed his gaze, watching the distant traffic move in streams of red and white.

"We could always run away," Miles suggested, though the lightness in his tone couldn't quite mask the underlying tension. "I hear Bora Bora is nice this time of year."

"With what money?" I reminded him. "Besides, Dimitrov would find us. The man hired a private investigator to look into our past relationship. You think he wouldn't track us down if we disappeared?"

"Probably not," Miles admitted. "Though I'd look great in a straw hat and flip-flops."

Despite everything, I felt the corner of my mouth twitch. "You'd burn to a crisp on day one."

"True. I've never understood how you tan so beautifully while I turn into a lobster after two seconds in the sun."

I bit my lip, holding back words I knew I'd regret as soon as I said them. Too bad it didn't work. "We could always go through with it," I said, the words escaping before I could stop them.

Miles turned to look at me, his expression carefully neutral. "With what?"

"The wedding."

I couldn't meet his eye, instead focusing on the city skyline. "People get married for practical reasons all the time. Green cards, health insurance, tax benefits."

"Protection from the Russian mob," Miles added dryly.

"Exactly." I twisted the ring on my finger. "Between you and me, we could make it clear it's temporary. Get married, get you out of debt, get divorced once everything settles down."

"You want a temporary business arrangement?" Miles asked, his voice oddly flat.

"It would solve our immediate problem."

"No."

"No?" I frowned at him.

"No," he confirmed. "I won't do that to you, Vonnie."

"But—"

"You deserve better than a marriage of convenience to a guy who abandoned you eight years ago." Miles took a step closer, his eyes never leaving mine. "You deserve a real wedding, with a man you actually want to spend your life with. Someone who makes you happy, who deserves you."

"But your debt—"

"I'll figure this out." He reached out, hesitantly, his fingers brushing a strand of hair from my face with a gentleness that made my breath catch. "You won't have to sacrifice your future because of my mistakes."

"And if there's no other way?" I asked.

His hand dropped back to his side. "I know I've messed everything up, Vonnie. I know. But I'm trying to fix it. And I will. I promise."

Miles stood close enough that I could feel his warmth. As the moment stretched, my traitorous heart beat in tandem with the pulse that drew me nearer. My resolve wavered but held, and I stepped back just enough to regain my balance. My thoughts. My clarity.

Shit, I needed space. I couldn't fall for Miles again. No. I just... I just...

Clearing my throat, I glanced toward the terrace doors. "We should get back inside," I said in a steady voice, despite my racing mind.

"Right," Miles agreed, though he made no move to follow as I stepped toward the door. "You go ahead. I need a minute."

I paused with my hand on the doorknob, looking back at him. The moonlight caught in his hair, turning it silver at the edges, and for a moment he looked like a stranger; an older, more serious version of the man I'd once loved.

"Miles," I said, not sure what I wanted to tell him.

"Yeah?"

"Your jacket." I started to shrug it off, but he shook his head.

"Keep it. You look better in it than I do."

I pulled it tighter around me. "Thank you."

"Anytime."

WHEN YOUR LOAN SHARK BECOMES YOUR LIFE COACH

Chapter 10: Miles

My hands wouldn't stop shaking, which made checking my phone for the eighth time in two minutes tricky. The screen cast blue light across my white knuckles. Bank balance: still pathetic. Time: still ticking toward my doom. Devonna: still walking away from me in my jacket like she belonged in it, which was a problem I didn't have time to unpack.

The terrace stones were cold under my palms as I gripped the railing, trying to steady myself. One month to come up with money I didn't have, or marry the woman I'd already destroyed once. Christ, what kind of special talent did it take to fuck up this spectacularly twice in one lifetime?

I loosened my tie with jerky movements, the silk suddenly feeling like a noose. The night air should have helped, but instead of clearing my head, it just gave my panic more room to expand. My chest felt tight, like someone had wrapped steel cables around my ribs and started cranking.

The worst part? This was all my fault. Every bit of it traced back to one moment of spectacular stupidity eight years ago.

I could still see myself standing in that jewelry store, convinced I knew everything about love. Custom made, the ring had been perfect for

Devonna—beautiful setting, deep purple amethyst that sparkled like when she laughed. Nine months' salary wouldn't cover it, but I'd been young and desperate and stupid enough to think love conquered basic math.

"You need money, young man?" The elderly jeweler's accent had been thick, but his smile was kind. "My friend, he helps people like you. Good people who want to make their lady happy."

That cousin turned out to be Mikhail "The Peacock" Dimitrov, though I friend known his reputation then. Just that he offered loans to people who couldn't get them through banks. The terms seemed fair. The interest manageable.

I'd been such a fucking idiot.

What started as a simple loan for an engagement ring had snowballed into eight years of legal servitude. Mikhail liked having a lawyer in his pocket, especially one too proud to admit he was drowning. Every time I thought I'd paid off the principal, there was another favor needed, another fee attached, another reason why my debt kept growing instead of shrinking like normal people's debts.

And now Devonna was trapped because I'd been too embarrassed to tell her I'd borrowed money from a loan shark to buy her ring. Because admitting the truth would mean confessing that our entire relationship had been built on lies and borrowed cash from the start. God, I'd just wanted to give her the life she'd deserved.

Footsteps echoed behind me.

"There you are."

I spun around, my heart slamming against my ribs. Mikhail stood in the doorway, a crystal tumbler of what was probably hundred-dollar scotch in his manicured hand. Even in dim lighting, his expensive suit looked perfect, every thread in place. The man managed to look grandfatherly and terrifying simultaneously, which was probably what made him so effective at separating people from their money.

"Mikhail." I fought to keep my voice steady. "Great party."

"Yes, my Florence knows how to celebrate." He moved to the railing beside me, gazing out at the city lights like we were old friends admiring the view. "What are you doing out here?"

"Just needed some air."

"Mmm." He sipped his scotch. "You know, when I first met you eight years ago, you reminded me of myself at that age. So determined to provide for the woman you love."

My throat constricted. "Mikhail—"

"Such passion," he continued, ignoring my attempt to interrupt. "Such fire. You would do anything for her, yes? Even borrow money from a stranger to buy the perfect ring."

Heat crawled up my neck. The bastard knew exactly how deep his hooks were in me.

"That was a long time ago."

"Time has an interesting way of coming full circle," he mused, swirling his drink. "Here you are again, trying to protect the same woman. Trying to be a man worthy of her devotion."

"What's your point?"

His pale eyes fixed on mine with uncomfortable intensity. "My point is that some things are worth any price. Some people deserve any sacrifice."

I couldn't tell if that was a blessing or a death sentence. With Mikhail, it was usually both.

"The debt—"

"Will be settled." His voice carried the finality of a judge's gavel. "One way or another. But I think you already understand this."

"If there's another way—"

"There is always another way, Miles." He finished his scotch and set the empty glass on the stone railing with a soft clink. "The question is whether you have the balls to take it."

He moved toward the French doors, then paused to look back at me.

"Miss Onai, she is a strong woman. A good woman. She deserves a man who chooses her freely, not one dragged to the altar by circumstance." His mouth curved in what might have been a genuine smile. "You are a good boy, Miles. Try not to fuck this up again, yes?"

Then he was gone, leaving me alone with spiraling thoughts and the growing certainty that I was about to do exactly that. Again.

AN HOUR LATER, I stood outside Devonna's building clutching takeout containers like they might save my life. Chicken tikka masala, extra mild because she couldn't handle spice despite pretending otherwise. Garlic naan with cilantro that she claimed to hate but always devoured first. Basmati rice with saffron, the expensive kind that made her close her eyes and sigh like she was tasting sunshine.

I'd memorized her order year ago, and try as I might, I couldn't forget it along with about a hundred thousand other details. Damn, I really was pathetic.

The building's glass door was swinging shut as I approached, and I quickened my pace to catch it. That's when I saw him.

Garrett "the Hulk" emerged looking like he'd stepped off a catalog cover — hair perfectly tousled, button-down wrinkle-free, that satisfied expression men wore when they'd spent the evening exactly where they wanted to be.

My stomach dropped straight through the sidewalk.

"Miles, right?" Garrett seemed as surprised to see me as I was to see him, though he recovered faster. "You here for Dev?"

"I could ask you the same thing." The food containers felt heavy in my suddenly tense arms. My jaw ached from clenching it. "But I'm pretty sure I already know."

Here I was, trying to be a nice guy and bring my fake fiancée some comfort food after a stressful night with the Dimitrovs, and she was already relieving stress in another way. God, I was an idiot.

Understanding dawned across his features. "Oh man, no. It's not what you're thinking."

"Right." I shifted the food to one arm, reaching for the door handle before I did something stupid like drop dinner and rearrange his face. "I'm sure it's not."

"Miles, wait." Garrett caught the door before I could escape through it. "Seriously, it's not like that. She needed a security sweep."

The words cut through my jealous spiral. "What?"

"Surveillance equipment. Bugs." He held up a small device that looked like a button. "Found two of them. One in her office, one in her apartment."

If possible, my stomach dropped from where it previously lay on the sidewalk all the way down into the final ring of hell. The jealousy

I'd felt a second ago vanished and something colder and infinitely more dangerous replaced it. "Where?"

"Office one was under her desk. The apartment one was behind her clock in the living room." He pocketed the device. "Amateur stuff, but still creepy as hell. Apparently the loan shark you're paying back knew something he shouldn't have even with a private investigator, and she asked me to take a look for any listening devices. She was pretty shaken up when I found them."

Damn it. That calculating bastard had been watching her, invading her privacy, violating her space because of my debt. Because he didn't believe us. Because I'd dragged her into this mess.

My hands curled into fists around the takeout containers. "Thanks for helping her."

"Yeah, of course." Garrett studied my face with sharp eyes. "You look like you want to murder someone."

"Just processing." The understatement of the century. "Thanks again."

"No problem. I told her to call if she needs another sweep. I've got contacts who can do more thorough work."

I nodded and pushed through the door, leaving him on the sidewalk. The elevator ride felt endless, my mind churning with rage and guilt and bone-deep fear that I'd pulled her into something worse than I'd imagined.

When she opened her apartment door, stress was written across her features in tight lines around her eyes. Her makeup was gone, hair pulled into a different colorful silk scarf, wearing that oversized gray sweater that meant she was trying to comfort herself.

"Miles." Surprise flickered across her face. "What are you doing here?"

"You didn't eat at the birthday party. I brought dinner." I held up the containers, my voice rougher than intended. "Indian food. Your usual."

Her expression softened. "Oh, thanks."

"Yeah."

We stared at each other across her threshold, and I watched her decide whether to let me in or send me away. Finally, she stepped back.

"Come on, I guess. I'll get plates."

I set the food on her kitchen counter, watching as she moved to different cabinets and drawers, pulling out plates and forks like

105

we'd done this yesterday instead of nearly a decade ago.

"I ran into your fuckbuddy on his way out." Oops. Guess I couldn't hold back all the barbs threatening to fly at her.

"He wasn't here to—"

"I know. The Hulk told me about the bugs."

"Oh. Good."

"I'm sorry."

Devonna arched an eyebrow as she opened the first container. "For being an ass just now or for something else?"

"This is my fault. All of it."

"It's not—" She stopped herself, shaking her head as she portioned rice onto plates with more force than necessary. "Actually, you know what? It kind of is. Here."

She handed me a plate, and we sat across from each other at her small table, and for several minutes the only sounds were cutlery against ceramic and the soft hum of her refrigerator.

"Thank you for this," she said finally, tearing a piece of naan. "I didn't realize how hungry I was until I smelled it."

We finished eating in companionable silence, and when I stood to clear dishes, she didn't protest. It was strange, falling into the old rhythm. She rinsed, I loaded the dishwasher. She wiped counters, I stored leftovers.

Every accidental brush of fingers when passing dishes set my skin on fire. The way she had to reach around me to get the dish soap made my breath catch. When she stretched up to put glasses away, her sweater rode up just enough to show a strip of smooth brown skin that made my mouth go dry. With wet hands, readjusting my slacks would've left a giant wet spot with a neon flashing sign reading "he's hard for you."

"Do you think Garrett would be willing to give you some more security measures?" I asked, loading the last fork with hands that weren't entirely steady. "For your office and here, I mean. Not that I think you're in any physical harm, but—"

"Yeah." She handed me the damp dish towel, our fingers lingering a beat too long on the transfer. "I already asked him to. And he offered to take a look at your motel room too. Miles?"

"Yeah?"

"I don't want you to get hurt again."

106

Despite my stomach rolling around in celebratory somersaults, I flashed her my cheekiest grin. "I'm glad you care."

Devonna rolled her eyes, tugging the towel back so she could smack me with it. "I just don't want you showing up to my apartment and creeping in the dark again."

"You used to like it. Some of my fondest memories were lurking in the shadows waiting for you to find me."

"Creep."

"Yeah." I caught the towel when she tried to smack me a second time, and with a little tug, I pulled Devonna and the towel to my chest. Catching her around the waist, I grinned down at her. "Now what's your plan?"

Her hands came up to rest against my chest, and I could feel her pulse racing under my fingertips where they curved around her waist. "My plan for what?"

"Getting rid of me." I let my thumb trace a small circle just above her hip bone, gratified when her breath caught. "Because I have to warn you, I'm pretty comfortable right here."

"Are you now?" She tilted her head, studying my face with those dark eyes that had always seen straight through my bullshit. "What makes you think I want to get rid of you?"

"Your usual MO. Feed the stray, then send him on his way."

"You're not a stray." Her fingers curled into my shirt. "You're more like... a really expensive pest problem."

"Ouch." I pressed my hand flat against her lower back, thumb stroking over warm skin. "Here I thought I was being charming."

"Oh, you're being something." She shifted closer, and I could feel every soft curve pressed against me. "Question is whether it's working."

"Is it?"

"Jury's still out." But her voice had gone breathy, contradicting her words.

"What can I do to sway the verdict?" I leaned down until my mouth was close to her ear. "I'm very good at making compelling arguments."

"I remember." Her hands flattened against my chest, fingers spreading wide. "You always were persuasive."

"Was I?" My thumb found the strip of bare skin where her sweater had ridden up. "What else do you remember about me?"

"That you're insufferably cocky when you think you're winning."

"Am I winning?" I backed her up a half step until she was pressed against the counter, trapped between granite and my body, which I could've argued was also granite in that moment. Well, at least one part of me.

"Don't get ahead of yourself."

"Wouldn't dream of it." I cupped her face in my hands, thumbs stroking over her cheekbones. "Tell me, Vonnie, would you slap me if I kissed you right now?"

"Maybe." Her tongue darted out to wet her lower lip. "Are you willing to take the risk?"

"Right now?" My voice dropped to barely above a whisper. "I want to kiss you until you forget every reason this is a bad idea."

"That could take a while."

"I've got time."

She studied my face for a long moment, her dark eyes searching. "You always were trouble."

"The best kind, though."

Instead of answering, she reached up and loosened my tie, letting the silk slide through her hands. "Prove it."

"Prove what?"

"That you're the best kind of trouble." Her hands moved to the top button of my shirt, fingers working with maddening slowness.

I lifted her onto the counter in one smooth motion, stepping between her thighs. "I can't believe you've forgotten."

"Cocky ass." She wrapped her legs around my waist, pulling me closer.

"Confident," I corrected, my hands settling on her hips. "There's a difference."

"Is there?" She tugged my shirt free from my pants, her fingers finding the warm skin beneath. "Enlighten me."

"Cocky would be assuming you want me here." I traced the edge of her sweater with my thumbs. "Confident is knowing you do, but waiting for you to admit it."

"And what makes you so sure I want you here?"

I leaned down until my mouth was a breath away from hers. "The way you're looking at me like you want to eat me alive."

"Maybe I'm just hungry again."

"For what?"

Her smile was pure sin. "Guess."

Devonna grabbed me by the back of my neck and kissed me.

It wasn't gentle or tentative. It was fire and desperation and eight years of dreams I'd tried to forget. Her mouth moved against mine, her tongue sliding along my lower lip before delving deeper. I groaned into the kiss, one of my hands wrapped around her waist and dragged her closer while the other gripped the back of her neck as I tilted her head to get better access.

My head spun. My knees went weak. When she nipped at my bottom lip, I retaliated by pressing my hips more firmly against her so she could feel exactly what she was doing to me.

"Fuck," she gasped against my mouth, and I couldn't help but grin against her as I dropped my kisses to the exposed column of her neck.

"Is this what you've been imagining?" I asked, my voice husky as I dragged my mouth along her jaw.

"Among other things." She tilted her head to give me better access, and I tugged at the shoulder of her sweater, revealing her collar bone. God, she was perfect.

"What kinds of things?"

Her laugh turned into a moan when I found that sensitive spot just below her ear. She arched against me.

"Show me," I whispered.

GET ME OFF THE TAXI STRAIGHT TO FUCK TOWN

Chapter 11: Devonna

I kissed Miles Houston. My fucking dam combusted into dust and I couldn't stop the flood. His hands were everywhere. One tangled in the back of my sweater, pulling me ever closer. Pressing me against that goddamn erection of his that made me wet between my thighs. The other traveled over my body, moving just enough to keep me on edge and grinding against him. And goddamnit, he felt amazing.

When he groaned into my mouth, the sound vibrated straight through me, settling low in my belly. His tongue swept against mine. I could feel the desperate edge in the way he kissed me back, like he'd been starving for this, like I was oxygen and he'd been drowning.

"Christ, Vonnie," he breathed against my lips.

His mouth moved down my throat again, finding a spot below my ear that made me arch against him with a sound that was pure surrender. His hands slipped under my sweater, fingertips tracing fire across bare skin.

"Miles." I didn't recognize my own voice. His name came out breathless, desperate. "We shouldn't—"

"I know."

But his hands kept moving, thumbs brushing the underside of my breasts. I was both thrilled and horrified that I'd forsaken my bra when I'd changed out of my cocktail dress. On the one side, easy access. On the other, easy access. His damn wandering hands made rational thought impossible.

"Tell me to stop, Vonnie, and I will. You know I will."

I opened my mouth to do exactly that, but what came out instead was a moan when he found my pulse point with his teeth. My legs wrapped tighter around his waist, pulling him closer, and the friction made us both freeze for a heartbeat.

If I didn't have him right then and there, I was going to explode.

But if I did have him, I knew my heart would shatter again. Maybe not tonight. Maybe not tomorrow. But it would happen, and I wasn't sure if I'd be able to put the pieces back together again.

"Stop." I pressed my hands against his chest, pushing him back far enough to break the spell. "We have to stop."

He went still immediately, his hands settling on my hips without moving. "Okay. But did I…" His words trailed off, and he sighed, stepping back far enough to run a hand through his hair. "Did I do something wrong?"

My mind retorted a million different answers in less than a second. No. Yes. Of course he did. No he didn't. Damn straight. Not even a little. Everything was wrong. I was making the exact same mistake I'd made eight years ago, letting his touch and his voice and the way he said my name like a prayer from a man who could actually enter a church without being set on fire override every logical thought in my head.

"I can't do this." I slid off the counter on shaky legs, putting distance between us. "We can't do this."

"Vonnie—"

"No." I held up a hand to stop whatever he was about to say. "This is already complicated enough without adding sex to the equation."

Miles dragged both hands through his hair this time, leaving it completely disheveled. His shirt was partway unbuttoned and wrinkled where I'd grabbed it, tie hanging loose around his neck. He looked thoroughly debauched, and the sight made my pulse spike all over again.

"It was just a kiss," he said, but his voice was rough.

"That was not just a kiss. That was a taxi straight to fuck town, and we both know it." I smoothed down my sweater with hands that weren't entirely steady. "Look, thank you for dinner. For bringing my favorite order and helping with dishes and being... nice. But I think you should go."

Hurt flickered across his face. But he nodded and reached for the buttons I'd undone, fingers working to restore some semblance of order to his appearance.

"Right. Of course." He finished buttoning his shirt, tucked it back into his pants. "Wouldn't want to complicate things."

My traitorous gaze fell on his tattooed forearms, and it made me want to rip his clothes off all over again, but for a different reason. I wanted to study him; to learn what had changed about the artwork on his body since the last time I'd been naked with him. What stories were inked into his skin that I'd missed?

Instead, I silently watched him put himself back together, trying not to notice the way his hands shook. Trying not to think about how those same hands had felt touching me like they'd used to.

"Devonna," he said when he reached the door, and the use of my full name made my chest ache. Shit. Had I messed up? No. No, I'd done the right thing. "About what just happened—"

"Nothing happened. We got caught up in the moment. It won't happen again."

He studied my face for a long moment, like he was memorizing it. "If that's what you want."

"It is."

"Alright." He twisted the doorknob, then paused without turning around. "For what it's worth, I don't regret it. Not for a second. I'd never regret you."

Then he was gone, leaving me alone with the taste of him still on my lips and the scent of his cologne lingering in my kitchen. Damn him. How the hell was I supposed to sleep knowing I could've had him again?

I slumped back against the door and let out a shaky breath. What the hell was wrong with me? Why couldn't I just stay away? Why couldn't I just let him deal with his problems alone? Had I learned nothing from the first time he'd crashed through my life and left wreckage in his wake?

Apparently not, because all I wanted to do was call him back and finish what we'd started.

Which was exactly why I couldn't. I was smarter than this. Stronger than this. I'd built a good life without Miles, and I wasn't about to let a few heated kisses and the memory of his hands on my skin undo all that progress.

Even if those kisses had been the best I'd had in eight years, no offense to Garrett.

Even if I could still feel the echo of his touch burning across my skin.

Even if part of me was starting to wonder if I was being the idiot for a change.

My phone buzzed on the counter, jarring me out of my spiral. I grabbed it, half-expecting a text from Miles, but instead found messages from Mari that made me laugh despite everything.

MARI: CRISIS ALERT! My engagement party is in two nights and I'm having a fashion emergency of epic proportions. Help me before I show up in sweatpants and shame.

MARI: Also, did you know Anica and Callan have been using the office as a copulating area? I'm pretty sure they fucked on my fucking desk. I think we need to call an intervention.

MARI: ALSO also, I think I saw them coming out of your office yesterday.

I stared at the messages, grateful for the distraction. With a quick voice to text, I responded.

DEVONNA: Emergency shopping trip tomorrow. And what the actual fuck? Yes, there will be an intervention. God, I need disinfectant.

MARI: I say we just burn the desks and buy new ones. Yours isn't that sturdy anyway. Hudson and I almost broke it yesterday during your break.

DEVONNA:Never mind. I'm just going to light the building on fire. Thanks for the warning.

She sent a kissing emoji, and I sent her the middle finger.

Setting the phone down, I headed toward my bedroom, trying to ignore the voice in my head that wanted to picture Miles and me breaking my desk. Damn him. And damn my gutter-prone mind that kept replaying the way Miles had kissed me. Like I was everything he'd ever wanted. Like he'd been lost without me.

TWO NIGHTS LATER, I stood in front of my full-length mirror having what could generously be called a breakdown. I'd changed outfits four times. Four times. Like I was sixteen and getting ready for prom instead of a grown woman attending her friend's engagement party with her fake fiancé.

The black wrap dress I'd finally settled on struck the right balance between sophisticated and sexy, showing just enough cleavage to be interesting without crossing into inappropriate territory. The fabric hugged my curves in all the right places, and the way it swished when I moved made me feel feminine and confident.

Which was important, because confidence was the only thing standing between me and complete humiliation tonight.

Miles would arrive at my apartment any minute to pick me up, and I still had no idea how to act around him after what had happened in my kitchen. Should I pretend nothing had changed? Address the elephant in the room? Seduce him in the backseat of his car?

Okay, that last option was definitely off the table. Right? Yes. No. Goddamnit.

Thankfully, my buzzer rang before I could argue with my horny self longer. What had the man done to me that made me want to take Mari's advice and tap that? God, I should've slept with Garrett when I'd had the chance. Maybe then I could've gotten it out of my system, and wouldn't be putting it on Miles.

Damn it. I wanted to put it—all of it—on Miles.

I was so screwed.

I took one last look in the mirror, squared my shoulders, and went to answer the door.

Miles stood in the hallway wearing a black suit that looked like it had been tailored specifically for his body. Which it probably had. Whitney had probably helped. His hair was styled in that deliberately messy way, and when he smiled at me, my brain temporarily shut down.

"Hi," he said, his gaze traveling slowly from my face to my shoes and back up. "You look stunning."

"Thanks." I grabbed my clutch from the side table, needing something to do with my hands that didn't involve smoothing his lapels. "You don't look terrible yourself."

His mouth curved in that crooked smile that had gotten me into trouble before. "High praise coming from you."

In the elevator, I studied his reflection in the polished steel doors. There was a tension in the way he held himself, like he was bracing for impact.

"Nervous about tonight?" I asked.

"Should I be?"

"Well, Mari and Anica know this" — I gestured between both of us — "is bullshit, and so in reality, Hudson and Cal know too."

"Naturally." He nodded for me to continue.

"But nobody else knows, and there will be lots of people who know me. If we're going to sell this, we need to be convincing."

"Convincing," he repeated, like he was testing the word. "Right. Well in that case..." The elevator doors opened, and Miles placed his hand on the small of my back as we walked toward the exit. "Let me escort you to your ride."

"More like a death trap," I muttered as I glimpsed the Mustang parked next to an Audi.

"Miles," I started, then stopped. What was I supposed to say? That I'd been thinking about our kiss for two days straight? That I kept reliving the way his hands had felt on my skin? That I was terrified of how easy it would be to fall for him again?

"Yeah?" He asked, pausing next to the creaky door he opened for me.

"Nothing. We should get going."

The ride to the restaurant was quiet except for the soft jazz playing on the radio and the sound of Miles drumming his fingers against the steering wheel.

"You keep staring at my hands," he said without looking away from the road.

115

Heat flooded my cheeks. "I'm not staring."

"You're definitely staring. Should I be flattered or concerned?" He cast me a cheeky grin, one eyebrow quirked.

"You should concentrate on driving."

"For the record, I don't mind. Stare away." Miles turned back to focus on the traffic.

"I wasn't staring," I insisted, even as my gaze drifted back to his hands.

"Of course not. My mistake."

We pulled up to the restaurant, and Miles handed his keys to the valet. As we walked toward the entrance, he offered me his arm, and I took it without thinking. Big mistake. He was warm and smelled nice and made my damn ovaries spin in circles like pathetic begging dogs waiting for a treat.

"Remember," Miles whispered, bending down to speak level with my ear. We approached the door and his breath tickled the baby hairs on my neck. "We're madly in love and can barely keep our hands off each other."

"I think I can manage to look smitten for a few hours," I said, trying to ignore the way his cologne was making my head spin.

"Good. Because something tells me some of these people are the type who'd spot a fake relationship from across the room."

He wasn't wrong. Which meant I needed to get my act together and stop letting Miles's proximity turn me into a hormonal teenager.

We stepped inside the restaurant, and I immediately spotted Mari near the bar. She looked incredible in a deep pink cocktail dress that made her blonde hair shine like spun gold, and she was talking animatedly to Hudson, who was nodding along with that almost-smile I'd seen him wear around her lately.

They looked good together. Happy. Like they'd figured everything out. Lucky them.

"Devonna!" Mari spotted us and waved us over, her face lighting up. "You made it! And you brought Miles."

"Oh, god, here we go," I muttered under my breath, and I felt Miles chuckle beside me.

Mari air-kissed my cheeks with exaggerated enthusiasm, playing up the show for anyone watching while whispering, "You look gorgeous, babe. Engagement looks great on you!"

"Speak for yourself, Mar," I said, eyebrows raising as she went in for a hug with my fake fiancé.

"I'm so glad you came, Miles!" She squealed.

"Couldn't leave him home alone," I said, loud enough for nearby guests to hear. "He gets into trouble when unsupervised."

"It's true," Miles agreed, stepping back from Mari and sliding his arm around my waist. He leaned into the performance with a grin. "Last time she left me alone, I accidentally sold a kidney to a stranger on the street."

"You did not," I said, smacking him in the chest with the back of my hand.

"Nah, but a random guy sitting in an alley did ask me for one once." Miles shrugged, his thumb tracing small circles on my hip that made concentration impossible.

Hudson stepped forward, extending his hand. "It's nice to see you again, Miles. Congratulations on the engagement."

"Thank you," Miles replied, shaking Hudson's hand. "Same to you, man."

"Mari told me all about your whirlwind romance," Hudson said, his sharp eyes watching Miles carefully. "Quite the story."

Mari shot Hudson a look over her shoulder that clearly said, "Shut the hell up or you're using a sock tonight," before jumping back into hostess mode.

"Come on, let me introduce you to some people," she said, linking her free arm through mine. "There are some people here who'd love to meet Dev's mysterious fiancé."

As we moved through the crowd, I was acutely aware of Miles's hand on my back, the way he guided me through conversations with subtle touches and meaningful looks. The restaurant buzzed with the sounds of celebration—the clink of champagne glasses, bursts of laughter from various groups, the soft background music barely audible over the animated conversations.

"So what do you do, Miles?" asked a woman from one of the magazines Knot Your Average Wedding had been featured in several times. She held her pen already poised over her phone's notes app.

"I worked for a small law firm, as well as some consulting work," Miles replied. "Although I'm currently exploring new opportunities."

"Competitive field," she said, typing rapidly. "I imagine having a fiancée as accomplished as Devonna can be intimidating."

"I'm not intimidated at all. Vonnie is a fierce, capable woman and I'm just lucky she let's me worship at her feet. I couldn't be more proud of her." Miles pressed a kiss to my temple. I was fairly certain my lungs took a hiatus for at least five seconds before remember that they were, in fact, vital to my survival. Not that they cared.

Miles looked down at me with what appeared to be genuine warmth, his hand finding mine and threading our fingers together. "She's the reason I believe I can take risks. Makes me want to be better than I thought I was capable of being."

Just part of our performance. Not real. God, it felt real though. But no. He was supposed to say things like that. We were supposed to gaze at each other like we were desperately in love.

He should've been a fucking actor because he had me convinced it was all true. Damn, he was good.

"That's beautiful," the woman gushed, taking notes. "And when's the wedding?"

"A little less than a month," Miles said before I could panic. "The date got bumped up due to unforeseen circumstances."

The woman glanced down at my not-pregnant-at-all stomach and then nodding with a very incorrect knowing look. "Got it."

"No you don't," I said at the same time Miles snorted. "I'm not pregnant. The date was moved up because... because..."

"We were graciously given a chance to get married in a beautiful venue, but the dates were limited." Miles stepped in, and I could've kissed him right there in front of everyone. I didn't, but the relief that filled me at his quick thinking made me seriously consider it.

The woman asked for more details, but Miles managed to avoid them by insisting that we wanted to keep some things private. In another stroke of good luck, Mari appeared at my elbow with fresh drinks, her expression pure giddiness as she handed me a champagne flute.

"Have you seen the cake? It's huge!" she squealed. "Hudson surprised me by having it flown out from that bakery in Chicago."

"It's like he likes you or something." I bumped her with my shoulder.

"I know! It's so weird."

The next hour passed in a blur of introductions and small talk. Miles was devastating at playing the devoted fiancé; asking thoughtful questions about people's work, making them laugh with self-deprecating stories, remembering names and following up on previous conversations. He had that rare gift of making everyone feel like the most interesting person in the room while somehow making it clear that I was the center of his universe.

It was infuriating how good he was at this. How natural it seemed.

During a lull in conversation, I excused myself to the restroom, needing a moment to collect my scattered thoughts. The bathroom was blessedly empty. I was touching up my lipstick when Anica appeared in the mirror behind me.

"Dev," she said warmly, her cream dress making her look like she'd stepped out of a fashion magazine. "I was hoping to catch you alone."

I turned to face her. "You look gorgeous tonight."

"Thank you. So do you. That dress is perfect on you." She moved to the counter beside me, pretending to check her own reflection while lowering her voice. "So. How are things really going with your 'fiancé?'" She used air quotes in the mirror.

"Complicated," I said finally.

"The best things usually are." She turned to face me fully, her eyes kind but penetrating. "Want to talk about it?"

I looked toward the bathroom door, knowing Miles was out there charming everyone and being perfect and making it impossible for me to remember why getting involved with him was a bad idea.

"We kissed," I said quietly. "Two nights ago. And I can't stop thinking about it."

"That doesn't sound like a problem to me."

"It is when the man in question left you before you were supposed to get married eight years ago and is only back in your life because he owes money to a loan shark and his mobster wife." The words tumbled out in a rush. "So kissing him was stupid. Getting involved would be stupider. But I can't seem to stop myself."

Anica was quiet for a moment, her reflection thoughtful in the mirror. "That's complicated," she said finally. "But can I ask you something?"

I nodded.

"When he left you eight years ago, do you know why?"

"Because he got cold feet. Because he realized he didn't really want to marry me." It was the same explanation I'd told myself a thousand times over the years.

"Or maybe there's another reason. Have you really not asked him?"

"I—" I frowned. "No. I haven't. I don't want to have my heart broken all over again."

"That makes sense." Anica touched my arm gently. "And I'm not making excuses for him. But sometimes people run from the things that matter most because they're afraid of ruining them. Maybe you should drink some liquid courage and ask."

"It wouldn't change anything. He still left. He still broke my heart."

"No, it doesn't change the past," she agreed. "But maybe it changes how you look at the present. The question isn't whether he hurt you before. The question is whether what you have now—fake engagement aside—is real."

I stared at her reflection in the mirror. "What do you mean?"

"I mean, when I was falling for Cal, I kept telling myself all the reasons it was impossible. He was my client. He was supposed to marry someone else. We came from different worlds. But underneath all those logical objections, the feelings were real. And sometimes that's all that matters."

"And if he hurts me again?"

"Oh, he will. Men are idiots more than half the time. But would you rather he leaves your life again?" she countered. "What if you're both different people now? What if this time, it works?"

"I don't know if I'm brave enough to find out," I admitted.

"You're one of the strongest women I know. You built your dream life from nearly nothing. You took a risk moving here to help build something new. You put yourself out there every single day. That takes incredible courage."

"This is different."

"Is it?" She squeezed my hand. "Look, I can't tell you what to do. But I can tell you that when I stopped running from my feelings for Callan, everything changed. You and Mari helped me realize that when you meddled in my shit. And it wasn't because it was easy — god knows it wasn't — but because it was worth it."

I looked toward the door again, thinking about Miles waiting for me. Miles with his easy smile and gentle hands and the way he'd kissed me like I was everything he'd ever wanted. The way he remembered things from what felt like a different lifetime. The way that we still fit together like that skeleton key I used to wear; the same one tattooed over his heart.

"I'm terrified," I whispered.

"Good," Anica said with a smile. "Apathy would be a bad sign that none of this matters."

When we returned to the party, the energy had shifted into full celebration mode. Someone had proposed a toast to Mari and Hudson, and the crowd had gathered around the couple near the bar. Mari was glowing, Hudson's arm around her waist as he said something that made her laugh.

Miles found me immediately, his hand settling on the small of my back as we joined the crowd. "Everything okay?" he asked above the raucous noise.

"Fine," I said, hyperaware of his proximity, of the way other guests were watching us with knowing smiles.

"To Mari and Hudson," someone called out, raising their glass. "To new partnerships and second chances!"

The crowd echoed the toast, and I caught Mari's eye across the room. She winked at me, her expression full of mischief and affection, before turning back to Hudson with a smile that made my chest ache with longing.

As the evening wound down and we made our rounds saying goodbye, I watched every interaction between Miles and me through new eyes. The way he helped me with my coat, fingers lingering on my shoulders. How he kept his hand on my back as we walked to the car. The comfortable silence that settled between us during the drive home, punctuated only by the soft music still playing on the radio.

"Thank you," I said as he pulled up to my building. "For tonight. You were the perfect fiancé."

"Perfect *fake* fiancé, you mean."

"Yeah." I unbuckled my seatbelt but didn't move to get out of the car. "Miles?"

"Yeah?"

"About the other night—"

"You don't have to explain," he said quietly, his hands still gripping the steering wheel. "I understand why you pulled away."

"Do you?"

He turned to look at me fully, his eyes serious in the dim light from the streetlamp. "You're protecting yourself. From me, from this situation, from the possibility of getting hurt again. I get it, Vonnie. I really do. I ruined things before, and you're smart not to let me do it again."

The understanding in his voice made my throat tight. "And you're okay with that?"

"I'm okay with whatever you need to feel safe."

I stared at him, at the man who had once shattered my heart and was now offering to let me set every single boundary. The man who had spent the entire evening being everything I'd ever wanted in a partner. But it was Miles.

"Well, thank you again, Miles. Drive safe," I said, reaching for the door handle.

"Goodnight, Vonnie."

As I walked toward my building, I could feel him watching me go. And for the first time since he'd crashed back into my life, I found myself wondering what would happen if I turned around, walked back to his car, and asked him to come upstairs.

Instead, I kept walking. But as I reached the door to my building, I allowed myself one look back.

He was still there, waiting to make sure I got inside safely. When he saw me looking, he raised his hand in a small wave that made my chest ache. I waved back, then disappeared into the lobby, leaving him sitting alone in his car.

THE WORST PEP TALK EVER, COUPLES THERAPY, & HANGING ON BY A THREAD

Chapter 12: Miles

My phone buzzed with Alek's third call in two days as I sat in my car outside Christoff's office, staring at the second hand briefcase with the weeks work of work I'd managed to fit into a fourteen hour work day. I was fucking exhausted. The legitimate job offer was supposed to save me. Too little money, too late to matter.

"You've been avoiding me," Alek said when I finally answered.

"I've been fucking busy." I rubbed my temples, where a headache had taken up permanent residence. "What do you want?"

"A drink. The usual place."

"Alek I've been working since —"

"I don't give a fuck. Be there."

Twenty minutes later, I walked into the bar Alek favored, spotting him immediately at his usual corner table. He looked impeccable as always, scrolling through his phone and nursing a whiskey.

"You look like shit," he said by way of greeting, not bothering to look up from his screen.

"Thanks asshole. You always know exactly what to say to boost a guy's confidence."

"Someone has to keep you grounded." Alek finally set his phone aside, studying my face. "You're spiraling. I can tell."

I slumped into the chair across from him, already regretting this meeting. "I'm not spiraling. I'm just tired."

"Right. And I'm sure it has nothing to do with your ex-fiancée." He signaled a bartender with the kind of imperious wave that made me want to apologize on his behalf. "How's that working out for you?"

"It's fine."

"Fine." Alek repeated the word like it tasted bad. "You're fake-engaged to the woman you're still clearly hung up on, and it's just fine. That's either the biggest lie you've ever told me, or you're even more sexually frustrated than I thought."

The server appeared before I could respond, and I ordered a beer I didn't want while trying to figure out how much to tell him. Alek had always been brutally honest about my shortcomings. It was one of the things I valued about our friendship, even when it stung.

"She kissed me," I admitted once the server left.

Alek's eyebrows shot up with genuine interest. "Now we're getting somewhere. When?"

"About a week ago. After I brought her dinner." I traced patterns on the sticky table with my finger, avoiding his gaze. "It was... intense."

"Did you fuck?"

"Really man?"

"Well?"

"She pulled away. Said it was too complicated." I finally looked at him. "She's right. This whole situation is fucked up enough without adding sex to the equation."

"God, you're pathetic." Alek shook his head like I was a particularly slow student. "Do you hear yourself? You have a second chance with the woman you never got over, and you're worried about complications? Just get on top of her so you can get over her."

"It's not that simple."

"It never is with you. You always have to overcomplicate everything, turn it into some grand tragedy instead of just taking what's offered." He leaned forward. "You're doing that thing again."

"What thing?"

"That self-sabotage thing. The same pattern you had in law school when you talked yourself out of every good opportunity that came your way."

I wanted to argue, but he had a point. I'd always been my own worst enemy when it came to good things. Maybe that was exactly what I was doing with Devonna.

"If you really want an out, I could see if there's another job like that one in Dubai."

The server interrupted, bringing me my beer. I thanked her and returned my focus to Alek. "I don't want to run away."

"It's not running away. Tell Dimitrov you're going off to get the money for the debt and—"

"Leave Vonnie here to be antagonized by him? Hell no. I'm not leaving her until the debt is paid off, and she's not in his radar anymore."

Alek sat back and downed the rest of his whiskey with a hiss. "If you want my two sense—"

"I don't."

"Then you should fuck your ex, then peace out and take the job, Miles."

"I told you, I'm not leaving her. I don't want to hurt her again."

"Whatever man. You're sucky life, your choice." He checked his expensive watch. "Look, I have to run. I have two women waiting up for me in the penthouse. You could join if you want."

"I'll pass." I glared at the beer in my hand.

"Fine, but think about what I said."

He stood and dropped money on the table—more than necessary, like always—then paused.

"And Miles? That self-deprecating thing you do? It's not as charming as you think it is. Women don't actually want to fix broken men. They want men who have their shit together." He clapped me on the shoulder with enough force to sting. "Get your shit together."

DR. ANALISE ROTHERSBERG had the kind of office designed to make people feel safe enough to spill their deepest secrets. It was covered from floor to ceiling in soft earth tones, strategically placed tissue boxes, and classical music playing just loud enough to mask awkward silences. The couch was exactly the right distance from her chair, close enough to feel intimate but far enough to maintain professional boundaries.

It was exactly the kind of place Mikhail would choose for his psychological warfare. And maybe his own therapy sessions he took to get through his marriage with Florence.

"So," Dr. Rothersberg said, consulting her notes, "Mikhail tells me you're planning to marry in less than three weeks, but there are some unresolved issues from your past relationship that might benefit from professional guidance."

Devonna sat on the opposite end of the couch like she was ready to bolt, her purse clutched in her lap like a shield. She'd been quiet during the drive over, staring out the window clearly thinking too hard about something.

"That's one way to put it," she said, her voice carefully neutral.

"I'd like to understand the timeline. You were engaged eight years ago, correct? Can you tell me what happened?"

I felt Devonna's gaze boring into the side of my head, but I couldn't bring myself to look at her. The leather couch suddenly felt like a witness stand.

"Miles left," Devonna said with devastating simplicity. "Two days before our wedding. No explanation, no discussion. Just a short note and a half dead cactus."

"I see. And Miles, what would you say happened?"

This was the moment I'd been dreading and rehearsing for eight years. I'd practiced a dozen different versions of this conversation, but sitting here with both of them staring at me, the carefully crafted explanations felt inadequate.

"I got cold feet," I lied, shrugging.

"Did you?" Dr. Rothersberg asked, pen hovering over her notepad. "Or was there something else?"

I could feel Devonna watching me, could sense her barely contained anger radiating across the few feet of cushion separating us.

"Well, there were financial complications," I said finally, running a hand through my hair.

"What kind of complications?"

I glanced at Devonna, whose knuckles had gone white where she gripped her purse. Her jaw was set in a stubborn line.

"I owed money to…some people. Dangerous people." The words came out hoarse, like I was confessing to murder. "They came to collect, and I realized I couldn't drag Devonna into that mess."

"So you made the decision for both of you."

"Yes."

"Without discussing it with her."

"Yeah."

Dr. Rothersberg made a careful note, her expression giving nothing away. "Devonna, how does it feel to hear this?"

"Like bullshit," Devonna said, her voice flat and cold. "He had no right to make that choice for me."

The venom in her tone made me flinch. "She's right," I said, forcing myself to meet her eyes for the first time since we'd sat down. The anger there was preferable to the hurt I'd expected, but not by much. "I handled it wrong. I was scared and stupid and I took the coward's way out."

"What were you scared of, Miles?"

"I…" I choked on the words, the anxiety I'd felt all those years ago slithering its way back into the forefront of my mind. God, I'd been terrified then too. "I was scared they'd hurt her. Scared I'd drag her down with me. Scared she'd…scared she'd look at me the way she's looking at me now." I swallowed hard, my mouth dry as sand. "She deserved better than a guy who had to borrow money from loan sharks to buy her engagement ring."

Devonna went very still beside me. "You borrowed money for my ring?"

"From…a loan shark." I didn't mention Mikhail's name since Dr. Rothersberg knew him, and I wasn't sure how well she knew him. Mikhail didn't exactly appreciate people spreading the word of what he did in his free time. "That's how this whole nightmare started." The confession felt like pulling teeth, but once I started, I couldn't stop. "I wanted it to be perfect for you. I'd seen pictures on your phone, knew it was exactly what you wanted. But I was making shit money at my firm, and the ring cost more than I made in half a year."

"So you went to a loan shark," Dr. Rothersberg clarified.

"I was twenty-three and stupid and convinced that love conquered basic financial planning." I laughed bitterly at my own naivety.

"And when they came to collect?" Dr. Rothersberg asked, an eyebrow raised.

"They made it clear Devonna was part of the equation. That if I couldn't pay, they'd find other ways to get their money back." I could still remember that conversation, the casual way they'd mentioned knowing where Devonna worked, what time she left the office. "Ways that involved the people I cared about."

Devonna was quiet for a long moment, processing. When she finally spoke, her voice was razor-sharp. "So you decided to protect me by destroying me instead."

"It wasn't supposed to destroy you."

"What did you think would happen, Miles? Did you think I'd just shrug and move on? That our relationship meant so little to me that I'd be fine with you disappearing two days before our wedding? God, I loved you. And you fucking left!"

"I thought..." I ran both hands through my hair, feeling like I was drowning. "I thought you'd be better off without me."

"That wasn't your damn choice to make!"

The outburst surprised all of us, including Devonna. Her chest was heaving, her carefully maintained composure finally cracking.

"I'm sorry," she said to Dr. Rothersberg, pressing her palms against her thighs. "I didn't mean to —"

"It's perfectly natural to feel angry," Dr. Rothersberg said gently. "Miles made a unilateral decision that profoundly affected both of your lives. That represents a significant betrayal of trust."

"I know that," I said desperately. "I've known it for eight years. But look at her life now, look at what she's accomplished. She's successful, independent, stronger than she ever would have been with me holding her back."

"That's not the point!" Devonna snapped. "You don't get to decide what's best for me. You don't get to play god with my life and then congratulate yourself on the results."

"I'm not congratulating myself. I'm trying to explain—"

"You're trying to justify it. There's a difference."

Dr. Rothersberg intervened before the argument could spiral further out of control. "I think we've uncovered some important ground today," she said, making more notes. "It's clear there are deep feelings on both sides—both loving and painful. I'd recommend continuing these sessions to work through—"

"That won't be possible," Devonna said, already reaching for her purse. "Thank you for your time, Dr. Rothersberg, but I think we've said everything that needs to be said."

She was out the door before I could form a response, leaving me sitting in the therapist's office feeling like I'd been hit by a truck.

"Should I go after her?" I asked.

"Give her some space to process," Dr. Rothersberg advised. "This was clearly difficult for both of you. And thank you for your honesty today, Mr. Houston. You made progress, even if it doesn't feel like it."

"It feels like progress in the opposite direction," I muttered as I stood up from the couch. "Would've been easier to leave the lid on this damn can of shit-eating worms."

"Often times, we need to reopen wounds to get out the shards of glass hidden below the surface. It's painful, but it keeps infections from festering. It's a step towards healing. You did well."

"Thanks, Doc." I shook her hand when she stood. "I'll see if I can talk Vonnie into another session or two. Do I pay now or—"

"Mr. Dimitrov covered the cost. Said you two needed it. I have to agree."

Lovely. My loan shark was paying for my therapy. I wondered if that added to the total cost I owed him. I decided it should probably ask.

When I walked outside, Devonna was standing by my car with her arms crossed and murder in her eyes.

"We're getting food," she said without preamble. "And then we're going to my place to finish this conversation."

THE DRIVE TO pick up Thai food was silent except for Devonna's clipped directions and the sound of my heart hammering against my ribs. She sat rigid in the passenger seat, staring out the window like she was memorizing every building we passed for some future interrogation.

When we got back to her apartment, I barely had time to set the food on her kitchen counter before she rounded on me with eight years of accumulated fury.

"Eight years," she said, her voice shaking. "Eight years I've wondered what I did wrong. What I could have done differently. Whether I was too needy or not supportive enough or if there was something fundamentally unlovable about me that made you run."

"Vonnie—"

"Don't." She held up a hand like a traffic cop, her dark eyes blazing. "I'm talking. For eight years, I blamed myself for not being enough. For not seeing the signs. For being stupid enough to believe someone could actually love me that much."

This was exactly what I'd been trying to avoid; this moment where she looked at me and catalogued all the ways I'd failed her.

"You were enough. You were everything. That's why I had to leave."

"That's the biggest load of bullshit I've ever heard." She started pacing, pausing midway to toss off her high heels, which clattered against the floor. "You left because you were a coward. Because when things got complicated, you decided it was easier to run than fight."

"Did you not hear me? I was trying to protect you!"

"From what? Dimitrov? He fucking loves me. Did back then too. So if not him, were you protecting me from having a choice? From being treated like an adult who could make her own decisions?"

"From me!" The words exploded out of me louder than I'd intended. "From my mess, my mistakes, my complete inability to take care of the woman I loved without fucking everything up!"

"So you decided to take care of me by breaking my heart instead. God, you fucking idiot!" She was struggling not to cry.

"I thought you'd move on," I said weakly. "Find someone better. Someone who deserved you."

"Move on." She laughed, but there was no humor in it, just raw hurt that made my chest ache. "You want to know what happened after you left?"

I nodded, even though I knew.

"I spent a month in bed. Couldn't eat, couldn't sleep, couldn't function. My mother had to drag me to therapy because I was having panic attacks every time I left the apartment. And then she got sick, then she died. And you... You weren't there. I was alone. Fucking alone." Her voice broke slightly on the last word. "I thought it was my fault. That I'd driven you away somehow."

"Jesus, Vonnie. I'm so sorry."

"Sorry doesn't fix all those years of therapy bills. Sorry doesn't undo the damage you did to my ability to trust anyone." She stopped pacing and faced me fully, her expression raw with pain. "Sorry doesn't give me back the life I could have had if you'd just talked to me instead of making decisions for both of us."

She was right. She was absolutely right, and there was nothing I could say that would make any of this better.

"You want to know the worst part?" she continued, her voice dropping to barely above a whisper. "The worst part is that I still fucking love you. After everything you put me through, after eight years of trying to forget you existed, you showed up in my damn apartment and my first thought was 'shit, he finally came back to me.' It's fucking stupid. I'm still a big enough idiot to be in love with a man who thinks so little of me that he couldn't trust me with the truth."

She loved me. Present tense. Despite everything I'd done, despite all the pain I'd caused, she still loved me.

"I don't think little of you," I said, taking a step toward her. "I think the world of you. I always have."

"Don't." She backed away, but I could see the tears she was trying not to cry. "You don't get to comfort me. Not after this."

"Then tell me what I can do. Tell me how to fix this."

"You can't!" The words came out as a sob that tore something loose in my chest. "Don't you get it? There's no fixing this. You broke something in me that can't be repaired."

"That's not true."

"Isn't it? Look at my life, Miles. Really look at it. I haven't had a serious relationship since you. I can't trust any man enough to let them get close. I built my entire existence around being

131

independent because you taught me that the people I love will leave when things get hard."

"You've dated. Garrett—"

"Garrett is a fuckbuddy. Garrett is safe because he doesn't care. We're friends who fuck around because we both want no attachments and to still orgasm." Her voice was steadier now, like she was explaining something obvious to a child. "He's nice and uncomplicated, but he's not you. He was never meant to replace you. None of the men I've fucked have been."

"I didn't mean to cripple your love life. I never meant to hurt you. I just wanted to keep you safe."

"You decided my feelings didn't matter enough to consider."

"I—I'm sorry."

We stood there staring at each other across her living room, the takeout containers growing cold on the counter.

"I would have stayed," she said quietly, her voice raw from shouting. "If you'd told me the truth, if you'd trusted me enough to let me choose, I would have stayed and faced whatever came next. We could have figured it out."

"I know that now." I put my hands in my pockets and slumped back against the counter. "What do you want from me, Vonnie? What can I do to make this better? To fix this?" I watched her struggle with an answer.

"I want you to stop making choices for me," she said finally. "I want you to trust me enough to let me decide what I can handle."

"Okay."

"I want you to stop treating me like I'm made of glass."

"Okay."

"And I want..." She took a shaky breath, her hands clenched into fists at her sides. "Damn it. I want you to stop running. I want you to stay and fight for this, even when it gets hard." A war of emotions played out on her face; anger and love and fear all fighting for dominance.

"I'm not going anywhere," I said, meaning it more than I'd ever meant anything. "Not unless you tell me to go."

She studied my face like she was looking for cracks in my resolve. Whatever she saw there must have satisfied her, because she took a step toward me, then another, until we were close enough to touch.

"I'm still angry at you," she said, her voice soft but firm.

"I know."

"I don't forgive you. Not yet."

"I know."

"But I love you. And I'm tired of pretending I don't."

"I love you too," I said, reaching up to cup her face in my hands. "I never stopped."

She leaned into the touch, her eyes fluttering closed. "Don't make me regret this."

Instead of answering with words, I kissed her. Soft and careful at first, like she might disappear if I pushed too hard. But when she kissed me back, her hands fisting in my shirt, something fundamental shifted between us.

This wasn't the desperate, heated kiss from a week ago. This was deeper, more honest. When we broke apart, we were both breathing hard.

"Bedroom," she said, her voice rough, her pupils dilated.

"What?"

She shoved me once towards her bedroom door. "Bedroom. Now."

"Are you sure?"

"Yes," she said, tugging on my shirt. "The question is whether you're finally ready to stop running."

I answered by lifting her off her feet, her legs wrapping around my waist as I carried her down the hallway. We kissed the entire way, desperate and hungry and eight years overdue.

When I set her down beside her bed, she immediately went to work on the buttons of my shirt, her fingers steady despite the heat in her eyes.

"Just want one more confirmation," I said, covering her hands with mine.

Her smile was pure sin. "I want you naked. Now."

I shrugged out of my shirt, and her hands immediately went to my chest, fingers tracing the tattoos I'd gotten before, during, and after her. Devonna's touch burned like a brand, and I had to bite back a groan when her nails scraped lightly over my nipples.

"Fuck, Vonnie," I breathed, my hands going to her waist. "Eight years, and you still know exactly how to wreck me."

133

"Good," she said, her voice husky as she worked my belt buckle. "Because I plan to completely destroy you tonight."

When her fingers brushed against the bulge in my pants, I nearly came apart right there. Eight years of celibacy had left me wound tight as a spring, and every touch felt magnified tenfold.

"Easy," I said, catching her wrist. "I'm hanging by a thread here."

"Are you?" She palmed me through my pants, and I saw stars. "How close are you to losing control?"

"Shit. Closer than I've been since I was seventeen," I admitted, my voice strained.

"Good." She pushed my pants down, and I kicked them away, standing before her in just my boxers. "I like you desperate."

She hooked her thumbs in the waistband of my boxers, slowly dragging them down. When my cock sprang free, already hard and leaking, she made a soft sound of appreciation that nearly killed me.

"Christ, I'd forgotten how gorgeous you are," she murmured, her fingers ghosting along my length. "All of you."

The barely-there touch had me jerking in her hand. "Vonnie, if you keep that up, this is going to be over before it starts, and then I'd die of embarrassment and you'd have to finish all by yourself."

She continued stroking my dick, her eyes glittering as she tilted her face back to look up at me. "That would be a damn shame."

"Fuck, Dev-Devonna, I'm seriously going to come if you don't stop." I gritted my teeth together.

"Fine. We have all night," she said as she stepped back, giving me space to breathe. "Besides, it's my turn."

I watched, transfixed, as she slowly undressed, revealing inch after inch of smooth brown skin. When she let it fall to the floor, her chest rose and fell, her nipples hard against the black lace of her bra.

"You're so fucking beautiful," I said, my hand drifting to my dick. "I used to dream about this. About you."

"Just dream?" she asked, reaching behind herself to unclasp her bra.

"Among other things." I swallowed hard as the lace fell away, revealing breasts that were even more perfect than I remembered. My hand tightened over my dick. "I jerked off to the memory of you more times than I can count."

134

Her cheeks flushed at my admission, but her eyes darkened with heat. "What did you think about?"

"Everything." I took a step toward her, then stopped myself. "The way you taste. The sounds you make when you're close. How tight you get when you're about to come."

She shivered at my words, her hands going to the zipper of her skirt. "What else?"

"How you used to beg me to use my mouth on you. How you'd pull my hair when I found that perfect spot." I watched her slide the dress down her hips, taking the matching panties with it. "How you'd fall apart on my tongue and then pull me up to kiss you so you could taste yourself."

She was naked now, standing before me like a goddess, and I felt like I was dying from want. I wanted to fall to my knees and worship her.

"Do you still remember how?" she asked, moving to the bed.

"Some things you never forget." I followed her, catching her wrist and pulling her against me. "Let me show you."

I kissed her then, deep and demanding. She responded with equal fervor, her tongue sliding against mine, her body pressing flush against my chest. Her nipples hardened more against my skin.

"I need to taste you," I said against her lips. "I've been starving for you."

"Do it," she whispered, lying back on the bed. "Make up for lost time."

I kissed my way down her body, reacquainting myself with every curve and hollow. When I reached her breasts, I took one nipple into my mouth, sucking hard enough to make her arch off the bed.

"Shit," she gasped, her hands tangling in my hair. "More."

I lavished attention on both breasts until she was writhing beneath me, her hips rolling in search of friction. Satisfied with her moans, I continued my journey south, pressing open-mouthed kisses to her ribs, her stomach, the sharp jut of her hip bones.

"Please," she breathed when I settled between her thighs. "I need—"

Her words cut off in a sharp cry when I dragged my tongue through her folds. She was already soaked, her taste flooding my mouth like the sweetest addiction.

"Fuck, I missed this," I groaned against her, pulling her legs over my shoulders. Her heels dug into my back, pinning my face to her pussy. "Missed how you taste, how responsive you are."

I worked her with my tongue and lips, alternating between broad strokes and focused attention on her clit. She was trembling beneath me, her thighs quaking around my head as I pushed her higher and higher. When I pressed my middle finger inside her, she damn near suffocated me with how hard she clenched her thighs. I was in fucking heaven.

"Don't stop," she panted, her fingers pulling at my hair. "Right there, just like that. Oh shit, Miles. Shit."

I doubled my efforts, adding two fingers to stretch her while I sucked on her clit. She was so tight around my fingers, her walls fluttering as she got closer to the edge.

"Come for me, honey," I said, curling my fingers to hit that spot. "Let me hear you."

She shattered with a scream of expletives, her body bowing off the bed as waves of pleasure crashed over her. I worked her through it, gentling my touch as she came down from the high, boneless and satisfied.

"Holy shit," she breathed, her chest heaving. "I'd forgotten how good you are at that."

"It's my favorite hobby," I said, kissing my way back up her body.

When I reached her mouth, she kissed me hungrily, moaning at the taste of herself on my lips. Her hand wrapped around my cock, and I nearly blacked out from the pleasure of it.

"Condom," I managed, my voice strained. "Before I embarrass myself."

She reached for the nightstand drawer, pulling out a foil packet. I watched as she tore it open, then took it from her hands.

"Let me," I said, rolling it on with shaking fingers.

When I looked back at her, she was watching me with dark eyes, her legs spread in invitation. The sight of her like that—open and wanting and mine—undid me.

"Come here," she said, reaching for me.

I positioned myself at her entrance, the head of my cock sliding through her wetness. "God, I missed you," I said, my voice breaking slightly.

"I missed you too," she whispered. "Now fuck me, Miles."

I pushed inside her, inch by torturous inch, watching her face as she adjusted to me. She was so perfect that I had to stop and breathe before I lost control completely.

"Move," she demanded, her nails digging into my shoulders. "Damn it, Miles. Fucking move or thrust...or...or...do something. Shit!"

I started with shallow thrusts, building the rhythm gradually. She felt incredible around me, like silk and fire and everything I'd been missing. When she wrapped her legs around my waist, pulling me deeper, I thought I might come apart.

"Harder," she gasped, meeting my thrusts with her own.

I gave her what she wanted, driving into her with increasing force. The sound of skin slapping against skin filled the room, along with our harsh breathing and the little sounds she made every time I hit just the right angle.

"Fuck, Vonnie," I groaned, my forehead pressed against hers. "So fucking perfect." Shit. This was not going to last as long as I wanted it too. Already the pressure at the base of my spine was building. But there was no fucking way I was going to finish before she got a second chance.

To speed up the process, I reached between us, my thumb finding her clit and circling it in tight patterns. Her walls started to flutter around me, and she clawed at my back as I pistoned into her. The added stimulation was all she needed, she came with a cry that went straight to my soul, her body clenching around me.

"Oh thank fuck," I muttered, satisfied that she was satisfied.

The feeling of her coming apart beneath me was too much. I followed her over the edge with a groan that seemed to come from my very core, spilling into the condom as my body trembled.

We collapsed together, breathing hard and holding each other. When I finally found the strength to move, I rolled to the side, pulling her with me.

"Shit, Miles."

"Better than I could've ever remembered," I said, pressing a kiss to her sweat-dampened temple. "And I remembered it being pretty fucking incredible."

"I'm still mad at you," she said, but her voice was soft, sated.

"I know. But I hope that doesn't mean there won't be a round two after I drink some electrolytes."

She shoved against me with a chuckle, and I tugged her closer.

"You're an ass," she said against my chest, her voice muffled.

"An ass who got some of the finest ass in New York."

"Damn straight."

MAYBE THE MUSTANG CAN STAY...

Chapter 13: Devonna

The first thing I noticed when I woke up wasn't Miles's arm draped possessively across my waist, or the way his hair was doing its best impression of a tumbleweed, or even the fact that we were both naked enough to scandalize a European beach.

It was that my left boob was completely numb.

I'd been sleeping on my arm for what felt like seventeen hours, and the entire appendage had apparently decided to file for divorce from my nervous system. When I tried to move, my arm flopped around like a dying fish, completely useless and making weird slapping sounds against Miles's back.

"What the hell," I muttered, trying to shake feeling back into my limb while simultaneously attempting to extract myself from beneath Miles without waking him up. This proved to be roughly as graceful as performing surgery with oven mitts.

I managed to roll sideways, which resulted in me tumbling directly off the bed and onto the floor with a thud that probably registered on seismic equipment.

Miles bolted upright like he'd been shot from a cannon. "What? Where? Are we under attack?"

"No," I said from the floor, my dead arm still flopping around like I was doing some kind of interpretive dance about stroke symptoms. "I just fell off my own bed because my arm decided to quit its job."

He blinked down at me, taking in my naked, disheveled state sprawled across my bedroom floor like I'd been dropped there by a very lazy tornado. "Are you okay?"

"Physically? Debatable. My arm feels like it's been replaced with a pool noodle." I struggled to sit up, which was significantly harder with only one functional limb. "Emotionally? I'm having what you might generously call an existential crisis."

"About your arm?"

"About everything." I gestured wildly with my good arm while the useless one continued to flail around independently. "About this. About last night. About the fact that I just had mind-blowing sex with my fake fiancé who is my ex real fiancé and then fell off my own bed like some kind of sexual slapstick comedy."

Miles ran both hands through his hair, which only made it stick up more. "Vonnie—"

"Don't 'Vonnie' me. I need coffee before I can process whatever this is." I finally managed to stand, pins and needles shooting through my arm as circulation returned. "And you need to put some clothes on before my neighbors call the police about the naked man in my apartment."

"I don't think they can see me from here."

"Miles. You're six-foot-something of pale naked-ass white man. Your moon is visible from the actual moon, it's glowing so much. So put some damn clothes on."

"Or..." He drew out the word and looked me up and down. "Round three?"

"Shut up. It's too early for your shit." I grabbed the first clothes I could find, yesterday's dress and what I really hoped were clean underwear, and fled to the bathroom before I could do something even stupider, like ask him to stay for breakfast or take him up on round three or spontaneously combust from embarrassment.

Twenty minutes later, I emerged dressed and caffeinated, staring at the cold take out food containers on my counter like they held the secrets to the universe. Evidence of our fight, our reconciliation, our spectacularly poor decision-making skills.

My phone vibrated with a text from Mari, and I nearly wept with relief at the distraction.

MARI: EMERGENCY OF EPIC PROPORTIONS! Chicago venue disaster. Need you on next flight. Ani approved you coming. Please save my sanity and possibly our careers.

I'd never been so grateful for a work crisis in my life.

DEVONNA: Booking flight now. What's the damage?

MARI: Think Bridezilla meets natural disaster meets actual lawsuit. Will explain everything when you get here. HURRY.

I scribbled a quick note for Miles, and left it next to the coffee maker where he'd see it.

Emergency in Chicago. Back in a few days. Please lock up when you leave. -D

Then I grabbed my laptop bag and fled my own life like it was on fire.

"THANK GOD YOU'RE HERE," Mari said when she picked me up from O'Hare. She looked like she'd been through a blender set to 'chaos'—hair escaping from its ponytail, mascara streaked under her eyes, and that particular wild-eyed expression that came from dealing with wedding emergencies for too long without adequate caffeine. "This is officially the wedding apocalypse."

"Scale of one to ten?" I asked, buckling my seatbelt as she pulled away from the curb with the kind of aggressive driving that suggested she'd been living on energy drinks, quite possibly tequila, and pure panic.

"Seventeen. With potential for nuclear fallout." Mari navigated traffic like she was fleeing zombies. "The venue double-booked us with a medical conference and the wedding is tomorrow. The bride is threatening to sue everyone including the guy who delivered the flowers. The groom showed up drunk at noon, and our local coordinator locked herself in a supply closet and won't come out."

"How drunk?"

"Needs-to-be-carried drunk. Like, someone should probably check his pulse drunk."

"Jesus. What about backup venues?"

"Everything's booked solid. I've called every place in the greater Chicago area that can hold more than fifty people. Even the sketchy ones that smell like old cheese."

We spent the next twenty hours performing wedding miracles that would have impressed Moses. The Art Institute had a last-minute cancellation, the caterer agreed to relocate for roughly the cost of a small country's GDP, and I managed to talk the bride down from homicidal rage to mere felony assault charges.

By ten PM the next night, we were collapsed in my last-minute hotel room with Chinese takeout and a box of wine.

"I don't know what I would have done without you," Mari said, raising her glass in an exhausted toast. "You're officially my patron saint of wedding disasters."

"Just returning about fifty favors," I replied, taking a gulp of wine that tasted like liquid salvation. "Besides, fleeing to Chicago was exactly what I needed."

Mari's eyes lit up. "Ah, now we get to the good part. What happened with the fake fiancé that had you running across state lines?"

"How do you know something happened?"

"Because you have that very specific look. I can't tell if it's the I-got-fucked look or the I'm-fucked look. I get them mixed up, surprisingly." Mari gestured with her wine glass, sloshing slightly. "Also, you've been checking your phone every thirty seconds like you're expecting either a love letter or a court summons."

I buried my face in my hands. "I fell off my bed yesterday morning."

"What?"

"I woke up next to Miles, panicked, and literally fell off my own bed because my arm had gone numb." I looked up at Mari through my fingers. "It was like my subconscious was trying to physically eject me from the situation."

"So you did sleep with him."

"My arm filed for unemployment because I was lying on it for too long after having the kind of sex that should come with a warning label."

141

Mari nearly choked on her wine. "That good?"

"Mari."

"What? It's a legitimate question." She tilted her head and gave me puppy dog eyes. "Come on. You never share the fun stuff. I've barely heard anything about your sex life and I'm getting bored hearing about all the different places and ways Ani and Cal do it. Give me something to spice up my life."

"I thought that was what Hudson is for."

"Yeah, but come on, Dev! Please?"

"That's not— Okay, fine." I pulled my knees up to my chest. "I slept with Miles and then woke up by falling off my own bed like some kind of disaster. What does that say about my life choices?"

"That you're human? That you're attracted to the man you never got over?" Mari set down her wine and turned to face me. "Dev, you've spent eight years punishing yourself for loving someone who hurt you. Maybe it's time to consider that people can change."

"But what if he hasn't? What if this is just physical for him, and I'm setting myself up to get destroyed all over again?"

"What if it's not? What if he's just as scared as you are?"

I stared at her, processing the possibility. "I don't know how to do this, Mari. I don't know how to trust someone who already broke me once."

"You don't have to figure it out all at once. But you also don't have to run away when you feel something real." She reached over and squeezed my hand. "Besides, any man who can make you fall off your own bed from sheer sexual satisfaction is probably worth taking a risk on."

"You're terrible."

"I'm practical. Now, give me details. How big is his dick?"

I SPENT TWO more days in Chicago, helping Mari with a few other weddings and training local staff. It was good to stay busy, to focus on problems that had solutions instead of the mess I'd made of my personal life.

But Miles texted me every day, and despite my best efforts to remain detached, I looked forward to his messages.

MILES: *Hope the crisis is manageable. Miss having you around to act as a shield from Florence.*

MILES: *Pretty sure I left my boxers at yours, just so you know.*

MILES: *Mikhail asked about wedding timeline. Told him everything was on track. Hope that's still true?*

I kept my responses brief and professional, but something warm bloomed in my chest every time his name appeared on my screen.

When I finally flew back to New York, I felt like I'd gained some perspective. Maybe Mari was right. Maybe I was letting fear drive my decisions instead of hope or logic or whatever normal people used to navigate relationships.

Garrett texted me as I waited for my luggage at JFK.

MILES: *Haven't heard from you in a while. Free tonight? I have some interesting stories to share about an event I covered in Vegas.*

I stared at the message, waiting for the familiar spark of interest. Instead, I felt nothing. Not curiosity about his work, not attraction to his sharp intellect, not even mild interest in our usual arrangement. I responded to him.

DEVONNA: *Can we meet for coffee tomorrow? Something I need to discuss.*

MILES: *Sounds serious. Everything okay?*

DEVONNA: *Yeah. Just some things I need to sort out.*

The next morning, I met Garrett at our usual spot near his office. He looked as gorgeous as ever, but instead of attraction, I felt like I was having coffee with a friend. The non-sex kind of friend.

"So," he said, settling into the chair across from me. "Your text sounded ominous."

"I think we should end our arrangement," I said without preamble.

Garrett raised his eyebrows but didn't look particularly surprised. "Miles?"

I nodded, grateful he wasn't going to make this more complicated than necessary.

"Fair enough." He leaned back, studying my face with the analytical expression I'd once found attractive. "For what it's worth, I think you're making the right choice."

"You do?"

"Dev, whether you realize it or not, you lit up the moment you first saw him in your apartment."

"That was rage, Gar."

"This was always just an arrangement to blow off steam. But I think you and him have potential. He seems to genuinely care for you, and that's all that I could ask for."

"I'm sorry if I wasted your time."

"You didn't waste anything. We both got what we needed from this arrangement." He finished his coffee and stood. "I hope things work out with Miles. You deserve to be happy, Dev. Really happy, not just safely satisfied."

After he left, I sat in the coffee shop for another hour, processing the conversation. Garrett was right. I had been settling. For years, I'd chosen safe, uncomplicated men who couldn't hurt me because they didn't matter enough to hurt me. But Miles? Miles had every knife in the world in his hands, and they were all directed towards my heart.

THE WEDDING THAT Saturday should have been simple. Intimate ceremony, garden reception, reasonable budget. Instead, I got Bridezilla Supreme and her mother, the Dragon Lady of Long Island, who between them had managed to turn a sweet celebration into a three-ring circus of demands, complaints, and threats to ruin everyone's Yelp ratings.

"The flowers are completely wrong," The Dragon Lady announced the moment I arrived at the venue, her whiny voice reaching me before I was all the way out of my Uber. "These are clearly peonies, not garden roses."

I looked at the centerpiece in her hands, which was definitely David Austin garden roses, exactly as specified in our contract and confirmed in three separate emails. "Mrs. Dunmore, these are garden roses. The specific variety you selected during our final walkthrough."

"Don't tell me what I selected. I know what I chose, and this isn't it." She gestured at the arrangements like they'd personally insulted her mother. "Do you understand the difference between peonies and roses?"

I took a deep breath and reminded myself that difficult clients were part of the job, and that her check had already cleared. "Would you like me to call the florist and see if they can bring additional options?"

"I want you to fix this catastrophe. That's what we're paying you for."

Before I could respond to this completely reasonable request, I heard a familiar voice behind me.

"Actually, those are some of the most beautiful garden roses I've ever seen."

I turned to see Miles walking toward us, looking unfairly handsome in a black button-down shirt and that godforsaken elephant tie I'd gotten him a long time ago. My traitorous heart did a little skip-rope routine at the sight of him.

"Miles," I said, trying to keep my voice professional despite the way my pulse had decided to throw a small parade. "What are you doing here?"

"I came to help," he said, his eyes warm as they met mine. "And maybe be someone to carry heavy things or intimidate difficult vendors."

Mrs. Dunmore looked between us. "And you are?"

"Miles Houston," he said, extending his hand with that charming smile. Shit, was I jealous of the Dragon Lady? Oh, I was definitely jealous that she was getting that smile. Damn it. "I'm Devonna's fiancé. I hope you don't mind me crashing the party. I wanted to see her work her magic."

"Fiancé?" Mrs. Dunmore's entire demeanor shifted from hostile to ingratiating faster than a politician during election season. "How wonderful! When's the big day?"

"Soon," Miles said, slipping his arm around my waist. "We're still working out the final details."

"Well, you're a lucky man. Devonna is clearly very talented."

I blinked, wondering what had happened to the woman who'd been questioning my basic competence thirty seconds earlier.

"She's the best," Miles agreed, placing a kiss against my temple. "I don't know how she makes it all look so effortless."

For the next three hours, Miles stayed by my side as I coordinated vendors, managed timelines, and solved the inevitable crises that popped up at every wedding like whack-a-moles. He didn't interfere or offer unwanted advice. He just existed as a steady, supportive presence that somehow made everything feel more manageable.

When the bride had a meltdown about her lipstick not matching her bouquet, Miles distracted the photographer with questions about lens options. When Mrs. Dunmore started complaining about the band's sound levels, Miles engaged her in a conversation about her own wedding that lasted forty-five minutes and ended with her showing him photos on her phone.

When the florist arrived with replacement roses that were identical to the originals, Miles complimented Mrs. Dunmore's discerning eye for floral arrangements.

"You're dangerously good at this," I said during a rare quiet moment as guests filtered in for the ceremony.

"At what?"

"Being supportive without taking over. Helping without mansplaining. Charming difficult people into submission."

"I'd like to charm you into submission."

"Miles."

"Right. Thank you." Something shifted in his expression, becoming more serious. "I'm trying to be better. At a lot of things. Vonnie, when you were gone, I missed having you around and —"

"Excuse me, Miss Onai?" One of the catering staff interrupted. "We need approval on the dessert station placement."

"Be right there," I said, then looked back at Miles. "Thank you. For being here. For not trying to fix everything yourself."

"Thank you for letting me stay."

The ceremony went off without a hitch, and the reception was flowing smoothly when Mrs. Dunmore cornered me near the bar during the father-daughter dance.

"I owe you an apology. I was horrible to you earlier, and you didn't deserve that."

"Wedding planning is stressful for everyone," I said, nodding once.

"It's not an excuse. You've done an incredible job with everything, and I was taking my anxiety out on you." She glanced over at Miles, who was chatting with the groom's father about sports. "Your fiancé seems wonderful. Very supportive."

"He is," I said, a soft smile lifting my lips.

"Hold on to that one. Men who understand what we do are rarer than good wedding venues in Manhattan."

As the evening wound down and the last guests filtered out, I felt the familiar satisfaction that came with another successful event. Another couple launched into married bliss, another crisis or eight averted, another day of proving I was good at what I did.

"Ready to get out of here?" Miles asked, appearing beside me as I finished my final checklist.

"God, yes. I'm pretty sure I haven't eaten anything since breakfast."

"Come on then. Let me drive you home and feed you something that doesn't come from a cocktail napkin."

We walked through the venue's elegant foyer in silence, but the guilt that had started bubbling up as soon as I'd seen him appear like a knight in tattooed armor started to fester. There was so much I needed to apologize for, and yet couldn't bring myself to speak. I'd fled to Chicago the morning after we'd slept together. He'd shown up here today to support me without being asked. He hadn't even seemed mad that I'd left him for several days. Why the hell wasn't he mad? I would've been pissed. Fuck, I was pissed at me.

And it didn't help that every time he'd touched my lower back or smiled at me during the reception, heat had pooled low in my belly.

The parking garage was dimly lit and nearly empty, our footsteps echoing off concrete walls. When we reached his Mustang, I was lost in thought and automatically headed for the passenger side, but Miles caught my wrist before I could reach for the handle.

"What are you doing?" he asked, his thumb tracing over my pulse point.

"Opening the door?" I said, confused by the intensity in his expression.

"That's my job," he said, but he didn't move to open it. Instead, he stepped closer, backing me against the car door. "Vonnie, about Chicago—"

"I'm sorry," I said quickly, the words tumbling out before I could stop them. They'd clearly been waiting for the opportunity to make their great escape. "I'm sorry I ran. I'm sorry I left that stupid note and fled like a coward the morning after we slept together." I looked up at him, taking in his slightly mussed hair and the way his tie was askew after a long day. "I panicked, Miles. I woke up next to you and all I could think was that I'd made a terrible mistake."

He frowned, and I regretted my words right away. "A mistake?"

"I thought maybe, but..." I took a shaky breath. "But the real mistake was what I did. I spent that entire night calling you out for running away eight years ago, for making decisions for me without talking to me first. And then what did I do? I turned around and did the exact same thing." I pressed my palms against his chest. "I ran without hardly an explanation. I made the decision for both of us that it was a mistake without even giving you a chance to weigh in. That's not fair, and it makes me a hypocrite."

"You're not a hypocrite, Vonnie. You had to go for work, and you came back. I'm not upset."

"You're not?" I studied his face in the fluorescent lighting, noting the way his eyes had gone dark, the tension in his jaw.

Something shifted in his expression. "No. But I missed you."

Instead of responding, I reached up and straightened his tie, letting my fingers linger against the silk. "Why do you still have this tie?"

He reached up and pressed his hand over my left one, and lifted it to his mouth, where he kissed the top of my engagement ring. "Because you gave it to me."

I watched as he pressed another kiss to the top of my hand before placing it back on his chest. "I realized something while I was in Chicago," I said without preamble.

"What?"

"That I've been lying to myself about a lot of things." I smoothed my hands over his lapels, feeling the solid warmth of his chest beneath the fabric. "Including how I feel about this ridiculous car."

Miles's hands came up to frame my face. "And how do you feel about it?"

"I hate that I love it," I admitted, my voice barely above a whisper. "I hate that you look so damn good driving it. All confident and in control, with your sleeves rolled up to show your ink and that satisfied expression you get when you're enjoying yourself."

He leaned down until his forehead touched mine. "What else?"

"I hate that it reminds me of all our old dates. How you'd pick me up, and I'd pretend to complain about the engine noise while secretly loving how proud you were of this stupid machine." My hands slid up to tangle in his hair. "I hate that every time I see a Mustang on the street, I think about you."

"Just the car?" he asked, his mouth barely an inch from mine.

"No." I pulled his head down until our lips were almost touching. "I think about you. About us. About how good we were together before everything went to hell."

"We're still good together," he said against my lips.

"Are we?"

Instead of answering, he kissed me. Soft at first, almost hesitant, like he was giving me a chance to change my mind. When I kissed him back, pressing closer and making a soft sound of approval, the kiss deepened into something hungrier.

His hands slid down to my waist, pulling me against him, and I could feel the evidence of how much he wanted me pressing against my hip. The knowledge sent heat shooting through my veins.

"Miles," I breathed against his mouth, and he responded by pressing me more firmly against the car, his thigh sliding between my legs in a way that made me gasp.

"God, I missed you," he said, his mouth moving to my neck. "And I'm glad you like my car."

"Miles," I said, my hands clutching at his shoulders. "I want you."

"Here?" he asked, his teeth grazing my pulse point. "In a parking garage where anyone could see us?"

"I don't care." And I realized I meant it. The proper, professional part of me that worried about appearances and maintaining decorum had apparently left the building. "I've been thinking about this all day. Watching you charm difficult clients and carry flower arrangements, being supportive without trying to take over. Shit, I was jealous when you winked at Mrs. Dunmore. Fucking jealous. Do you have any idea how sexy that was?"

"Tell me," he said, his hands sliding down to cup my ass, lifting me slightly so I was pinned between him and the car.

"Sexy enough that I've been wet since you made Mrs. Dunmore laugh about her own wedding photos." I nipped at his earlobe, enjoying the way he sucked in a sharp breath. "Sexy enough that I kept imagining dragging you into the coat closet and having my way with you."

"Why didn't you?"

"Because I'm a professional," I said, then slid my hand down between us to palm him through his pants. "But I'm off the clock."

Miles groaned, his hips bucking into my touch. "Christ, Vonnie. Fuck."

"That's the plan," I said, working his belt buckle with fingers that were steadier than I felt. "I want to make you lose control the way you make me lose control."

"You already do," he said, but his protest died in his throat when I finally got my hand inside his pants and wrapped my fingers around him.

He was hard and hot and perfect in my hand, and when I stroked him slowly from base to tip, he made a sound that went straight between my legs.

"Fucking hell," he breathed, his forehead dropping to rest against mine. "That feels so good."

"Just good?" I asked, adjusting my grip and twisting my wrist the way I remembered he liked.

"Perfect," he corrected, his voice strained. "You're perfect."

"Damn right."

I established a rhythm, watching his face as I worked him with my hand. His eyes were closed, his breathing harsh, and there was something incredibly powerful about being able to affect him this way. I pressed open-mouthed kisses along his jaw.

"Vonnie," he said, his hand covering mine to still the movement. "If you keep that up...shit, fuck."

I slipped my hand out from under his, then took both his wrists and pressed them against the car on either side of me. "Stay," I said, my voice a hoarse whisper.

He obeyed, his breath coming in ragged pants as I held his gaze and deliberately sank to my knees. I kept my eyes on his as I spat on his cock. His pupils dilated at the sight. I worked him with my hand, feeling him grow even harder as I tightened my grip.

"Vonnie," he rasped, his hips jerking. "You don't have to—"

"Shh," I hushed him, then leaned forward and took him into my mouth.

His taste was familiar, salty and warm, and I reveled in the way his breath hitched as I swirled my tongue around his tip. I took him deeper. Shit, he was larger than I remembered. I gagged. Very ladylike. In my defense, he easily hit the back of my throat, and his hands clenched into fists against the car.

"Fuck, Von," he groaned, his voice echoing in the empty garage. "Fuck."

I hummed in approval, the vibration making him jerk in my mouth. I worked him in combination with my hand and mouth. I continued to take him as deep as I could. His hips moved in time with my movements, his breath coming in harsh pants.

"I'm close," he warned, his voice strained. "Vonnie, I can't—oh fuck—"

I didn't stop, didn't slow down. Instead, I redoubled my efforts, my hand gripping him tighter, my mouth taking him deeper. He came with a harsh groan, his cock pulsing in my mouth, and I choked, surprised by the force of it. For a second, I panicked, my eyes watering, but I managed to swallow, my mouth still around him.

Miles was breathless, his chest heaving as he looked down at me with an expression that was equal parts satisfaction and hunger. But something shifted in his demeanor. He tilted his head, dropping one hand down to cup my chin. "Damn perfect. Now get in my fucking car. This isn't over," he commanded, his voice low.

"We should probably—"

Before I could react, he reached down and hauled me to my feet, his mouth crashing against mine in a fierce kiss. He backed me against the car, his hands roaming over my body, touching and squeezing.

"Car. Now." He captured my mouth in another kiss, this one desperate and demanding. Miles reached around me to open the back door.

The space was cramped, designed more for show than practicality, but I didn't care as I crawled inside and turned to face him as he followed me. The door slammed shut, encasing us in the dim, leather-scented interior. His hands were on me instantly, rough and demanding, pulling me onto his lap. I straddled him, my knees pressing against the soft leather seats. His cock, still slick from my mouth, was hardening again against my thigh.

"Condom?" I gasped, grinding against him.

"Glove compartment."

I scrambled off him, reaching between the seats for the glove compartment. There was a box of condoms waiting for me when I opened it, and I grabbed two loose ones.

"What a fan-fucking-tastic view," Miles crooned from behind me. A second later, he smacked my ass, and I yelped. Before I could scold him, his hands were on my hips, steading me and holding me in place.

I arched into his touch, a soft moan escaping my lips. His hands were rough, possessive, as they squeezed and teased. He pinched my nipples through the fabric of my dress, sending a jolt of pleasure straight to my core.

One hand dropped to my thigh, slowly sliding up until it reached the hem of my dress. He pushed it up, exposing my bare ass to the cool air of the car. His fingers traced the edge of my lace thong, teasing the sensitive skin beneath.

"What are you—Oh shit, fuck, Miles!"

He pulled down my thong and ran his tongue up my center. I clung to the condoms, my other hand bracing me against the drivers seat.

Miles's tongue was relentless, licking and sucking like he was a man starved. My knuckles turned white as I gripped the seat, my breath coming in ragged gasps. He didn't tease or play; he devoured, his hands gripping my hips so tightly I knew there'd be bruises. I didn't care. I wanted the reminder of this moment tomorrow.

"Fuck," I gasped, my body trembling as he slid two fingers inside me. He curled them, pumping them in and out. "Fuck, fuck, fuck—"

He didn't let up, his fingers moving in and out of me while his tongue worked my clit. The sounds coming from me were desperate, needy, and I didn't give a damn. I was so close, my body tensing, my breath hitching.

"I'm—I'm—" I managed to choke out, and then I was shattering, my body convulsing around his fingers, my cries echoing in the enclosed space.

Before I could catch my breath, Miles was pulling me back, hauling me onto his lap. I turned to face him, straddling him on the back seat. His cock was hard again, pressing against my thigh, and his heart pounded in his chest.

"Put it on," he rasped, pointing to one of the condoms in my hand.

My hands were shaking, but I managed to tear open the packet and roll the latex down his length. He was thick and hard, and I couldn't resist giving him a few strokes, loving the way his breath hitched.

"Vonnie," he growled, his hands gripping my hips. "Now."

I lifted up, positioning him at my entrance, but I didn't sink down right away.

"Say please."

"Please."

"Actually, I want you to say —"

"Devonna Inez Onai, if you don't fucking sit on my dick right now —"

"You'll what?" I interrupted, admiring his flushed face below me. "Fuck!"

He thrust up, filling me in one smooth stroke. I cried out, my body stretching to accommodate him. The sensation of him filling me was intense.

"That," he said, his breath short. "I'll do that." Miles pulled out, air filling his lungs as his eyes rolled back in his head.

I chuckled as I sank down slowly, taking him inch by inch. We both groaned as I settled fully onto him, his cock filling me completely. The angle was different in the cramped space, deeper somehow, and I could feel every inch of him stretching me.

"Fuck, you feel good," he breathed, his hands sliding up to cup my breasts. "So fucking good."

I started to move, lifting up and then sliding back down, finding a rhythm that had us both gasping. I leaned forward, my hands on his shoulders, my body moving faster, harder. The car rocked with our movements, and I was grateful for the relative privacy of the empty garage.

His hands guided my movements, lifting me, pulling me down, setting a pace that was fast and hard. He reached up, one hand gripping the back of my neck, pulling my head back. The other hand slipped around to my front, his fingers finding my clit, circling, pressing. I moaned, my body tightening around him.

"Miles," I panted, my body tightening again. "I'm close. I'm — oh god —" My body clenched around him, my cries filling the car. He followed me over the edge, his cock pulsing inside me, his groans mixing with my own.

I collapsed against him, my body limp, my breath coming in satisfied gasps. His arms came around me, holding me close, his heart pounding against mine.

"Fucking hell, Vonnie," he breathed, his voice rough.

"Yeah, fuck. I think I do love this car," I said with a giggle, resting my forehead against his shoulder.

"You fucking better. I'm never getting rid of it now."

THE REHEARSAL DINNER FROM HELL

Chapter 14: Miles

I fucked up the wine glasses thirty seconds into dinner. Not just any dinner. Our rehearsal dinner. Mikhail's spectacle at Le Cirque, where the waiters moved like ballet dancers. I'd googled "formal dining etiquette" that morning like some desperate teenager cramming for a test, but apparently knowing the theory and executing it under pressure were two different animals.

The toast began, and I grabbed what looked like a perfectly reasonable wine glass. Crystal caught the light, champagne bubbled prettily, and I felt almost confident until some wretched old lady friend of Florence's audibly gasped.

"That's the water goblet," she whispered loud enough for half the room to hear.

Heat crawled up my neck as every eye turned toward me. God, you would've thought I'd shown up to a black-tie event in work boots and a hard hat from the looks they were giving me. Devonna smoothly switched our glasses while launching into some story about her latest bridezilla, her laugh bright. Professional damage control at its finest.

Under the table, she squeezed my knee. "No one noticed," she murmured against my ear.

But they had. All of them. Mari hid a giggle behind her napkin while Hudson narrowed his eyes at her. Anica shot her intimidating billionaire tech genius husband, Callan, a look that said *poor guy doesn't have a clue.* Even the waiter paused, uncertain whether to correct me or pretend nothing happened.

I kept my mouth shut through the bread course, following Devonna's lead like a kid shadowing his mom at a grown-up party. Pick up the butter knife this way. Break the bread like that. Don't reach across anyone. Simple rules that everyone else seemed born knowing.

The entrées arrived looking more like mini art installations than food. Some French creation I couldn't pronounce involving duck and what might have been edible flowers. When the waiter explained the preparation in his practiced monologue, I made my second tactical error.

"So it's basically a fancy version of the duck sandwiches my dad used to make?"

The silence stretched long enough for me to realize I'd stepped in it again. Mikhail's eyebrows climbed toward his hairline. Anica choked slightly on her wine. Even Mari, who usually seemed game for anything, looked like she was fighting between amusement and secondhand embarrassment.

"Doesn't he have such a refreshing perspective on cuisine?" Devonna asked, her smile so bright it could've powered the restaurant.

Refreshing perspective my ass. She'd just turned my foot-in-mouth moment into something that sounded almost sophisticated. I watched her work, watched how effortlessly she translated my screw-ups into charming quirks, and felt something twist in my chest that wasn't gratitude.

It was a shame.

"Tell us about your work, Miles," Mari said, probably trying to steer conversation toward safer ground.

"I work for Christoff Law. It's a larger firm than the nonprofit I was working at previously," I said.

"Oh, a lawyer! My parents wanted me to study law. I said no thank you. But that's great that you were working for a non-profit." Mari said without a hint of pity. "Why'd you switch?"

Devonna glanced at me wide eyed over her wine glass, tilting her head towards Florence and Mikhail, who sat to the right of her.

156

"I, um, I decided it was time for a change."

"Change can definitely be a good thing," Hudson said, leaning over to kiss Mari on the temple. She beamed up at him. "Are you happy with your knew job?" He asked me.

"Fuck no." I froze, wishing I could swallow the words, but it was too late. Everyone around me stopped moving too. "Er, I, uh mean. It's not what I want to do long-term." Glancing at Devonna, I begged her with my eyes to help.

"We rarely start out in the jobs we are going to turn into careers, right?" She said, shrugging and beaming until everyone continued what they were doing.

Mikhail raised an eyebrow as he drank his brandy. Thankfully, though, he remained silent and didn't add to the stream of questions.

I flexed my fingers under the white tablecloth, suddenly aware of how out of place I felt. I made it through the main course without major incident, mostly by nodding at appropriate intervals and letting the conversation flow around me. They talked about art openings I'd never heard of, restaurants with year-long waiting lists, business deals that involved more money than I'd see in a lifetime. Each reference felt like a test I was failing without knowing the questions.

When Mikhail started discussing some gallery acquisition, I tried to contribute by mentioning a car show I'd attended. The way everyone paused told me I'd misjudged the room again.

Dessert arrived; some architectural chocolate creation. I was actually managing to eat it without embarrassing myself when Devonna's phone buzzed. She glanced at it, then at me, and I saw something flicker across her face.

"Excuse me for just a moment," she said, slipping away toward the restroom.

That's when Alek materialized beside my chair. I'd invited him to dinner not expecting him to show up.

"Hey man," I said, nodding towards him. "Glad you could make it."

"Hell of an evening," he said, settling into Devonna's vacated chair without invitation. "Must be something, getting to play in the big leagues." He said this in a lower voice, but by the frown on her face, Anica had heard him.

157

"It's been nice," I said carefully, not liking his tone.

"Nice?" He chuckled. "Miles, man, I watched that whole performance. The wine glass thing, the duck sandwich comment, the way you just sat there while they talked about things you've never heard of."

My jaw clenched. "Your point?"

"My point is" — he leaned closer to whisper — "that you looked like a fish out of water. And worse, so did she." He gestured toward where Devonna had disappeared. "Did you see her face every time you opened your mouth? The way she kept jumping in to translate what you meant?"

I had seen it. The quick recovery smiles, the smooth redirections, the way she'd worked overtime all evening to make me seem like I belonged.

"Yeah, but it's not like she was embarrassed," I said, rubbing the back of my neck. Mikhail was whispering to Florence, his attention across the room, thank goodness. Hudson, Mari, and Callan were in a discussion together. That left only Anica, who was clearly eavesdropping. I wasn't sure if that was a good thing or not.

"Wasn't she?" Alek leaned forward, his voice somehow dropping even lower. "Look, I'm not trying to be cruel here. But that woman is trying to build something in this world. Look at her friends, man. They're lightyears ahead of you. Devonna is trying to make a name for herself among people who matter. And you..." He gestured at me like I was evidence in a case he was making. "You're a complication she has to manage."

"Fuck you."

"I'm trying to help you see reality." His tone turned almost gentle, which somehow made it worse. "She's brilliant, educated, connected. She belongs here. And you? You drive a rusty Mustang and think duck sandwiches are fine dining conversation."

I wanted to hit him. Wanted to grab his perfectly knotted tie and slam him against the wall until he took back every word. But I couldn't, because underneath the rage was a cold recognition that he might be right. He was always right.

"Think about tonight," Alek continued. "How many more dinner parties like this can she handle? How many times can she cover for you before it starts affecting her reputation? Before people start wondering what someone like her is doing with someone like you?"

158

"Yeah, but she...she chose me," I said, but the words sounded hollow even to my ears.

"Did she? Or did circumstances choose for her? You're the one who showed up and guilted her into this. But you don't have to trap her in a world she doesn't want, man." He pulled out his phone, scrolled through something, then showed me the screen. "I told you about this before, but you turned me down. But there's another chance, and you're running out of time. That position in Dubai. It's opening up again. Apparently the guy they chose went missing. It's only a ten-year contract. Just the starting bonus is enough to pay of the big guy and set free the woman you're dooming to a life in the gutter with you. Miles, it's good money. Really good money."

I stared at the job posting, my heart hammering against my ribs. Alek was right. Again. The starting bonus was more than enough to pay off Mikhail and then some. Enough to start fresh somewhere new, somewhere Devonna wouldn't have to explain my existence to her sophisticated friends.

"Think about it," Alek said, pocketing his phone. "You could solve your money problems and give her the space to find someone who actually fits in her world."

"Why do you care?" I whispered back, noting that Anica was watching me, though I doubted she could hear what we were discussing. I prayed that was the case.

"Because I'm your friend. I'm looking at for you, and by extension, her. And Miles, watching her slowly realize she's made a mistake?" He shook his head. "That's not going to be good for anyone." He tapped the table twice before standing up. Alek straightened his jacket and shrugged. When he spoke, it was still quiet, but clearly Anica was listening again. "The job's real, Miles. I could make a call, have you on a plane by tomorrow afternoon. Clean break, no messy explanations needed."

I didn't respond.

"Think about it man," he said smoothly. "And congratulations to you and Devonna. Enjoy the party."

He walked away before I could respond, leaving me sitting alone with his words echoing in my head and the taste of expensive chocolate turning to sludge in my mouth.

"What was that about?" Anica asked as soon as Alek was gone. She leaned forward and raised and eyebrow. "Are you two friends or something?"

For some reason, her comment set me on edge and I narrowed my eyes at her. "Yeah, he's my best friend. And he's just looking out for me."

"Then why is he suggesting you get on a flight tomorrow? You're wedding is tomorrow." She matched my expression, frowning at me. "Your wedding to one of my best friends."

"He's just —"

"You're not going to leave her again, are you?" Anica whispered, making sure no one was listening at the table. They weren't.

"No," I shook my head and downed the rest of my wine. "Of course not."

Anica looked over her shoulder at the direction Alek had left, and when she looked back, her nose was wrinkled. "He may be your best friend, but he talks to you like shit, Miles. Take his advice with a grain of salt. Or a whole salt shaker, if you're smart."

"No offense, Anica, but you don't know Alek and you hardly know me." I tossed my napkin onto my plate and stood, walking away from the table. I needed air.

It just so happened that Devonna returned at the same time I was leaving. She was walking towards me, and I almost turned to go a different direction when I noticed the redness on her nose and a smudge of mascara under one eye. Shit. She'd been crying.

Every protective instinct I had flared to life. Whatever Alek had said, whatever doubts were eating at me, none of it mattered when I saw her like this. I closed the distance between us in three strides.

"Hey," I said softly, reaching for her elbow. "What's wrong?"

The moment I touched her, she crumpled. Just completely fell apart, stepping into my arms and burying her face against my chest. Her shoulders shook as she tried to muffle her sobs against my shirt.

"Vonnie?" I wrapped my arms around her, one hand stroking her back. "Honey, what happened?"

Over her head, I saw Mari and Anica pushing back from the table, concern written across their faces. I held up a hand, shaking my head slightly. Whatever this was, Devonna didn't need an audience.

160

"Is there somewhere private we can go?" I asked a hovering waiter, who looked like he'd rather be anywhere else.

"There's a family restroom down the hall," he said, pointing toward the back of the restaurant.

I guided Devonna away from the dining room, her hand clutched in mine, her breathing still uneven. The family bathroom was small but clean, with a locking door and enough space for both of us. I flipped the lock and turned back to her.

"Talk to me," I said, pulling some toilet paper from the roll and pressing it into her hands. "What's going on?"

She dabbed at her eyes, trying to compose herself, but fresh tears kept coming. "It's Garrett," she managed between hiccups. "He was... God, Miles, he was shot."

My spine stiffened, my throat constricting as I tried to process her words.

"Is he...?" I couldn't finish the question.

"He's in emergency surgery. They don't know if..." She pressed the toilet paper to her mouth, her whole body trembling. "His sister called me. She thought we were still... she didn't know about us."

I pulled her back into my arms, letting her cry against my shoulder while I stroked her hair. "I'm so sorry, honey. I'm so fucking sorry."

"He's in San Francisco," she whispered. "I can't even... there's nothing I can do."

"We could get you on a plane," I said immediately. "Tonight. I'll call—"

"No." She pulled back, wiping her nose. "No, there's nothing I can do there either. His family is with him. I just... I just need a minute to pull myself together."

I handed her more toilet paper, watching as she tried to repair the damage to her makeup. But her hands were shaking too badly to be effective.

"Let's get out of here," I said. "I'll tell them you're not feeling well, we'll go home—"

"We can't leave." She looked at me like I'd lost my mind. "It's our rehearsal dinner, Miles."

"So what? You're upset, you need—"

161

"I need to go back out there and finish dinner like a normal person." She straightened her shoulders, trying to pull herself together. "I can't fall apart in front of Mikhail and Florence."

"Why the hell not?" The words came out harsher than I'd intended. "Why do you have to perform for them?"

"I'm not performing—"

"Bullshit." I ran both hands through my hair, pacing the small space. "You've been performing all night. Covering for me, translating my mistakes, making excuses. And now you're trying to pretend you're fine when you're clearly not."

"What are you talking about?"

"I'm talking about the fact that I don't belong out there!" The words exploded out of me. "I don't belong at fancy dinners or gallery openings or whatever the fuck else your world requires. I use the wrong fork, I say the wrong things, and you have to spend all your energy making me seem normal."

"It's our rehearsal dinner," she said again, her voice rising. "Our dinner, for our wedding—"

"It's not just the dinner, Vonnie. It's your life. Your whole fucking life." I stopped pacing, facing her. "God, Von. You deserve better than this. Better than me."

"Don't you dare—"

"Answer me something," I interrupted. "And be honest. If I could pay off Mikhail's debt tomorrow, if we didn't have to get married, what would you choose?"

Alek's proposition came back to me, and I was pacing again. Shit, I couldn't stop. I needed to know. Was he right?

She stared at me. "What kind of question is that?"

"An important one." I stepped closer. "If you had a choice—really had a choice—would you marry me anyway? Knowing we'd be poor while I try to pay him back? Knowing you'd have to keep covering for me at every fancy event for the rest of your life?"

"Miles, you're scaring me. Where is this coming from?"

I ignored her question. "Answer me, Devonna. What would you choose?"

"I... I don't understand why you're asking me this."

162

"Because I need to know." My voice cracked. "I need to know if you're with me because you want to be or because you have to be. Because I made you when I showed up like an ass in your apartment and set your world on fire."

"Where the hell is this coming from?" she demanded, her tears forgotten in the face of her anger.

I took a deep breath. "There's a job. In Dubai. Ten-year contract. The signing bonus alone would be enough to pay off Mikhail and set us both free."

The silence stretched between us.

"And you're considering it." Her voice was flat.

"I'd leave tomorrow."

"You son of a bitch." She shoved me, hard enough that I stumbled back against the wall. "You're thinking about leaving me again."

"I'm thinking about setting you free—"

"By abandoning me? Again?" Her voice climbed higher. "God, you're exactly the same as you were eight years ago. The moment things get complicated, the moment you have to actually fight for something, you run."

"This isn't running—"

"Like hell it isn't." She was in my face now, eyes blazing. "You get spooked at one dinner party and suddenly you're ready to disappear for ten years?"

"It's not about the dinner party—"

"Then what? What's so terrible about your life here that you'd rather spend a decade in the desert?"

"You are!" The words tore out of me. "You're too good for this, Vonnie. Too good for me. You should be with someone like Garrett, someone who belongs in your world, someone who doesn't embarrass you every time he opens his mouth."

"Garrett got shot tonight!" she screamed. "He's fighting for his fucking life in a hospital three thousand miles away, and you're standing here telling me I should be with him instead of you?"

"I didn't mean—"

"You meant exactly that." Tears were streaming down her face again, but these were angry tears. "You meant that I'd be better off with anyone else. Anyone who isn't you."

"Wouldn't you be?"

"I don't know!" The admission seemed to shock her as much as it did me. "I don't know, Miles, because you never give us a real chance. Every time we get close to something real, you decide I deserve better and you disappear."

"Maybe because you do deserve better."

"Maybe you should let me decide that for myself." She wiped her face with the back of her hand. "But you won't, will you? You'll just make the decision for both of us, pack your bags, and leave me to clean up the mess of my broken fucking heart. Again."

"Devonna—"

"No." She held up a hand. "Just... no. I can't do this right now. My friend is dying, and you're talking about abandoning me, and I just... I can't."

She reached for the door handle, but I caught her wrist. I wasn't expecting her free hand to fly up and slap me across the cheek. Stumbling back, I covered my burning face where she'd hit me.

"Fuck you, Miles. If you want to be free from me so bad, then fine. Take the fucking job. Get out of my fucking life." Devonna spun on her heels and stormed out of the bathroom.

"Goddamnit," I muttered, and then with a frustrated growl, I turned around and punched the wall. The solid brick wall. "Fuck!"

Guess Garrett wasn't the only one going to the hospital.

MEN ARE IDIOTS. PERIOD.

Chapter 15: Devonna

The wedding dress hanging on my closet door mocked me as I stared at it from my bed, where I'd been lying for the past hour, trying to convince myself that yesterday's fight was just a nightmare. That Miles was in my kitchen making coffee like he had since he'd started staying over the last few weeks, cursing at the coffee maker like it wasn't operator issues causing it not to work. That we'd figure out how to apologize to each other and get married in four hours like we were supposed to.

Instead, the apartment felt hollow. Empty in a way that had nothing to do with the early morning quiet and everything to do with the Miles-shaped absence that seemed to echo from every corner.

"Miles?" I called out, even though I already knew. He hadn't come home last night. I hadn't expected him too.

Still though, the silence that answered me felt like a slap.

I dragged myself out of bed, my head pounding from crying and too much wine and the kind of exhaustion that settles into your bones when your life implodes. The taste in my mouth was stale alcohol and regret. My dress from last night clung to me, wrinkled and smelling like the expensive restaurant.

His side of the bed was untouched.

He'd left me. Again.

The night before our wedding day.

Before I could stop myself, I twisted off the engagement ring and hurled it across the room, where it bounced pathetically off the wardrobe and rolled under the bed.

"Are you fucking kidding me?" I screamed at my empty apartment, my voice cracking on the last word. "Are you fucking kidding me?"

I sank down on my floor, pressing my back against the bed frame, and tried to breathe. The cold wooden floor felt good against my flushed skin, but they couldn't stop the way my chest felt like it was caving in on itself.

Eight years ago, he'd disappeared without explanation, leaving me to figure out what I'd done wrong. This time, he'd at least had the courtesy to tell me why. Progress, I guess.

My phone rang, and for one desperate second, my heart leaped. Maybe it was Miles, calling to tell me he wasn't running away. That he was choosing me. Choosing to stay.

Instead, Anica's name flashed on the screen.

I stared at it, letting it ring. I'd ignored her calls all morning, along with Callan's, Mari's, and Hudson's. I wasn't ready to explain what had happened. Wasn't ready to admit that Miles had left me again.

But the phone kept ringing, and I knew Anica well enough to know she'd show up at my apartment if I didn't answer soon.

"Hello?" My voice came out as a croak.

"Devonna! Jesus Christ, finally. I've been calling you for hours. We all have. What the hell happened last night? You came out of the bathroom crying and just disappeared from the restaurant without saying anything to anyone."

I pressed my free hand against my eyes, trying to stop the tears that threatened to start again. "Miles left."

"Left? What do you mean left? Left the restaurant? We saw him leave right after you, but then neither of you answered your phones—"

"Left left, Anica. As in, packed his stuff and got on a plane to Dubai. There's no wedding."

The silence on the other end stretched so long I thought the call had dropped.

"He did what?" Her voice had gone dangerously quiet.

"There was a job. He decided to take it. He chose to pay off Dimitrov instead of marrying me. He spewed some bullshit about setting me free." I laughed, but it came out broken. "Setting me free, Anica. Like I'm some kind of prisoner in my own life."

"That motherfucking coward. I could tell he was off after his asshole friend came and talked to him."

"Asshole friend?"

"That other lawyer guy whose totally full of himself and speaks more passive aggressively than a preteen daughter to her mother."

"Alek?"

"Maybe. I don't remember. All I know is he came to talk to Miles while you were taking that phone call, and from what I could hear, they were talking about a job and a flight and it all sounded suspicious as hell."

I heard rustling in the background, then Callan's voice, distant but audible. "What's wrong? Is Devonna okay?"

"Miles left her," Anica said, her voice muffled like she'd covered the phone. "He's gone."

"He did what?" Callan's voice was loud enough that I could hear it clearly. "Where is he? I'll kill him. I'll actually fucking kill him. Actually, I'll hire someone. Do we still have that guy Andrew's phone number?"

"Cal, not now," Anica said, then came back to me. "Dev, honey, I'm so sorry. We're coming over right now."

"You don't have to—"

"Like hell we don't. Mari and Hudson are already on their way. They gave up trying to call. We've all been worried sick since you both disappeared last night without explanation." Her voice softened. "What happened? The last thing I saw was you two going to the bathroom after you were crying, and then Miles left and looked like someone had punched him in the gut, and then you were both just gone."

I closed my eyes. "We had a fight," I said quietly. "A bad one. About him not belonging in my world, about the Dubai job, about everything. I told him..." I swallowed hard. "I told him to take the fucking job and get out of my life."

"But you didn't mean it."

"No. Yes. I don't know." I sank back down onto the floor, pulling my knees to my chest. "I was angry and hurt and scared about Garrett, and I just... I said things I shouldn't have said."

"What about Garrett?"

"Garrett was shot yesterday. In San Francisco. His sister texted me this morning that he came out of surgery alright, but hadn't woken up yet. It's going to be a long recovery. But last night we didn't know if he was going to make it, and Miles was talking about leaving, and I just lost it."

"Oh, honey." Anica's voice was full of sympathy. "That's a lot to handle all at once."

"Miles asked me what I'd choose," I said, the words tumbling out. "If he could pay off Mikhail's debt, if we didn't have to get married, what would I choose? And I never got to answer because everything went to hell, and now he's just... gone."

"What would you have said?" Callan's voice was closer now, like he was leaning over the phone.

"That I choose him," I whispered. "Poor, awkward, doesn't-fit-in-my-world him. I choose us."

"Then we're going to fix this," Anica said firmly. "We're coming over right now with coffee and a plan."

"There's nothing to fix, Anica. He's already gone. Probably already on a plane."

"It's not over until you say it's over."

"I'm saying it's over." I stood up, walking to the window where I could see people going about their normal Saturday morning routines. "Miles Houston has officially run away from me for the last time. I'm done chasing men who don't want to be caught."

"Fuck chasing. The only one who is going to be chasing is him. We'll make sure of it. That man is going to grovel his fucking heart out or you're going to be the one to walk. If you want him in your life, then he's going to be in your life. The man clearly loves you, and he's lost his goddamn mind. We'll be there in twenty minutes. Don't go anywhere."

She hung up before I could protest, leaving me staring at my phone and wondering what exactly she was planning.

I burst into tears. Not the pretty kind of crying you see in movies, but the ugly, snotty, gut-wrenching kind that leaves you gasping for air and questioning every life choice that led you to this moment.

The makeup artist was supposed to be at my apartment in an hour. The photographer at noon. Guests would start arriving at the venue by three, expecting to witness the happily ever after that was currently shattered all over my apartment floor along with my dignity.

I was still crying when Mari called five minutes later.

"Anica just told me," she said without preamble. "Hudson and I were already on our way, but we're stopping to get enough coffee to caffeinate a small army. Don't move. Don't do anything stupid. Just wait for us."

"Mari, I—"

"That piece of shit," she continued, her voice getting higher with each word. "That absolute piece of garbage. I knew something was wrong when you both disappeared last night, but I thought maybe you'd just gone home to... you know, boink or something. Not this."

"There's nothing you can do—"

"Like hell there isn't. Hudson! Hudson, get your ass in gear! We have a crisis!"

She hung up too, leaving me alone with my tears.

Twenty minutes later, my apartment had been transformed into what looked like a crisis management center. Mari arrived first, armed with coffee. Hudson followed close behind, carrying pastries and looking like he was ready to commit murder on my behalf. Anica and Callan appeared ten minutes later with tequila, tissues, and matching expressions of barely contained rage.

"For later," Anica explained, setting the tequila on my counter. "When we're done making a plan."

"We're not making any plans," I said from my position on the couch, where Mari had deposited me with a cup of coffee and stern instructions not to move. "I just got abandoned at the altar."

"Technically, you got abandoned before the altar," Hudson pointed out. "Which is somehow worse."

"Not helping," Mari hissed, smacking his arm.

"I can make some calls," Callan offered, settling into my armchair. "I know people who specialize in making other people's lives very difficult."

"Cal," Anica warned, but she didn't sound entirely opposed to the idea.

"What? I'm just saying. If someone hypothetically wanted to ensure that Miles Houston never worked in law again, I could probably arrange that. Hypothetically."

Despite everything, I felt a laugh bubble up in my chest. "While I appreciate the billionaire mob boss energy, maybe we should start with the basics. Like canceling the wedding."

"I've got Caroline working on it," Mari said, not looking up from her phone where she was furiously typing. "I already called the venue, the caterer, the photographer. Everyone's been notified or being notified as we speak."

"What about Dimitrov?"

"Oh, he knows," Anica said, making a face that did little to settle the unease in my stomach.

"Yeah," Callan echoed, making the same face as his wife. "He knows, and he's pissed as hell."

"Not at you, of course," Anica said, though her words did little to comfort me.

"Shit," I whispered, staring wide eyed from Anica to Callan. "Is he going to kill Miles?"

"I don't think so," Callan said, scratching his chin. "He did say he was going to hunt him down, but his wife clarified that he was just going to sit Miles down for a chat."

"So he's going to lack kneecaps then?" Mari asked, rubbing her own kneecap.

"Depends on if he can find him," Callan said, still typing on his phone. "I offered to help. From what I can tell, Miles is at a motel downtown."

"Starlight?" I asked, the coffee in my mug already starting to go cold as I ignored it.

Callan glanced down at his phone, then nodded. "Yeah."

"You're stalking Miles?" I raised an eyebrow.

"I'm assuring Mr. Dimitrov gets to speak to him before he leaves."

"At least he's not on a plane yet, right?" Mari asked, and Anica nodded.

My phone buzzed with a text from Garrett's sister, whom I'd added to my contacts after last night.

ANNABELLE: Garrett just woke up. Doctors say he's going to be fine. Full recovery expected. Thank you for caring about him. - Annabelle (Garrett's sister)

Relief flooded through me so fast it left me dizzy. At least one person I cared about wasn't broken beyond repair.

"Garrett's okay," I announced to the room. "He made it through surgery fine."

"Thank god," Anica said, sinking into the chair next to me. "One less thing to worry about."

"Who is Garrett?" Hudson asked, pulling apart one of the pastries and popping it into his mouth.

"Devonna's old fuckbuddy. He ended up in the hospital last night," Mari said, stealing a piece of the pastry from her fiancé before settling down on the other side of me. "So the venue is canceled, the guests have been notified, Garrett isn't dead, the loan shark is in theory not going to commit murder right away. What else?"

"Nothing. We're done here. I'll deal with the repercussions of cancelling this wedding and Miles will go off to Dubai if Dimitrov doesn't kill him, and shit will eventually fall into a new normal," I said firmly. "Guys, Miles made his choice. He chose running away over staying and fighting for us. Again. And I'm done."

"Men are idiots. Period," Mari said matter-of-factly. "Present company excluded most of the time," she added, nodding toward Hudson and Callan. "But Miles is a special kind of idiot. The kind who needs to be told he's being an idiot so he can be less of an idiot."

"Well, I'm not going to tell him he's an idiot," I said, slumping back on the couch. "Somebody else is going to have to do that."

ALEX ROMANO GETS WHAT HE DESERVES

Chapter 16: Miles

For the first time in a long time, I'd made the right move and wasn't a complete fucking idiot. At least, that's what I kept telling myself as I sat on the edge of the motel bed, staring at the Dubai job offer spread across the scratched nightstand. I'd printed it out, along with the one-way plane ticket to Dubai, which left in six hours.

My duffel bag sat packed by the door, containing everything I owned that mattered. Which, it turned out, wasn't much. Some clothes, my laptop, a few books.

My broken hand throbbed where I'd punched the bathroom wall last night, the cast the urgent care doctor had put on it doing little to ease the pain. Every pulse reminded me of the look on Devonna's face when she'd slapped me. The way she'd told me to take the fucking job and get out of her life.

The skeleton key tattoo over my heart ached worse than my hand.

My phone buzzed with a text from Alek.

ALEK: On my way over with some good whiskey. We should toast to your smart decision.

I didn't want to toast to anything. I wanted to crawl under the thin motel blanket and pretend none of this was happening. But Alek had been the one to bring me the job offer in the first place, and he'd been nothing but supportive through this whole mess.

The least I could do was let him bring me a drink.

Twenty minutes later, Alek knocked on my door carrying a bottle of expensive whiskey and wearing a concerned expression that made him look like a worried older brother.

"Miles," he said, stepping into the room and immediately surveying the damage; the job offer I'd been staring at, my packed bag, the general sense of a man who'd hit rock bottom. "Jesus, you look like hell. How are you holding up?"

"I've been better," I admitted, closing the door behind him.

"I can imagine." Alek set the bottle on the nightstand and turned to face me, his expression serious. "Look, I know this is hard. Ending things with Devonna, leaving everything behind. But I want you to know how proud I am of you for making the tough choice."

"Proud?"

"Hell yes." Alek twisted the cap off the whiskey and poured two glasses using the plastic cups from the bathroom. "It takes real strength to walk away from something that's not working, even when it hurts."

"It *was* working," I muttered as I ran my good hand through my hair.

"Was it, though?" Alek handed me a glass, his voice gentle. "Man, I've been watching you struggle for weeks. You've been stressed out of your fucking mind, and out of your fucking depth."

I took a sip of whiskey, letting it burn down my throat. "Yeah, but—"

"You just didn't work," Alek interrupted. "You don't belong with her. And the way Devonna had to constantly manage you, explain your... quirks to her friends..."

"She didn't mind."

"Didn't she?" Alek settled into the room's only chair, leaning forward. "Miles, I care about you. We've been friends for years. And as your friend, I have to tell you, you just aren't it for her."

I set down my glass, suddenly not wanting the alcohol. "What do you mean?"

"She didn't love you the way you went nuts for her. She's an eleven, and you're a three on a good day. I'm not trying to hurt you," Alek continued, his voice soft with false sympathy. "But you have to

173

admit, there were signs. I mean, just last night, the way her friends looked at you at that rehearsal dinner..."

"What about them?"

"The pity, Miles. Pure, undiluted pity. They felt sorry for her, having to babysit a grown ass man."

My hands clenched into fists, pain shooting through my broken fingers. "That's not—"

"Face it, man. You just don't deserve her."

"You're wrong."

"Am I? Think about it, Miles. Really think about it."

I stood up, pacing to the small window that looked out onto the motel's parking lot. A neon sign flickered outside, casting red and blue shadows across the wall. "She chose me," I said, but even to my own ears, it sounded desperate.

"That's bullshit and you know it." Alek's voice was getting closer. I could hear him moving behind me. "You showed up at her apartment, created this whole mess with Mikhail, backed her into a corner where marriage was the only way out. That's not really choosing, is it?"

"She could have said no."

"Could she? With a loan shark breathing down your neck and her business potentially at risk? Come on, Miles. She's too good a person to let you get your kneecaps broken, even if staying with you was slowly killing her."

I turned around to face him, and the satisfied gleam in his eyes made my stomach clench. "What the hell is that supposed to mean?"

"I'm just saying, this is the best thing for both of you. You get to start fresh in Dubai, make real money, build a life where you actually fit in. And she gets to find someone who..." He paused, pretending to search for the right words. "Someone who doesn't need constant management."

"Someone like who?"

"Someone sophisticated. Someone who can easily fit into the life she's worked so hard to create." Alek's smile was growing sharper. "Someone who can actually contribute to her world instead of just dragging her down."

The red haze of anger was building behind my eyes, but I forced myself to stay calm. "And I suppose you have someone in mind?"

"Well, now that you mention it..." Alek straightened his tie, and something about the gesture made my skin crawl. "I've always thought Devonna was remarkable. Beautiful, intelligent, successful. The kind of woman who deserves a man who can match her ambitions."

"A man like you?"

"I didn't say that." But his smile said everything he wasn't saying out loud. "I'm just pointing out that there are men who could appreciate what she has to offer. Men who wouldn't embarrass her at business dinners or make her friends cringe with secondhand embarrassment."

My vision was starting to tunnel, but Alek wasn't done.

"I mean, let's be honest here, Miles. What do you really bring to the table? You've basically done charity since you got out of law school. You were top of our class, and you chose to forsake a paycheck for lame kids fucking up on the streets. Meanwhile, I make seven figures a year, and look good doing it. You live paycheck to paycheck. You don't know art from your ass, and you think a nice restaurant is anywhere that doesn't have a drive-through window."

"Careful," I said quietly.

"I'm just being realistic. Devonna has built something real at Knot Your Average Wedding. She's got connections, ambition, class. And you..." He gestured at me dismissively. "You're a pathetic lawyer with tattoos up his ass who thinks fancy means wearing an elephant tie."

"Stop talking."

"She needs someone who can elevate her, not someone she has to constantly apologize for. Someone who can take her to gallery openings and charity galas without making her worry about what he'll say or do wrong."

"I said stop."

"Someone who can make her come in seconds just by —"

"Shut the fuck up." I shoved him back with my good hand.

"Oh, hit a nerve?" Alek's mask slipped, revealing something ugly underneath. "Face it, Miles. You've known you weren't good enough for her from the start. God, the amount of times you came to me as an insecure little douche...I literally lost count."

"Get out."

"The truth hurts, doesn't it? That beautiful, successful woman lowered herself to your level, and now she's finally free to find someone worthy of her. Someone who won't drag her down to his level. Someone who can show her what a real man can do when he fucks her senseless and has her—"

I hit him before he could finish the sentence.

My fist connected with his jaw with a satisfying crack that sent pain shooting through my broken hand. The cast certainly helped pack that punch. Alek stumbled backward, knocking over the chair, blood trickling from his split lip.

"You son of a bitch," I said, advancing on him. "This was never about helping me, was it? This was about getting me out of the way so you could move in on her."

Alek scrambled to his feet, backing toward the door. "You're making a mistake—"

"The only mistake I made was trusting you." I grabbed him by his expensive shirt and slammed him against the wall. "How long have you been planning this? How long have you been working to break us up?"

"Miles, you're being paranoid—"

"Oh, don't start scrambling now, Alek. Not when you can gaslight me into hanging on your every word. God, you're a fucking piece of shit. Every conversation we had about Devonna, what did you say? That I wasn't good enough? That she'd be better off without me? That I should leave?" I shoved him harder against the wall, never more grateful for the few inches I had on him than I was now. Fuck, he actually looked nervous. Good. "You've been manipulating me from the start."

"I was trying to help you see reality—"

"You were trying to clear the field." I let go of his shirt and stepped back, disgusted. "Well, congratulations. You got what you wanted. I'm leaving."

Alek straightened his shirt, wiping blood from his mouth. "You'll thank me for this someday. When you're in Dubai making real money and she's moved on to someone who actually deserves her, you'll realize I did you both a favor."

"Get the fuck out."

"Thanks for clearing the way, man."

Before I could knock his two front teeth out, he grabbed his bottle of whiskey and bolted for the door, pausing only to look back at me with something like pity. "You were always going to lose her. I just helped speed up the inevitable."

The door slammed behind him, leaving me alone with my rage and the growing realization of what I'd done. What I'd let him do to me.

Goddamnit. Anica had been right. She'd heard just a snippet of the way Alek had spoken to me last night and pegged him perfectly. I should've listened to her.

I sank back onto the bed, cradling my throbbing hand. Punching Alek had felt good, but it hadn't changed anything. I'd still left Devonna. I'd still chosen running over fighting.

I'd still proven that maybe he was right about me after all.

A heavy knock on my door made me freeze. Three sharp raps, then silence.

"Open up, son," came a voice from the other side. Russian accent, calm and pleasant. "We need to talk."

Mikhail

As if this day couldn't get any fucking worse.

There was more movement in the hallway. Other footsteps, murmured voices.

Double fuck.

He hadn't come alone.

I could pretend I wasn't here. Stay quiet and hope he'd go away. But the Starlight Motel's walls were thin, and I'd just had a shouting match with Alek. Odds were not in my favor. He probably knew I was in here.

"Houston," the voice came again, still polite but with an edge of impatience. "Don't make this more difficult than it needs to be."

I stood up with a resigned sigh, my broken hand throbbing, and walked to the door. Through the peephole, I could see Mikhail in his expensive suit, flanked by Shane and Erik.

I opened the door.

"Mikhail," I said, stepping back to let them in. Why fight the inevitable?

"Miles." Mikhail swept into the room like he owned it, his gaze taking in the packed duffel bag, the job offer on the nightstand, the general aura of a man who'd hit rock bottom. "Interesting accommodations you've chosen."

Shane and Erik filed in behind him, Erik closing the door with a soft, definitely not ominous at all, click. The small motel room felt even smaller with three large men in expensive suits filling the space.

"Please, sit," Mikhail said, gesturing to the bed like this was his office instead of my janky motel room. "We have much to discuss."

I sat, mainly because my legs didn't feel entirely steady. Mikhail took the room's only chair while Shane and Erik positioned themselves by the door.

"So," Mikhail said, his voice conversational as he straightened his cufflinks. "You left my daughter-in-law the night before her wedding day."

"She's not your—"

"She's family the same way I'd consider you family," Mikhail cut me off, his tone never changing but his eyes going hard. "Which makes this a family matter."

I swallowed hard, my broken hand throbbing. "Look, I'm taking a job in Dubai that will more than cover my debt to you completely."

"Your debt?" Mikhail chuckled and pinched the bridge of his nose. "You think this is about money?"

"Isn't it?"

"Son, let me tell you a story." Mikhail leaned back in his chair, getting comfortable. "Eight years ago, a young man came to me looking for a loan. Desperate, heartbroken, completely destroyed by love. You remember this day?"

I nodded reluctantly.

"This boy, he could barely speak coherently. Just kept saying this girl's name over and over. Devonna, Devonna, Devonna. And I thought to myself, 'Mikkie, you remember this feeling. You remember what it was like when you first saw Flo.'" His eyes went distant. "The most beautiful woman I had ever seen. Her father, he was very protective of his little princess. When I first asked to court her, he laughed in my face. Said I was nothing but a street thug with delusions of grandeur. But I persisted. I sent flowers, wrote letters, learned to dance because she loved dancing. Her father, he kept testing me. Made me prove I was worthy of his daughter. And you

178

know what? I was grateful for those tests, because they made me become the man she deserved."

"That's... nice," I said carefully. "But I don't see what this has to do with—"

"Everything," Mikhail said firmly. "Because when you came to me eight years ago, broke and desperate, I saw the same love in your eyes that I had felt for Florence. The kind of love that makes a man do stupid things. Brave things. The kind worth fighting for."

"So you... helped me?"

"I gave you extensions. Opportunities. Time to get your shit together and win her back." Mikhail's smile turned predatory. "And when that didn't work, I decided to... apply some pressure. Even that didn't work. But I had need of a talented lawyer like yourself, and there still seemed to be hope that one day you two might find each other again."

"You... you wanted me to be with Von?" I frowned, smoothing my uninjured hand over the top of my pants.

"I am not an idiot, despite what my daughter might think. I know Shane has been fucking my daughter for the better part of two years. I know they are," —he wrinkled his nose— "in love, or whatever."

By the door, Shane stiffened, his eyes going wide. "What?"

"Shut up. I'll deal with you later. Right now, we are focusing on a different idiot." Mikhail didn't even look at Shane. "I know that my daughter wanted to distract me as things got more serious between the two of them. Irina, along with everyone in the Dimitrov family, knows how head over ass you've been for Miss Onai. My daughter also knows how fucking stupid you are and how much money you owed me. Also knew that I'd consider you an adopted son, despite how stupid you can be. So she thought she'd play me. Suggest that I have the two of you married, knowing you would never agree. But in that disagreement, I'd be distracted and she and Shane could do whatever the fuck it is they do."

"So... you knew I'd refuse too?" I glanced at Shane as I asked Mikhail the question. Irina's beau had turned a similar shade of discolored off-white as the motel walls. "But you had these goons hold me upside down off a balcony until I said I was engaged."

"Engaged to whom, exactly?" Mikhail asked with a gleam in his eye.

"Devonna."

"Ah, you're catching on." Mikhail nodded approvingly. "You see, my daughter Irina, she is a very clever girl. But she gets her cleverness from me. The plan was simple once Irina started the ball rolling. Create a crisis, force you to contact Miss Onai, let nature take its course."

"But it didn't work," I said.

"Didn't it? You got the girl. You had her. The wedding was today." Mikhail's expression darkened. "And then you decided to be a fucking idiot."

"I was doing the right thing—"

"The right thing?" Mikhail stood up, beginning to pace in the small space between the bed and the window. "The right thing would have been to fight for her. To stand by her side and prove you belonged there. Instead, you ran away like a coward."

"She deserves better than me."

"According to who? You? That piece of shit who was just here filling your head with poison?" Mikhail's eyes flashed dangerously. "Oh yes, I know about your friend, Mr. Romano. I never liked that asshole."

"Yeah, he really is," I grumbled, my hand throbbing in solidarity.

"Mr. Romano was trying to get you out of the way so he could move in on your woman," Mikhail said bluntly. "And you were too stupid to see it."

"I know."

Mikhail stopped pacing and fixed me with a stare. "And you handed her to him on a silver platter by leaving her last night."

"I didn't... she wouldn't..."

"Wouldn't she? Think about it, son. You've left her broken-hearted, and what would be an excellent way to get back at you? Sleep with your best friend, perhaps?"

"Fuck," I whispered.

"Now you're getting it through that fucking skull of yours," Mikhail said. "Your woman doesn't want perfect, you dumb asshole. She wants someone who'll stand there with her when everything goes wrong. She wants you."

"How do you know?"

"Because I did what I do best. I watched her these last several weeks. I've seen the way she looks at you, the way she defends you, the way she lights up when you walk in a room. That girl is head over

180

heels for you, flaws and all. Just like Florence was for me, even when I was nothing but a street thug with big dreams."

"But I left her," I said, choking on the words. "I left her the night before our wedding."

"Yes, you did. And now you need to decide if you're going to compound that mistake by staying gone, or if you're going to grow a pair and go get her back."

I stared at him, my mind racing. "She'll never forgive me. Not for this."

"Maybe not," Mikhail agreed. "But you'll never know unless you try. And if you don't try, if you get on that plane to Dubai today, then you really are the coward I was afraid you might be." He slid his hands into his pockets and gave me a terrifying grin. "And I'll break your kneecaps." He headed for the door, Shane and Erik falling in behind him. Shane still looked shell-shocked by the revelation about Irina.

"One more thing, Miles," Mikhail paused at the door. "If you do decide to go crawling back to her, you better be prepared to grovel like your life depends on it. Because it does."

"And if she won't forgive me?"

Mikhail's smile was sharp. "Then you better find a way to make her. Because if not, I will be very disappointed. And you don't want to disappoint me. Only a fucking idiot would do that."

Yeah. I was a fucking idiot.

THE MAN REMEMBERS EVERYTHING

Chapter 17: Devonna

In the quiet hum of the office, I buried myself under a mountain of seating charts and caterer contracts. Anica and Mari were off attending some wedding planning seminar, leaving me alone with Caroline, who was manning the phones and the lobby. It gave me the freedom to hide in my office and sulk.

Unfortunately, an hour before the end of the workday, a knock interrupted my sulking. Caroline poked her head in, her fiery curls pinned back.

"Devonna, there's someone here to see you," she said with a smile. However, the crease between her brows whispered something wasn't right.

"Unless it's a client with a seven-figure budget or a Spice Girl, tell them I'm unavailable," I replied, focusing on my laptop as though its screen held the secrets of the cosmos.

Caroline hesitated, and an odd tone crept into her voice. "Well... he's kind of insistent. I told him your were busy, and—"

"Devonna, you'd make time for an old friend, right?" drawled a familiar voice, dripping with arrogance. Full marks for persistence went to the man stepping into my office, sporting an air of superiority.

Alek Romano.

"Romano," I muttered, resisting the urge to chuck a stapler at his smirking, punchable face. God, he really was the human equivalent of a paper cut soaked in lemon juice, evidenced when he shooed Caroline away. I rolled my eyes, then nodded once. Caroline mouthed "good luck" and shut the door.

"What do you want?" I asked, raising an eyebrow as I looked him up and down. He was holding a box of expensive-looking cookies and wearing what I assumed was meant to be a sympathetic expression.

"I heard about what happened," he said, stepping farther into my office without invitation. "I wanted to check on you."

A dark purple bruise had formed along his jawline. Clearly, he'd tried to cover it with concealer, but hadn't quite managed to hide it.

"What happened to your face?" I asked.

His hand moved instinctively to the bruise. "Nothing. I walked into a door. Anyway, I brought these for you. I know how much you love those little French cookies from Ladurée."

I did not, in fact, love cookies from Ladurée.

"That's thoughtful," I said carefully, not taking the box. "But unnecessary."

"Devonna, I know this must be incredibly difficult for you." Alek settled into the chair across from my desk like he belonged there. "Having someone abandon you like that, especially someone you trusted."

When Mari helped alert the guests that the wedding was off, she hadn't given specifics. So unless Miles had told him what happened...Something cold settled in my stomach. "What exactly are you here for, Alek?"

"I'm here as a friend. Miles... well, Miles has always been impulsive. Quick to make decisions without thinking them through." He leaned forward, his expression earnest. "I tried to talk him out of it, but you know how he is when he gets an idea in his head."

I raised an eyebrow. Anica had been very clear over what she'd heard Alek and Miles discussing. I knew he was partially to blame for Miles leaving. Still though, I was interested what his purpose was for interrupting my day.

"Do I?"

"Come on, Devonna. You've seen how he operates. The way he jumps into things without considering the consequences. And now he's just... gone."

"What's your point?" I asked.

"My point is that maybe this is for the best." Alek's voice was gentle, like he was delivering difficult but necessary medicine. "I know it hurts now, but Miles was never really... stable enough for someone like you."

"Someone like me?"

"Successful. Driven. Gorgeous. You're building something real here, and you've always needed a partner who can match that ambition. Someone who won't drag you down or embarrass you at important events."

"Alek, hun, I don't *need* a partner. I may choose to have one, but I don't *need* one." I stared at him, watching the way he leaned forward with false concern, the practiced sympathy in his eyes. The bruise on his jaw was starting to make sense. "How did you say you got that bruise again?"

He shrugged. "A door."

"Uh, huh." I leaned back in my chair. "Did Miles give you that bruise?" I asked.

Alek's hand flew to his face again. "I told you, I walked into —"

"Bullshit." I stood, crossing my arms. "You went to see him, didn't you? Probably to gloat about how right you were, how he was doing me a favor by leaving. I know you were talking to him about that Dubai job last night. Did you encourage him to leave?"

"Devonna, you're upset, and I understand that, but —"

"Get out."

"What?"

"I said get out of my office." I walked to the door and held it open. "And take your manipulative gaslighting with you. Maybe it worked on Miles, but it sure as hell won't work on me. Now get out."

Alek stood, his mask slipping. "You're making a mistake. When the shock wears off, you'll realize I'm right. Miles Houston is a liability, and you're better off without him. And then, when you need someone to hold you, I'll —"

"Call my girls. Now get the fuck out of my office."

"Entitled bitch," he muttered under his breath. Thankfully, though, he left without further argument.

After he was gone, I sat back down at my desk and stared at the cookies he'd forgotten to take with him. My phone buzzed with a text from Mari.

MARI: *Emergency at Central Park. Bethesda Fountain. Can you come quickly?*

I sighed and responded with a quick "be right there," and grabbed my keys, heading for the door.

"I have to go check on Mari, so I'm going to head out early," I said to Caroline as I fixed the collar of my jacket. "If that douche comes back, call security."

"Will do," she said, giving me a two-finger salute.

Central Park in the late afternoon was busy with joggers and tourists, but as I approached Bethesda Fountain, the crowds seemed to thin out. Mari was nowhere to be seen, but there was a trail of white rose petals leading away from the fountain toward the lake.

"Are you kidding me right now?" I muttered, but I followed the petals anyway.

The trail led to a secluded spot by the water where someone had set up what looked like a scene from a fairy tale. String lights hung between the trees, casting a warm golden light over a small area that had been transformed with white flowers, flickering battery-operated candles, and a blanket spread on the ground.

And sitting on that blanket, looking nervous as hell, was Miles.

He was wearing the same clothes he'd worn the day we met here nine years ago. Jeans, a dark green sweater that made his eyes look impossibly bright, and that leather jacket he'd probably owned since college. His hair was messed up like he'd been running his hands through it, and there was a white cast on his left hand.

"Hi," he said, starting to stand.

"Why aren't you on a plane right now?" I asked, taking a step back when he moved. My arms crossed automatically over my chest. "What are you doing here?"

He sank back down onto the blanket, his hands falling to his lap. "I wanted to talk to you."

"Really?" I stayed exactly where I was, several feet away from his fairy tale setup. "Right. Because that's what you do when you want to talk to someone. You disappear with a plan to run away to Dubai, and then ambush them in a park."

"Vonnie—"

"No." I held up a hand. "You don't get to 'Vonnie' me. You lost that privilege when you decided to make life-altering decisions for both of us without bothering to consult me."

Miles winced, his shoulders hunching. "You're right. I fucked up."

"Which time? When you left eight years ago, or when you left the night before our wedding? Because I'm having trouble keeping track of your various exit strategies."

He looked down at his cast, flexing his fingers. "Both times. All of it."

"Helpful." I shifted my weight, deliberately not sitting down despite the obvious invitation of the blanket. "So what's this supposed to be? Some grand romantic gesture that's going to make me forget that you abandoned me again?"

"It's not supposed to make you forget anything." His voice was quiet. "I don't want you to forget. I want you to remember why we were good together before I screwed it up."

I let out a harsh laugh. "Before you screwed it up? Miles, you've screwed it up twice. That's not a pattern, that's a personality trait."

"I know."

"Do you?" I took another step back, putting more distance between us. "Because from where I'm standing, this looks like the same old Miles. The one who thinks he can fix everything with the right gesture, the right words, the right—" I gestured at the surrounding setup, "—romantic lighting."

Miles was quiet for a long moment, just looking at me with those piercing eyes that had always been my weakness. But I wasn't feeling weak right now. I was feeling angry.

"You're not going to sit down," he said finally. It wasn't a question.

"Nope."

"You're not going to make this easy for me."

"Did you think I would?" I cocked my head, studying him. "Did you really think you could just show up here with some fairy lights and I'd fall into your arms?"

"No." He ran his good hand through his hair. "I hoped, but no. I know I don't deserve easy."

"You don't deserve anything from me right now. You made your choice, Miles. You chose to leave. Again."

"I chose wrong." He shifted on the blanket, leaning forward. "I've been choosing wrong for eight years."

"And now you want another do-over?" I shook my head. "That's not how this works. You don't get to keep hurting me and then show up with apologies when it's convenient for you."

"It's not convenient—"

"Isn't it?" I cut him off. "And now you're back because what? You got lonely? You realized Dubai isn't as appealing as you thought?"

Miles was quiet, his jaw working like he was trying to find the right words. The silence stretched between us, filled with the distant sounds of the city and the gentle lapping of water against the shore.

"I didn't get on the flight because I realized I was being a coward," he said finally.

"Congratulations. You figured out what I've known for years." I kept my voice steady and controlled. "What do you want, a medal?"

"I want you to yell at me." The words came out rushed, desperate. "I want you to tell me exactly how much I hurt you, how stupid I've been, how I don't deserve a second chance. Or a third chance. Or whatever number we're on now."

"Why?"

"Because at least then you'd be talking *to* me instead of talking *at* me." His eyes searched my face. "You're doing that thing where you go cold and professional. Where you shut down."

He wasn't wrong. I could feel the familiar walls sliding into place, the ones I'd built after he left the first time. The ones that kept me safe but also kept me separate.

"Maybe that's what you deserve," I said quietly.

"Maybe it is." Miles pushed himself up to his knees, not quite standing but no longer sitting either. "But it's not what I'm hoping for."

"What are you hoping for?"

"Honesty." He looked directly at me, not flinching away from whatever he saw in my expression. "I'm hoping you'll tell me what you're really thinking instead of hiding behind that professional mask you wear when you're protecting yourself."

I *was* hiding. I *was* protecting myself. And I hated that he could still read me so easily.

"You want honesty?" I asked, my voice dropping dangerously low.
"Yes."

"Fine." I took a step closer, close enough that he could probably see the anger burning in my eyes. "I think you're selfish. I think you're a coward who runs away the moment things get complicated because it's easier than doing the work. I think you tell yourself you're being noble when really you're just scared of failing."

Miles absorbed each word, but he didn't look away.

"I think," I continued, my voice gaining strength, "that you don't actually love me. You love the idea of me. You love having someone to rescue and protect and make decisions for. But you don't love me enough to trust me with the truth. You don't love me enough to let me choose."

"You're wrong about that last part," he said quietly.

"Am I?"

"Yes. I love you enough to let you choose right now. To walk away if that's what you want. To tell me to go to hell and mean it. But I had to come back. I had to give you that choice."

I stared at him, searching his face for signs of manipulation, for the careful calculation I'd seen in Alek's expression earlier. But all I saw was raw honesty and the kind of fear that came from putting everything on the line. Some of the anger in my chest fizzled out.

"And if I do?" I asked. "If I tell you to go to hell?"

"Then I'll go. Shit, I'm already half way there." His voice was steady despite the tremor I could see in his hands. "And I'll spend the rest of my life regretting that I wasn't brave enough to fight for you when it mattered."

For the first time since he'd started talking, I found myself wanting to sit down. So I did. I looked around at the setup, taking in the details. A bottle of Macallan 18 sat next to two glasses. A bag of black truffle chips like the imported ones he'd eaten when he'd first reappeared in my life. White roses, not red, because I'd told him red roses were cliché. And sitting in a small jewelry box, a delicate gold chain with a skeleton key pendant.

"What is that?" I asked quietly, transfixed by the necklace.

"I remember everything about you." His voice was rough. "The way you take your coffee. How you always order the same thing at restaurants but read the entire menu anyway. That you hate surprises but love thoughtful gestures."

My breath caught. "Miles—"

"I know what you're going to say. That this is too much, that grand gestures don't fix what I did. And you're right. But I needed you to know that leaving you was the biggest mistake of my life. Both times."

"What if I can't trust you not to leave again?" I asked.

"Then I'll spend however long it takes proving that I won't." He reached for the skeleton key necklace and held it up between us. "I got this made for you. Same design as the one you used to wear, the one tattooed over my heart." He pushed the jewelry box towards me.

"Miles," I said, my voice barely above a whisper.

"I love you, Devonna. I've loved you for years, through every stupid decision and every moment of cowardice. I love your sharp tongue and your terrible morning breath and the way you get that little wrinkle between your eyebrows when you're concentrating." He cupped my face in his hands. "I love that you don't need me to rescue you, but that you let me support you anyway. I love that you're strong enough to call me on my bullshit and patient enough to let me grow."

"And if I say no?" I asked, though I was already leaning into his touch. "If I say this is too little, too late?"

"Then I'll respect that. I know you don't need me. You don't need anyone to be completely successful and fulfilled in your life. But I want you to want me. I want to find ways to make your life easier, not harder." His thumb traced across my cheekbone. "I want to earn your trust back every day."

I closed my eyes. He was asking me to risk everything again, to trust that this time would be different.

The smart thing would be to say no. To protect myself from another heartbreak. To find someone stable and reliable who wouldn't run away when things got complicated.

"Well?"

"I…"

CONDITIONS, CONDITIONS, CONDITIONS

Chapter 18: Miles

Her eyes were closed, her face soft in my hands, and I was pretty sure I'd stopped breathing entirely.

"I..." she'd said, and then nothing. Just silence. Her skin was warm against my palms, and a slight tremor passed in her jaw. Shit. I couldn't tell if that was a good sign or a bad sign.

Every instinct I had was screaming at me to say something, to fill the silence with words or promises or more apologies. But I'd learned something over the past few days about shutting the hell up and letting her lead.

So I waited. Even though my heart was trying to beat its way out of my chest.

Even though my hands were shaking.

Even though years of mistakes and a bit of clarity had led to this single moment where everything could go either way.

A tear slid down her cheek.

"Shit," I whispered, brushing it away with my thumb. "Vonnie, don't cry. I didn't mean to make you —"

"You didn't make me do anything," she said, but her voice was quiet. "That's the problem."

"What do you mean?"

"I mean you can't make me forgive you. You can't make me trust you again. You can't make me choose you." She leaned into my touch, closing her eyes again briefly.

My stomach dropped. "And?"

"And..." She took a shaky breath. "And I'm terrified."

"Of me?"

"God, no. Of us. Of doing this again and having you decide to leave again when things get complicated." She opened her eyes, looking directly at me. "Of falling in love with you all over again just to watch you run away when I need you most."

I didn't let go of her face. Couldn't let go. "What if I promised that wouldn't happen?"

"You can't promise that."

"I can—"

"Miles." She caught my wrists, holding my hands against her cheeks. "You can't promise me you'll never get scared again. You can't promise me you'll never make mistakes or hurt my feelings or do something stupid. And I can't promise you the same thing."

"Then what now? Von, I love you."

She was quiet for a long moment, studying my face like she was trying to memorize it. "We can promise to try. We can promise to stay and fight instead of running when things get hard. We can promise to have the ugly conversations instead of making assumptions."

"I can do that."

"Can you? Because the next time you start spiraling about not being good enough for me, the next time some asshole like Alek gets in your head and makes you doubt yourself, what are you going to do?"

"I'm going to tell you about it."

"Even if it makes you look weak or insecure or needy?"

I thought about the motel room, about sitting there convinced I was doing the noble thing while really just being a coward. About all the conversations we could have had over the years if I'd been brave enough to be honest about my insecurities.

"Especially then," I said.

"And if I tell you that your fears are bullshit and you're being an idiot?"

191

"Then I'll listen to you. Because you're usually right about these things." I managed a small smile. "Even when it hurts to hear."

"Damn right," she agreed, and there was a hint of her old sass in it that made my chest feel lighter.

"So is that a yes?"

"It's a maybe leaning toward yes with conditions."

"I'll take it." I started to lean forward to kiss her, but she pressed a finger against my lips.

"Conditions first, kissing later."

"Yes ma'am."

"First condition: no more grand gestures to fix problems. If you fuck up, you apologize with words and changed behavior, not fairy lights and expensive whiskey. Well, maybe the whiskey…"

"Noted."

"Second condition: we take this slow. Like, actually slow. Dating, getting to know each other again, figuring out if we even like the people we've become."

"I already like the person you've become."

"You say that now, but wait until you see how much I work. Wait until you realize how precise I am about the way I like my apartment."

"I already know you color-code your closet, so that's a good start."

"Third condition." Her voice got softer. "You have to be patient with me while I learn to trust you again. I'm going to be scared sometimes. I'm going to test you sometimes. I'm going to need reassurance."

"As much as you need."

"And fourth…" She paused, biting her lip. "You have to let me take care of you too. Not just financially or practically, but emotionally. When you're hurting or scared or feeling like shit about yourself, you have to let me in."

"That's the hard one," I admitted.

"I know. But it's important. We can't build something real if it's just you taking care of me and me pretending you don't need anything."

I nodded, understanding what she meant. The old version of us had been unbalanced that way. Me trying to be the strong one, her trying not to be too much trouble. Both of us performing instead of just being.

"Okay," I said. "Those are fair conditions."

"All of them?"

"All of them."

"Even the slow part? Because I mean slow, Miles. Like, not-sleeping-together-for-a-while slow."

I groaned, dropping my forehead against hers. "You're going to kill me."

"I'm going to make sure we get it right this time," she corrected. "Besides, the anticipation will be good for you. Build character."

"I have plenty of character."

"You have plenty of charm. Character is something different." She was smiling now, really smiling, and it was like watching the sun come up. "So? Do we have a deal?"

"We have a deal." I brushed my thumb across her bottom lip. "Does this mean I can kiss you now?"

"This means you can kiss me now."

I didn't need to be told twice. I leaned in and kissed her softly. If she wanted slow, I'd give her slow. She could control the wheel and the gas pedal. Devonna kissed me back with the same gentleness.

When we broke apart, she was looking at me with an expression I couldn't quite read.

"What?" I asked.

"Nothing. Just..." She shook her head, smiling. "I forgot how good you are at that."

"At kissing?"

"At making me believe in us again."

I felt my throat get tight. "I won't let you down this time, Vonnie. I swear."

"You might," she said simply. "We both might. But we'll figure it out as we go. I love you too, you know." She picked up the skeleton key necklace from the blanket, holding it up between us. "Help me put this on?"

My hands were steadier this time as I fastened the clasp, the key settling against her chest right where it belonged. She touched it gently, looking down at it.

"It's perfect," she said.

"You're perfect."

"I'm really not. But I appreciate the compliment."

I caught her hand, lacing our fingers together. "So what happens now?"

Devonna scrunched her nose and glanced down at the chip bag and whiskey. "I eat that bag of chips you owe me and we crack open that whiskey." She looked me up and down, and then grinned. "And you tell me all about the tattoos you got while we were apart, starting with that wedding cake."

"Funny story. There's this gorgeous woman who works for a wedding planning company call Knot Your Average Wedding…"

ONE YEAR
LATER

Epilogue: Devonna

I
t was funny, really. I'd helped plan hundreds of weddings over the years, and yet I was more stressed about our house warming party than I ever had been about any angry bridezilla or picky monster-in-law. I sat perched on our marble kitchen counter, stress-eating mini quiches while Miles bustled around the living room, rearranging cushions and straightening picture frames that didn't need straightening.

"You know, if you keep eating those at that rate, we won't have any left for the guests," Miles commented, glancing at me with a raised eyebrow.

"Then you'll have to make more," I mumbled through a mouthful of pastry. "Besides, I'm checking the quality. It's control testing."

Miles chuckled, walking over to the kitchen island and snagging a quiche for himself. " Quality control, huh? And how are they faring?"

"Delicious," I admitted, popping another one into my mouth. "You outdid yourself, and I will be expecting these every Sunday morning for the rest of our lives."

With a smirk, he brushed away a crumb on my cheek and pecked my lips. "Deal." Miles looked around the house with a satisfied smile. "It looks good, doesn't it?"

I followed his gaze, taking in the cozy living room, the dining table set with mismatched plates and cutlery, and the string lights casting a warm glow over everything. Our house. It still felt surreal sometimes.

"It does," I agreed. "But I still think we should have gone with the grey throw pillows instead of the blue."

Miles rolled his eyes. "You only say that because you lost the coin toss."

"I maintain that the coin was rigged," I grumbled. In truth, I loved the blue pillows. I loved our house, with its quirks and compromises. I loved the life we were building together.

The doorbell rang, and I nearly choked on what was left of my quiche. "They're here!" I squeaked, brushing crumbs off my white lace sundress.

Miles laughed as he helped me down from the counter, pressing a quick kiss to my forehead before heading to the door. "Ready?"

"Let's do this."

The first small wave included Mari and Hudson, who immediately started walking around the house exploring, and Anica and Callan, who'd apparently brought enough wine and champagne to supply a small restaurant.

"This place is gorgeous," Mari gushed, spinning around to take in the living room. "The lighting, the flowers, the way you've arranged everything... Wait. This doesn't look like a normal housewarming party."

"What do you mean?" I asked innocently, accepting a hug from Anica.

"I mean this looks like..." Mari studied the white flowers arranged in small bouquets, the fairy lights strung at exactly the right height, the way we'd moved all the furniture to create an open space in the center of the room. "This looks like—"

"Like what?" Hudson interrupted, hands casually in his pockets. He raised an eyebrow.

"Nothing," Mari said quickly, but her eyes narrowed. "Just very... intentional."

Callan appeared beside us with champagne glasses. "Whatever this is, I approve."

Before anyone could respond, the doorbell rang again, and Miles went to answer it. This time it was Mikhail and Florence, followed by Shane and Irina, who were practically glowing with happiness.

"Devonna, sugar!" Florence exclaimed, enveloping me in a cloud of expensive perfume as she hugged me. "The house is absolutely beautiful."

"Thank you," I said, shooting a glance at Miles, who was helping Mikhail out of his coat. "We wanted something cozy."

"Very cozy," Mikhail agreed, a small grin on his lips.

Irina glided over to me, holding up her left hand to show off the engagement ring Shane had given her the month before. "Can you believe it? We're finally engaged!"

"Congratulations," I said, glancing at Mikhail, who stood with his gaze narrowed at the back of Shane's head. Hopefully Shane would still have his kneecaps by the end of the wedding planning stage. "When's the wedding?"

"Next spring," Shane said, wrapping his arm around Irina's waist. "Maybe you could help us plan it?"

Florence cleared her throat, and Irina rolled her eyes. "With my mother's help, of course," Irina said.

"I'd love to," I replied.

The doorbell rang again, and this time it was Garrett with Catrina, his girlfriend of eight months. They'd met when he was in San Francisco, and from what little I'd been told, it was a crazy start to their relationship. She'd been the one he'd been protecting with his security company when he'd been shot.

"Look at this place," Garrett said, whistling appreciatively. "Well done, Devonna. Good to see you, Miles." He shook Miles's hand, clapping him on the back. Miles winced, but grinned.

"Thanks, Hulk." Miles nodded towards Catrina. "You must be his girlfriend. It's nice to meet you."

"You can call me Cat," Catrina said, holding out her hand to Miles. "You two have a lovely home."

"What's with the..." Garrett gestured vaguely at the excessive decorations and flowers.

"Just wanted the place to look nice for the party," I said, but I could feel my cheeks heating up.

"Well it's beautiful," Catrina said. "Is there a bathroom?"

"Unfortunately, the house came without one, but we make do with a bucket in the—"

"Down the hall to the left," I said, smacking Miles in the chest.

As more people arrived and the house filled with conversation and laughter, I settled into the role of hostess. It was fun, even more so as Miles joined me, helping to refill drinks and take trash.

But the longer it went on, the more I started to get anxious. Miles noticed and interlaced his fingers with mine.

"Ready?" He whispered in my ear. "If so, I'll go get Mikhail."

"I think so. My stomach is just not cooperating."

He kissed me on the temple. "Must be the revenge of the mini quiches. If you need a minute, I'll—"

"No, let's do this. I'm ready." I squeezed his hand for courage.

"I'll find the Peacock then and we'll get this party started." He let go of me and made a beeline for Mikhail, who stood across the room with his arm around Florence. Mikhail looked up expectantly when Miles approached. They exchanged a few quiet words, and then Mikhail's face broke into an even wider grin than he'd been wearing all evening. He nodded and began moving toward the center of the room, Florence beaming beside him.

"My friends," Mikhail announced, his voice carrying easily across the apartment, "if I could have your attention please."

The room quieted, everyone turning to look at him with varying degrees of curiosity. Miles returned to my side, taking my hand and squeezing it reassuringly.

"Miss Onai and Miles have asked me here tonight for a very special reason."

Anica's eyes went wide. "Oh my god."

"This is not just a housewarming party," Mikhail said, his grin growing impossibly wider. "This is a wedding!"

The room exploded.

Mari's scream was so loud that I was pretty sure the neighbors next door heard it. Anica hugged Mari, and they both charged me and enveloped me into their hug. Callan started laughing and couldn't stop. Hudson just stood there with his mouth open, staring at us like we'd announced we were joining the circus.

"You magnificent, sneaky, wonderful people," Callan said, shaking his head in amazement. "How did you manage to keep this a secret from my wife?"

198

"And more impressively, *my* wife," Hudson muttered as he shook Miles's hand.

"We're just that good," I said, high-fiving Miles over Mari's head.

"Wait, wait, wait," Anica said through her happy tears as she pulled away from our three-way hug. "You're getting married right now? Here? Do you have rings? A license?"

"We have everything," Miles said, pulling our marriage license from his jacket pocket.

"And the rings are safely with me," I added, patting one of the pockets in my sundress, "because someone has misplaced his keys three times this week."

"I temporarily misplaced them in creative locations," Miles corrected.

"They were in the fridge once."

"Oh my god, this is happening," Anica said, changing the subject. "You're actually doing this. Right now. In your new living room."

"With Mikhail officiating," Miles added.

"Of course I am officiating," Mikhail said proudly, straightening his tie. "Who else should marry my children? I am the one who brought them together, after all."

"Nothing like the threat of a good weighted swim in the river to get the ball rolling," Florence pointed out fondly.

"It worked, did it not?" Mikhail patted Miles on the shoulder. "I'm proud of you, Miles."

"I thought you said he was a loan shark?" Catrina whispered to Garrett from somewhere behind me. It was quiet enough that I doubted Mikhail had heard it, since his focus was on Miles. But I still glanced over my shoulder in time to see Garrett shushing her with wide eyes.

"Later," Garrett replied. "I'll explain it later."

"How long have you been planning this?" Irina asked loud enough to pull my attention back to what was happening in front of me.

"Two months," I admitted. "We decided two months ago, got the license, asked Mikhail to officiate, and planned everything while pretending to argue about paint colors."

"The paint color arguments were real though," Miles said. "We genuinely couldn't agree on whether the bedroom should be sage green or seafoam."

"We went with sage," I added. "Just so everyone knows."

"Okay, everyone," Mikhail said, shifting into officiant mode. "If we are doing this, we do this properly. Miss Onai, Miles, please, come up here with me. Everyone else, move to that side."

As our friends and family arranged themselves around us, Miles leaned over and kissed my cheek. The nervousness I'd been carrying all evening melted away, replaced by a warmth that spread from my chest to my fingertips.

"Any regrets?" he asked quietly.

"Only that we didn't think of this sooner," I replied.

Mikhail cleared his throat, and the room settled into expectant silence. "My friends, we are gathered here today to witness the marriage of Devonna Onai and Miles Houston. Two people who have taught me that sometimes love requires a little... encouragement."

"A little?" Florence muttered, earning chuckles from a few people.

"They have chosen to write their own vows," Mikhail continued, his voice taking on a surprisingly ceremonial tone. "Miles, you go first, and try not to cry too much. Save some tears for your bride."

Miles cleared his throat, pulling a folded piece of paper from his jacket pocket. "I wrote this down because the last time I tried to wing an important speech about my feelings for you, I ended up on my knees in Central Park begging for forgiveness."

"That worked out pretty well though," I pointed out.

"True." He unfolded the paper, then looked directly at me. "Vonnie, a year ago, you gave me a list of conditions for being together. You wanted honesty, communication, and the promise that I'd stop making decisions for both of us without consulting you first. Today, I want to add my own promises to that list," Miles continued. "I promise to show up for you every day, not just when it's easy or convenient, but especially when it's hard. I promise to choose you, and us, and this beautifully chaotic life we're building together, every single day for the rest of my life. Even when you steal all the covers."

"Especially when I steal all the covers," I corrected, making everyone laugh.

"I love you, Devonna, and my only regret in this life is that I did not marry you sooner. I can't wait to live the rest of my life with you, and I will strive every day to make your life better than it was the day before. Thank you for choosing me."

"Your turn, Miss Onai," Mikhail said to me when Miles finished.

I didn't have notes. Every time I'd tried to write something down, it felt too formal, too planned. So instead, I just looked at Miles and spoke from my heart.

"Miles, you are the reason I get to laugh and feel joy every day. Your memory is a steel trap, and I love that you remember details about me, about us, that I so easily forget. It shows me how much you truly do love me. You have a kind heart and everyone who meets you loves you instantly. I couldn't help but do the same. We haven't always made the right decisions, and I doubt we always will. But you and I, we belong together. I think that was something I knew ten years ago, and I certainly know it to be true now. I cannot wait to live my life with you by my side. You are my best friend and the first person I want to talk to when something happens. You make me feel more confident, more beautiful, and more loved than anyone I've ever met. I promise to be your partner in crime until the end."

I reached up and touched the skeleton key necklace I'd worn every day since that night in the park. "A year ago, you gave me this key and told me it represented something you'd been too scared to fight for. Today, I want to give that back to you. Not the necklace, but what it represents. My trust. My heart. My future."

I could see him trying not to cry, which was making it harder for me not to cry.

"I promise to be patient when you're learning how to let me take care of you. I promise to call you on your bullshit, but also to support you when you're struggling. I promise to choose you, every day, even when you're being impossible. Especially when you're being impossible, because that's when you need me most." I finished, and Miles squeezed my hand.

"Do you have the rings?" Mikhail asked.

I handed him the small box, and he opened it to reveal two simple gold bands. Nothing elaborate, nothing that would overshadow the significance of what they represented.

"Miles, do you take Devonna to be your wife, to love and cherish, to support, for as long as you both shall live?"

"I do," Miles said, sliding the ring onto my finger with hands that were somehow steadier than mine.

"Devonna, do you take Miles to be your husband, to love and cherish, to support, for as long as you both shall live?"

"I do," I said, managing to get his ring on despite the slight tremor in my hands.

"By the power vested in me by the state of New York and several very expensive online courses," Mikhail announced with a grin, "I now pronounce you husband and wife. Miles, kiss your bride."

Miles cupped my face in his hands and kissed me, soft and sweet and full of all the promises we'd just made to each other. Our friends and family erupted in cheers around us, and I could hear Mari sobbing happy tears somewhere behind me.

When we broke apart, Miles rested his forehead against mine. "Hello, Mrs. Houston."

"Hello, Mr. Houston," I grinned up at him. "How does it feel to be married?"

"Like the best decision I've ever made."

"Even better than punching Alek that one time?"

"That one has officially been bumped down to second best decision I've made. You are first. Always first."

As our friends swarmed us with hugs and congratulations, I caught sight of Mikhail wiping his eyes with Florence's handkerchief while she rubbed his back consolingly.

"You okay over there, Mikhail?" I asked.

"I am excellent," he replied, clearing his throat. "I am just very proud of my children. Look at the beautiful wedding I have performed!"

"We're not actually—" Miles started to say, but I elbowed him.

"Thank you," I said instead. "For everything. We wouldn't be here without you."

"Damn right," Mikhail said.

"Damn right," I echoed.

Later, after the champagne had been finished, the wedding cake I'd been hiding in the garage had been cut and consumed, and the guests had all departed, Miles and I sat on our couch and stared at the fire place.

The last guest had left an hour ago, the front door clicking shut behind Mari and Hudson after they insisted on staying to help clean up no matter how many times we told them to go home. Now, the house was quiet except for the faint hum of the dishwasher and the occasional crackle from the fireplace Miles had insisted on lighting despite the mild weather.

I sunk my tired toes into the plush carpet we'd argued over ("It's too expensive," I'd said. "People are going to walk barefoot on this, Vonnie," he'd countered. "Do you want them stepping on something cheap?").

Miles flopped onto the couch beside me, letting out an exaggerated groan. "Married," he announced, like he was testing the word.

"Married," I confirmed, curling into him. His arm draped over my shoulders.

Miles's fingers traced absent patterns along my bare arm. "You think Florence cried more or less than Mari?"

"Oh, definitely more. Mari was just louder."

He chuckled and turned his head, his lips brushing my temple. "You tired?"

"Exhausted." I tilted my face up toward his. "But not too tired."

Slowly, deliberately, his fingers slid from my shoulder down to my wrist, tracing the inside of my arm. "Not too tired for what?"

I shifted, turned fully toward him, and pressed my knee between his thighs. "Use your imagination."

He exhaled, grip tightening before he moved, lifting me onto his lap so I straddled him face-to-face. His hands settled on my hips, thumbs pressing into the dip of my waist. "Imagination's got nothing on reality."

I rolled my hips forward, just enough to feel him harden beneath me. His groan was thick, swallowed when I kissed him. His tongue met mine and his fingers tangled in my hair, pulling just enough to make me gasp.

"Bedroom," I managed between kisses.

"Too far." He gripped my thighs, lifting me as he stood. I wrapped my legs around his waist, arms locked around his neck. He carried me the few steps to the dining table we'd spent three weekends refurbishing. The wood was smooth under my palms as he set me onto the edge, shoving plates and stray champagne glasses aside without ceremony.

Miles stepped between my thighs, hands skimming up my bare legs beneath the sundress, pushing it higher until his fingers ran into lace. He paused, gripped the fabric, and tore.

I yelped—part laughter, part gasp—as the delicate panties gave way beneath his hands.

"Miles!"

"We could've afforded the nicer ones," he muttered darkly, fingers already dragging through wet heat. "But you insisted on the sale rack."

I choked on a laugh that dissolved into a moan when his thumb pressed firm against my clit. "You—fuck—you don't get to mock my underwear choices when you're the one"—His fingers slid inside, curling just right, and I arched, hands grabbing fistfuls of his shirt—"when you're the one destroying them."

"You love it," he murmured against my neck, teeth grazing the sensitive skin below my ear. "Tell me you don't."

I didn't. Couldn't. Not when his fingers worked me so mercilessly, not when his free hand tugged my dress down to bare my breasts, his mouth closing over one nipple in filthy, sucking strokes.

"You gonna come like this?" His voice was ragged against my skin. "Or should I bend you over this table and ruin you properly?"

I rocked into his touch, already close, but— "Both."

He laughed and pulled his fingers free to grip my hips instead, turning me roughly until my palms flattened against the table. His knee nudged my legs wider as he dragged my dress up over my ass. Cool air hit my heated skin before his hands replaced it, kneading, possessive.

Then he dropped to his knees behind me.

I heard him inhale before his tongue licked a long, torturous stripe through my center. My fingers scrambled at the table's edge. "Oh my god—"

He hummed, licking into me, hands gripping my hips to keep me still even as I rocked back against his mouth. It was obscene, the noises—his tongue, my breaths, the slick, filthy sounds of him devouring me like he was starving for it.

"Come on," he urged between laps, fingers digging into my thighs. "Come on Vonnie, let me feel it."

204

I shattered with a cry, pleasure rippling through me in shuddering waves. Still, his mouth didn't relent—sucking my clit until I squirmed, oversensitive.

Only then did he rise, hands smoothing over my hips as I turned to face him again. His lips glistened, smug. "Good?"

In answer, I reached for his belt, unbuckling it before dragging his jeans low enough to free his cock. His breath hitched as I stroked him, thumb swiping over the head, spreading wetness down the length.

"Better now," I murmured.

He swallowed roughly, watching my hand on him. Then his gaze flicked up, dark with intent. "Get on the table."

I didn't need to be told twice. My fingers curled around the edge of the table, hoisting myself up onto the smooth surface with a quickness that made Miles's lips twitch. The wood was cool against my bare thighs, but the heat radiating from him as he stepped between my legs burned away any lingering chill.

"You're wearing too much," I murmured, dragging my nails down his chest through the thin fabric of his shirt.

His hands settled on my knees, spreading them wider. "And?"

I smirked, hooking my fingers into the collar of his shirt and yanking him closer. "Fix it."

Miles didn't hesitate. His shirt and tie disappeared and then the rest of his clothes. When he stood like a tattooed god before me, he turned his attention to me. His hands slid up my thighs, bunching the fabric of my dress until he could shove it over my hips. The lace of my ruined panties—what was left of them—was still damp, clinging to my skin. He made a low sound in his throat as his fingers traced the torn edges, his touch feather-light but deliberate.

"These were my favorite," I lied, just to see his eyes darken.

"Bullshit," he muttered, tearing the last scrap away with a sharp tug. "You bought them because they were cheap."

I laughed, but it dissolved into a gasp when his fingers slid through me, testing, teasing. His thumb pressed against my clit, circling just hard enough to make my hips jerk.

"So fucking wet," he murmured, watching his fingers work me.

"So fucking ready," I breathed, rocking against his hand.

Miles smirked, withdrawing his touch to fist his cock. He was already hard, flushed and leaking, and my mouth watered at the sight.

I reached for him, but he caught my wrist, pinning it to the table beside me. "Uh-uh. You don't get to touch yet."

I arched a brow. "Bossy."

"You love it."

I did.

His free hand gripped my hip, fingers digging in as he guided himself to my entrance. The first slow push stole my breath—the stretch, the heat, the way his jaw clenched as he sank into me inch by inch. The moment his cock slid into me, I lost all capacity for coherent thought.

"Fuck," he hissed, his forehead dropping to mine. "Fuck, Vonnie—"

"You going to be slow the whole time?" I taunted, though I was still out of breath. I shifted to take him deeper.

His grip on my hip tightened. Miles didn't ease in the second time—he gripped my hips and drove deep in one brutal thrust, forcing a choked cry from my throat as I arched off the table.

"Fuck, you feel good," he gritted out, dragging his fingers down my sides before slamming home again. "Like you were fucking made for me."

I could only manage a ragged gasp, nails scraping against the polished wood as he set a relentless pace. Every thrust stretched me fuller, deeper, until my vision blurred at the edges with the sheer too-muchness of it.

Miles hooked an arm under my knee, hitching my leg higher against his hip—"Jesus Christ," I whimpered, because the angle rubbed just right, just there, and suddenly I was shaking, sweat-slick and desperate.

He swore again, leaning over me, bracing one hand beside my head. "Look at you," he rasped, gaze raking down my body—my breasts bouncing out of the dress top with every rough snap of his hips, my flushed skin, the mess of wetness between my thighs where he pistoned in and out. "Goddamn, Devonna."

I reached up, fisting my hands in his hair and dragging his mouth down to mine. The kiss was messy, biting—more shared breath and teeth than actual finesse. I could taste myself on his tongue, and the depravity of it made my stomach flutter.

"Keep going," I panted when he broke for air, my thighs squeezing around him. "Don't stop—please—"

"Not fucking planning to." His fingers dug into my thigh as he hauled me impossibly closer. "You gonna come for me again?"

"Yes. Oh god, yes." The word fractured into a moan as he snapped his hips harder, the thick root of him grinding against my clit with every deep, unforgiving thrust. My spine curled off the table, my climax coiling tight, tightening—

Miles slid a hand between us, pressing his thumb in small, filthy circles. "There you go," he murmured, watching my face as I shattered, body clamping around him. "That's it, honey. Take it."

I came with a sob, back bowed, toes curling, and Miles didn't let up, fucking me straight through it, dragging the pleasure out until I was trembling and gasping.

"Fuck, fuck—" he groaned, hips stuttering. His grip on me went bruising-tight, and then he was spilling deep, pressing in with one final, shuddering thrust.

For a long moment, we stayed like that; him slumped over me, both of us breathless, his softening cock still buried inside me. His lips brushed my collarbone as he mumbled, "Married sex is damn brilliant."

I barked out a laugh, swatting weakly at his shoulder. "Oh, really? How so?"

"Mm. Because your fucking mine." He pulled out with a slow, satisfied hiss and scooped me off the table before I could protest, carrying me toward the bedroom like I weighed nothing. "Gonna have to test the theory again, though. Just to be sure."

I nipped at his jaw as he dropped me onto the mattress. "Better make it a thorough experiment."

Miles grinned, crawling over me with that look in his eyes; the one that promised trouble. "Oh, I plan to."

Read the First Chapter in
Anica & Callan's Christmas Novella

GUILT TRIP TO GRAM'S ESTATE

Chapter 1: Anica

The coffee maker gurgled in the kitchen, filling our apartment with the smell of dark roast. I stretched beneath the sheets, reaching for Callan's side of the bed and finding it empty but still warm.

"You awake?" Callan's voice came from the doorway. He stood there in boxer briefs and nothing else, holding two mugs of coffee and looking like every fantasy I'd ever had about domestic bliss.

"Getting there." I sat up, letting the sheet pool around my waist. He tracked the movement, lingering on my bare chest before meeting my gaze with a heat that made my pulse jump.

He set the mugs on the nightstand and crawled back into bed, his mouth finding mine before I could reach for the coffee. His tongue slid against mine as his hands traveled of their own accord around my body. I arched into his touch, my fingers threading through his hair.

"Good morning to you too," I said when he pulled back to trail kisses down my neck.

"Best way to start a Sunday. No work, no meetings."

I opened my mouth to agree, but his phone beat me to it when it started buzzing on the nightstand.

"Ignore it," he muttered. It stopped and then immediately started again.

I squirmed out from under him, ignoring his disgruntled sigh, and checked the screen. "It's Gram."

"Of course it is." He rolled onto his back with a sigh and swiped to accept, putting it on speaker. "Morning, Gram. What's the emergency?"

"Callan Anthony Burkhardt, don't take that tone." Her voice filled the bedroom. "I'm calling with wonderful news."

Callan and I exchanged a look. Gram's "wonderful news" usually fell several levels short of wonderful.

"The kind that requires lawyers?" he asked.

"The family kind." She spoke over his groan. "I've decided to host The Ultimate Burkhardt Christmas Experience at the estate this year. A week-long celebration starting tomorrow—Monday through Christmas Day. The whole family under one roof."

Callan frowned, rubbing his temples as he rested the phone on his bare chest. "That's a lot of planning on short notice."

"I have everything under control. Tree decorating, gingerbread competitions, caroling, an ugly sweater party, a charity auction—it'll be magnificent." She paused for effect. "Unless you're too busy, of course. I understand if my grandson, the CEO, can't spare time for his elderly grandmother during the holidays."

"Really? Guilt tripping? Isn't that beneath you at this point?"

"Clearly not. Will you come or won't you? Anica, I know you're there too. You want to come, right?"

"Hi Gram," I said, leaning onto Callan's chest to speak closer to the phone. "Do you mind if Cal and I discuss this for a second?" I didn't give her a chance to respond before I hit the mute button on Callan's phone. "Why are you being all dramatic? It sounds fun." I asked Callan, prodding him in the side.

"Sure. Forced family fun. The best kind of fun." He covered his face with his arm, and I curled up closer to him, draping a leg over his.

"I've only met Gram in the time that we've been married, but you've met almost all of my close and extended family. Wouldn't it be fair for me to get to meet more of yours?"

"I've been sparing you because I'm a good husband. Really, you should thank me. I'm like a knight in shining armor."

I snorted. "They can't be that bad."

"You've met Gram."

"And I love her."

I watched Callan's jaw clench, watched him try to say no. Finally, he closed his eyes. "Fine. If you want to go so badly, I will suffer through and be ready to say I told you so as a Christmas present." He unmuted the phone, and with a sigh and a glare at me, he spoke. "We'll be there."

"Wonderful! I knew I could count on you, Ani. I'll have your room ready." She disconnected before he could respond.

Callan stared at the ceiling, his breathing controlled but shallow. "Fuck."

"Hey." I touched his arm. "If you really don't want to go—"

"Too late now. It's fine." But his voice was flat, and he was already getting out of bed. "Gram wants a family Christmas. We'll give her a family Christmas."

He disappeared into the bathroom, and the shower started a second later. I lay there for a moment, staring at the same ceiling he'd been studying, trying to figure out if I'd made a mistake by pushing him.

BY THE TIME I'd showered and dressed, Callan was in the kitchen committing crimes against breakfast food.

"What are you doing to those eggs?" I asked, watching him poke at what looked like scrambled rubber with a spatula.

"Making breakfast." He didn't look up from his murder scene.

"That's a generous interpretation." I gently extracted the spatula from his hand and turned off the burner before he could set off the smoke alarm. "You're the one who usually cooks. What happened?"

"I got distracted." He refilled his coffee mug, gripping it with both hands like a toddler getting to use a grown-up cup.

I studied him while scraping his egg disaster into the trash. My husband was many things—brilliant, sarcastic, unfairly attractive at seven in the morning—but a terrible cook wasn't one of them.

"You're worried about Gram's," I said.

"I'm not worried." He took a long drink of coffee. "I'm mentally preparing for a week of 'fun festivities' with people I avoid contact with most of the year."

"You see Gram each month. We'll be fine." I plated the eggs and set them on the counter. "Now come eat before these get cold."

He listened, though he at standing up instead of sitting with me at the bar seating.

Eventually, his expression softened. "I know I'm throwing a hissy fit. Just know it's not towards you. I love Gram. She's the only family member who actually gives a damn about me. Plus, she's getting up there in years and claims to have injured her back from doing hot yoga, which we both know is complete bullshit, but whatever game she's playing, I want to make sure she's okay. And I want to make sure she has a good Christmas because I'm a good grandson. But damn it, I really don't want to go."

"You think the injury is fake?"

"Gram's back is fine. She does headstands for fun." He grabbed both our empty plates and moved to the sink. "And if she wants us there for Christmas, then we'll be there for Christmas. I'll smile, make small talk, and count down the days until we can leave."

"You make it sound like a prison sentence."

"More like a hostage situation with better food." He started loading the dishwasher. "There'll be the tree-lighting ceremony where we all stand around pretending to care about traditions. The gingerbread house competition, where one or two of my family members get weirdly competitive. The caroling expedition that's really just an excuse to bar hop through Manhattan while butchering Christmas songs. Oh, and someone will definitely ask us about babies at least twice a day."

I leaned against the counter, watching him aggressively organize dishes. "You've really thought this through."

"I've survived too many Burkhardt Christmases. I know what's coming." He closed the dishwasher and turned to face me. "The question is whether you're ready for it."

"I've handled bridezillas who fired me five times in one day and still wanted me at their wedding. I've mediated family feuds that make the Kardashians look friendly. One time, I prevented a groom's mother from wearing a white dress to the ceremony by 'accidentally' spilling red wine on it." I crossed my arms. "I think I can handle your family."

"You say that now." But he was almost smiling. "Wait until Aunt Mavis asks why you're 'still working' when you're married to a billionaire, or until Uncle Randolf makes some comment about how marriages in our family don't last, or until Uncle Brennan tries to sell you on his latest miracle product."

"I'll manage."

"I know you will." He pulled me close, his hands settling on my hips. "That's why I need you there. Someone has to keep me from saying what I'm actually thinking."

"I thought sarcasm was your default setting."

"That's polite sarcasm. There's a whole other level of rude sarcasm I reserve for family." He kissed my forehead. "You're my filter."

"So romantic. 'Darling, you complete me by preventing me from starting family feuds.'"

"Exactly." He grinned. "Now come help me pack."

Read the rest of Anica's and Callan's story in the next book...

SCAN OR CLICK THE CODE BELOW TO FIND
MERRY NOT INCLUDED ON AMAZON!

Acknowledgments

To my husband, who has mastered the art of nodding sympathetically when I explained why Miles absolutely had to recover that ring from the lake, even though it makes zero financial sense. Thank you for your unwavering support of my career choice to make fictional people fall in love while you handle the real-world responsibilities I forget about during deadline week. Your ability to say "That's nice, Rina" to my 2 AM plot revelations while half-asleep is a gift that keeps our marriage intact.

To my dogs, the CEOs of Distraction Incorporated, who believe every writing session should include mandatory snack breaks and quality control lap inspections. Thank you for your commitment to ensuring I never take myself too seriously, especially when you choose the climactic love scene as the perfect time to demand walkies.

To my grandmother, whose voice echoes in every page. Her belief that love stories matter (even the messy, complicated ones) gave me permission to write characters who make terrible decisions in the name of their hearts.

To my fearless beta readers—Lily M., Rachel H., Dani T., Sam P., Brittany B., and Tyler K.—thank you for your brutal honesty wrapped in encouragement. Special thanks to the beta who wrote "Florence is terrifying and I want to be her when I grow up" in the margins (you know who you are). Your insights made Devonna fiercer and Miles more worthy of redemption.

And to you, reader, thank you for believing in second chances and fake engagements that feel too real. Thank you for rooting for characters who should probably run in opposite directions but keep choosing each other instead.

If this book made you want to throw Miles in a lake (but fish him out again), scream at Devonna to just kiss the man already, or text your friends demanding they read this lovely little fake engagement book, please consider leaving a review. The algorithm gods are hungry, but more importantly, your words help other readers find their next book boyfriend and the chaos that comes with him.

Also, should I write Garrett and Cat's story? Or should I do Shane and Irina? Maybe I should let Caroline find someone next...

Until next time, lovely reader.

About the Author

Carina Walsh lives for three things: perfectly timed banter, the sound of readers gasping at plot twists, and telling stories where the guy gets the girl (or the other way around). She is very excited to share her Knot Your Average Wedding Romcom Series with readers. When she's not writing steamy romcoms, she can be found reading in her favorite chair, testing TikTok recipes in the middle of the night, or testing specific scenes from other spicy romcoms with her husband (for science). Carina currently resides in Boston with her husband and their two dogs, and is excited to continue writing sexy books with laugh out loud moments.

CHAPTER THIRTY-FIVE

Carrie's apartment had its own entry by means of an exterior stairway. Jack left his truck at the curb, since the driveway was too narrow for two vehicles.

Whistling, for some odd reason, "Summer in the City," he passed through the archway that separated the house from the garage and proceeded to the back. On the way Jack had tried to look at the less bleak side of his situation. If there'd been a plan to kill him and collect the insurance money, it was useless now, since the police knew Li wasn't his wife. Kelly and the rest would no doubt head for new territory and dream up a new scheme. At least the police had descriptions and were actively looking for them now.

Jack had been to Carrie's a few times to pick her up but had never actually climbed the stairs. Noting in passing that the lower floor was dark and quiet, he guessed Fournier was out for the evening.

He placed his feet carefully to avoid slipping. Though the staircase was roofed, a fine powder had blown in and lay in long parabolas on steps' outer edges. In some of them he saw the print of Carrie's boot. Shifting the six-pack of Coke he'd brought to his other arm, he approached the door. At his knock there was silence for a few seconds, then the sound of footsteps. Carrie opened the door, and the call on his lips for warm baked goods froze. Her face was ashen and her eyes were wide with fear.

"Carrie, what—" Then he saw movement behind her and understood.

"Come in, Jack," Greg Laughton invited.

Since there was nothing else he could do, Jack stepped inside. The door closed after him to reveal Sean Green standing behind it, holding a pistol. "I thought you'd be running like the dogs you are by now," Jack growled.

"I had to collect a few things." Jack glanced around the apartment. On the countertop to his left was a bowl of half-finished cookie dough. The smell of vanilla lingered from a bottle that had spilled into the sink when Carrie's work was interrupted. In the small living room an elderly man, Fournier, Jack guessed, lay unconscious on the couch, a trickle of blood running from a cut on his forehead. His hands and feet were bound with what looked like cords from Venetian blinds. The little plastic cup was still attached at one end. In a black Naugahyde chair in one corner sat Li, looking as perfect and unmoved as ever.

"We were in the process of transferring our operation to Florida when you stuck your nose in, Porter. Now that isn't possible."

"Sorry to have inconvenienced you."

"We'll survive." Green tilted his head toward his burly companion. "Laughton here wasn't pleased when you two dumped him in the bay."

"We didn't like his attitude." Jack made his bid for logic, knowing it was probably useless. "You're finished, Green. Cops are looking for you down the east coast, around the Gulf, and all over the Midwest. They know the whole story."

"Which is exactly why I sent my brother west to find us another house where we can squat for a while. New territory is always exciting, don't you think, Joker? I came to pick up the beautiful Li, get the money I stashed for emergencies, and—" His tone hardened. "—settle our score."

"A detective in Chicago knows everything."

Green tasted the cookie dough with a finger before answering. "But the cops are slow in sharing information, Joker. When you have your accident, the police in Chicago won't even hear about it for a week. We'll have time to erase our footprints, so to speak." Green's veneer slid away momentarily. "I never liked you or your poker face."

"So kill me. Let Carrie and the old man go."

Green only chuckled, and Laughton answered for him. "That's part of the fun, Joker. You watching your girlfriend die."

Glancing around the room, Jack sought an idea, a weapon, anything. The apartment was laid out simply, a large combination living/dining area, a short hallway with three doors, one on either side and one at the end. A half-completed jig-saw puzzle lay on the coffee table, the pieces turned face up and spread out on the surface of an old piece of paneling. He recalled Carrie saying she liked puzzles. This one had turned deadly.

As Jack's gaze passed to Carrie's white face, guilt flooded through him. He wanted to take her into his arms and reassure her, gaining strength from contact with her, as he realized he'd done for months now. He'd gotten her into this, had put her life in danger by assuming Green and Laughton would run once they were discovered. Now they would both die. Jack Porter—crippled, stupid detective. Why had he ever thought he could take on men like these and win?

Apparently, Carrie read his thoughts, because her brows furrowed and her eyes lit with a fierce answer. It was almost as if she said aloud: *Because you have to. Because we'll all die if you don't.*

Jack felt his mind begin to focus as he pushed self-doubt aside. Green and Laughton huddled together, discussing their next move. Li's eyes had taken in the exchange between him and Carrie. Something unreadable flashed across her face. Jack couldn't tell what she was thinking, but when he met her gaze steadily, she looked away.

When Laughton finished explaining the specifics of his plan to Green, he nodded agreement. "Put the old guy downstairs in his bed and untie him, so it looks like he was asleep." Moving to one of the doors, he examined it. "Good. We've got an old-fashioned house with real locks on every door. See if you can find the key for this one."

It didn't take long to find a wooden rack near the back door from which hung a selection of keys. Laughton chose several of the general shape he wanted and tried until he found the one that fit the lock on Carrie's bedroom.

"The detective and his pretty secretary have a thing going." Green reached out and touched Carrie's face, and Jack had to stop himself from slapping the hand away. "They retire to her boudoir. The old faggot is asleep downstairs. Then tragedy! The house explodes. The pilot went out and a spark ignited the gas. Terrible loss."

"Too bad Li can't collect on my insurance," Jack commented. "You'll be running."

"It's only a matter of time, my friend. New names, new lives, we'll manage, won't we, Li?" He moved to her side and stroked her silky hair. "Such a beautiful woman."

"She is," Jack agreed. "I remember the first time I saw her. Someone else had been impressed by her beauty."

"Really." Green wasn't interested, but Jack had the satisfaction of seeing Li's chin drop a little.

Laughton had been assessing Carrie's room as a temporary prison. "One window that doesn't open." He stopped with his hand on the doorknob. "Lock them in there. I'll get things set in the basement."

"Don't turn on any lights down there," Green cautioned. Laughton didn't reply, only made the clicking noise that conveyed both compliance and disdain.

***

Green accompanied Jack and Carrie into her bedroom, satisfying himself that they'd be secure. When he left, locking the door behind him, Jack immediately tried the window. It didn't open, and Carrie could have told him it was painted shut. Beyond it was a storm window. Even if they could manage to break both panes, the drop to the concrete driveway was too far to manage without breaking bones.

"We can signal for help through the opening." Carrie looked around for something they could use to break the glass. Her bedroom seemed to be all pillows and a fuzzy snake she'd won at a carnival. A shoe? She went to the closet and took out the sturdiest one she owned, a platform with a chunky heel. When she turned around, she saw Jack seated on her bed. He was taking off his pants.

"If I get Green back in here, can you put him on the floor with this?" As he spoke, he un-strapped his artificial leg, a combination of wood and metal she guessed would make a serviceable club.

No time to doubt herself. "Yes."

"Good. Give me that shoe and stand over there." Pulling his jeans back up, Jack swiveled his body to the opposite side of the bed so the empty pant-leg wasn't obvious. The prosthesis felt alien in her hands, and the top was warm where Jack's skin had rested on it. She took up a position at the side of the room, holding the leg behind her back in what she hoped was a natural pose. When she was ready, Jack hit the window with the heel of the shoe. The ancient glass made a satisfying crash as it splintered into a hundred pieces and clattered to the floor.

In seconds the key turned in the lock. Green appeared in the doorway, holding cords from another of Carrie's venetian blinds. "Li has my gun pointed at this door, so don't even think about leaving." He stepped into the room, shaking his head in mock disgust. "Look at the mess you made, Joker, and all for nothing. All you've done is make it necessary for me to tie you up." He stepped toward Jack. "Now put your hands around the bedpost. I wouldn't want to—"

As he moved past her, Carrie swung the leg with all her might. Green slumped forward with a low grunt of surprise. She pushed him toward Jack, who cradled him into the mattress as quietly as possible.

"Tie his hands," he ordered. Carrie used the cord Green had brought to tie his hands and feet, using the sailing knots her dad had taught her. He started to come to after only a few seconds, but she got a cloth belt from her closet and gagged him with it. When she finished she checked the knots. They were tight, and she hoped they hurt.

As she worked, Jack strapped the prosthesis back in place. When he was able to stand, they faced the question of what to do next. Li was outside the bedroom door, and she had Green's gun. Would she shoot them? Then there was Laughton to consider. How long before he returned? Motioning for Carrie to stay where she was, Jack stepped out into the hallway. Unable to stand not knowing, Carrie peeked out the doorway to see what would happen.

Li sat waiting to see who emerged from the room. The gun lay

221

in her lap, offering the opportunity to eliminate the threat they posed to her if she chose.

Jack stood motionless for a few seconds, and Carrie bit her lip as she witnessed an unspoken conversation. His question seemed to be *What will you do?* Li's answer was absolute stillness. She didn't raise an alarm. Neither did she offer help.

Carrie touched Jack's arm, pointing to a door at the end of the hall that opened onto interior stairs. Below was Fournier's home and another staircase that led to the basement. Laughton was down there, sabotaging the furnace. They had to descend those steps and get Dr. Fournier out of the house before he finished his murderous task.

Jack turned back to look at Li. Carrie didn't turn but stared at the wall, taking herself out of the situation as much as possible. She had no faith in this woman, who'd betrayed Jack in every way possible, but she trusted Jack's instincts. Jack seemed satisfied with what he saw. Giving Li an odd sort of salute, he gestured for Carrie to precede him.

They had tiptoed down only the first few steps when Laughton's voice came from below. "Green? It's time to get out." Silence. "Green?" The voice sounded ominous, and Carrie squelched the urge to move faster. Stairs were still difficult for Jack, more so going down than up. Worse, these steps were steep, and the old wood creaked at each shift of weight.

"Green!" Laughton was moving now, coming up the basement stairs. They reached the main floor, and Jack pulled Carrie into a dark corner of the large living room. They stood motionless as Laughton's footsteps crossed the landing and continued up to Carrie's apartment. Pulling her close Jack whispered in her ear, "Get the old man out then go to a neighbor's and call the police and the fire department."

"Come with me!"

"Get him out. Call for help." Jack repeated. "I have to stop Laughton."

"Jack, he'll kill you."

"He'll try." Jack was unlike himself—in fact he was unlike

anyone Carrie had ever encountered. She was meeting for the first time the soldier inside him, the one who could and would kill. He frightened her, and in the end, she tiptoed away to do as he demanded.

CHAPTER THIRTY-SIX

Carrie moved hurriedly through the living room, cranking the casement windows open as she went. She opened the French doors onto the patio, and freezing air rushed in at her. In the bedroom she found Doctor Fournier stretched out on the bed. When she shook him he moaned softly, and his head rolled on the pillow. She opened the bedroom window and approached again, whispering his name. He opened his eyes and tried to focus.

"Can you walk? We have to get out of here." The old man shook his head, but still he attempted to rise. She helped him sit up.

"Carrie?" His voice sounded loud in the still room.

"Shh! Please, Doctor Fournier, stand up." Putting her arm around his back, she pulled him to his feet. With agonizingly slow progress she led him into the hallway, wincing at each noise they made. As she turned toward the back door a thump upstairs made her pause. Laughton had discovered their escape. He'd probably freed Green, which meant both killers would soon be after them. Adjusting her hold on Fournier's waist, she spoke encouragingly. She'd get her landlord out. Then she'd find Jack.

***

Jack tried to imagine the layout of the downstairs. When he arrived, he'd noticed the formal front entrance was blocked by snow. That meant Carrie would be heading out the door at the back of the house, which was under the exterior staircase.

If he could bring Laughton down the interior stairs, which faced the front, she'd have time to get away. Kicking the bottom stair once, he waited a few seconds and then repeated the action. Laughton's shape appeared fleetingly in the doorway above then the upstairs lights went out, making the whole house dark.

At the same time, Jack heard heavy footsteps above. Someone was coming down the outside stairs. Laughton had freed Green and sent him to mount a rear attack. He hoped Carrie could avoid him.

Looking around the dark room, Jack searched for a weapon. He saw only the amorphous shapes of overstuffed chairs and oak tables. He was a cripple, facing killers, and he had nothing to defend himself with. What chance did he have?

The words Todd had said in a faraway hooch came to mind. "I'd rather know what kind of person I really am." Since Vietnam Jack had learned he was a survivor. He'd survived a bitter childhood, the chaos of war, a terrible injury, and his best friend's murder. He'd survive this.

Hell—he'd do more than that. He would prevail over these sorry examples of human beings.

The back door opened and closed with no attempt at quiet. Green was coming his way. He'd face both enemies at once, but at least Carrie had gotten away.

There was no sound on the dark stairway, but Laughton was a master at stealth. Jack figured he'd wait at the bottom while Green pushed Jack toward him. Then, still and deadly as any predator, Laughton would attack from behind. The plan to sandwich Jack between them was either his chance at life or his death sentence. It was a gamble, but so was life. The Joker would play the hand he'd been dealt.

Taking a position a few feet from the bottom of the steps, Jack held his breath and waited. Everything depended on choosing the right moment. Someone would go down, maybe one of his enemies, maybe Jack himself.

He sensed rather than saw movement across the living room. That was Green, and Jack hoped he was still shaken from the blow to the head Carrie had dealt him. Recalling the determination on her face as she'd swung the improvised club, he almost smiled. Carrie was a constant surprise.

The room fairly crackled as the energy of the hunt built. Jack forced himself to wait longer than he wanted to, longer than felt possible. He had to let the tension grow unbearable for his opponents in order to get them exactly where he wanted them to be.

When Jack actually felt the heat of a body inches from him and smelled the sweat of a man under stress, he went into action. Inches from Green's face he shouted, "Kelly!"

As he said it Jack dropped like a stone to the floor. In reaction to the perceived threat, Green fired twice at the spot where Jack had been. Laughton, who'd come up behind Jack, took both bullets full in the chest. A strangled sound came from his throat as he fought for breath and fell backward, crashing against the wall.

From his prone position, Jack grabbed the hems of Green's pant legs, pulling upward with all his might. The man's feet came out from under him, and he landed on his backside with a startled "Oomph!" The gun went off again, but the muzzle slewed wildly upward as he fell. Before Jack reached him, a slight form entered the fray, kicking at Green wildly as a flashlight beam waved crazily in accompaniment. The gun slid from Green's hand and Carrie kicked it away, raining punishment on the dazed man until Jack said, "Carrie, it's okay. We got him."

He heard a muffled sob as she helped him up from the floor. "Are you all right?"

"Fine." His hands trembled and his hip ached from contact with the hardwood floor, but he really felt fine.

"Shall I turn on the lights?"

"If Laughton has the gas set to blow, we need to get out of here." Grabbing Green's shirt, Jack helped him to his feet and pushed him ahead of them through the patio doors, the closest means of exit.

***

As they came onto the sidewalk in front of the house, a police car approached, lights flashing. In the distance a fire truck's siren wailed closer. Seeing the gun Jack carried, the officers took defensive positions behind their car doors. Jack dropped the gun on the ground and raised his hands, calling, "No threat, officers. The action's over." Doctor Fournier emerged from a house across the street and crossed to the police car, a wet cloth pressed to his head.

In minutes the story had been told—at least the short version—and Green was under arrest. A few minutes later an unmarked car pulled up. Bill Stevenson approached the first cop he met, and Carrie overheard their conversation. "I understand a girl named Caroline Walsh had some trouble here tonight."

"That's right," the cop replied.

Stevenson looked around in confusion. "I don't see her."

The cop pointed. "That's her, Detective. The good-looking chick."

Stevenson's knowledge of the case made things easier for Jack and Carrie, and Sean Green was placed under arrest with only a request that they give full statements the next day. The police found Greg Laughton's body inside after firemen had turned off the gas and proclaimed the place safe for entry. They advised the occupants to spend the night elsewhere and have the place checked thoroughly the next day before returning.

Li was nowhere to be found. Jack said nothing about her to the police, and Carrie followed his lead.

Once official procedures had been completed, they returned to the Eagle office, where Jack insisted Carrie take the couch while he dropped into the saucer chair in the reception area. They had little to say to each other, being unready to discuss the past and unable to consider the future. Sleep didn't come easily, but the comfort of Jack's closeness was restful, and eventually, Carrie drifted off.

***

Jack awoke the next morning feeling sore, unclean, unkempt, and relieved. The coffee was on, and he poured himself a cup, stirring in plenty of sugar for energy. He had a lot to think through, and he spent some time on Li, a cipher who had planned to profit from his death but had done nothing to stop their escape. He realized he didn't want Li punished. He simply hoped she was out of his life forever.

Carrie came to mind: brave, wonderful Carrie, who in two short months had become indispensable to the business and, Jack admitted, to him. Peeping in at the office couch, he saw that it was empty. Where had she gone so early? There was a new note propped on the phone: *Called Doctor F. He's fine. I'm going to see Mom.* Jack smiled. The last wall to be scaled before complete independence: looking at our parents through adult eyes.

CHAPTER THIRTY-SEVEN

Carrie drove out to Flushing in the agency truck. The sky was slate-gray again. November in Michigan meant few sunrises, few sunny days. She missed Florida, the little she'd seen of it.

Pulling into the concrete drive, she noticed a car parked on the street in front of the house. Newly acquired caution made her look around carefully as she approached her mother's house. Either she was beginning to have the instincts of a sleuth, she thought, or she'd become paranoid. Onalee greeted her at the door with a smile that seemed nervous.

"You look nice, Carrie. I wonder if I could wear my hair like that."

Glad for once to not be on the defensive she replied, "I can give you the number for my hairdresser."

"Come in." Onalee led the way to the kitchen, usually her least favorite room.

Sitting at the kitchen table was a neat gentleman with silver whitewalls and a stiff-upper-lip manner. He sipped tea from a Melmac cup, the bag laid out like a flag on the saucer. He seemed very much at home in Onalee's kitchen at eight o'clock in the morning. Almost as surprising as the guest was the scent of cinnamon rolls. Onalee was baking? It had to be Pillsbury, but it was still amazing.

"Honey, this is Mr. Williams. He moved in down the street a month ago. From England." Her possessive tone said more than her words. *Oh, my gosh. Mom has a boyfriend.*

"How nice to meet you, Caroline. Your mother neglected to mention how lovely you are." To Onalee he said, "I should have known a woman as attractive as you would have charming children."

Onalee purred, "You say the sweetest things, Bill." William Williams, good grief! Bill wore a sweater vest over a white dress shirt, slacks with a sharp crease ironed in, and--bedroom slippers. Carrie's expression must have betrayed her thought, because Mom's face turned bright pink. Bill, who had launched into a lengthy description of the business from which he'd recently retired, didn't notice.

Carrie made the visit as brief as was polite, telling the short version of her adventures and emphasizing that the worst of the criminals were either dead or under arrest. As she talked, she managed to put away two cinnamon buns when Onalee pulled them, warm and bubbly, from the oven.

When she left, Carrie's mother walked her out to the truck. "I meant to tell you about Bill that night I asked you to go to the movies. You couldn't go, and—anyway, we're engaged, so it's all right if he stays here." Onalee's eyes sought Carrie's approval.

"I think that's wonderful, Mom."

In response her mother gave her the only truly spontaneous hug Carrie could remember.

Onalee's last remark indicated she had been listening to Carrie's story. "What about Mr. Porter? Is he going to be okay after all this?"

Carrie pictured Jack as she'd left him, sleeping soundly in the saucer chair that had been Li's usual spot. His face had been relaxed, his sleep peaceful. "I think so," Carrie answered. "It'll take time, but I think he will."

ABOUT THE AUTHOR

Peg Herring lives in northern Lower Michigan, where she reads, writes, and loves mysteries. She and her husband enjoy travel and gardening, two great pastimes that don't coexist well. Peg also writes as her younger, hipper alter ego, Maggie Pill.

Dear Reader,

If you enjoyed this book, please consider placing a review somewhere others will see it. Authors rely on word of mouth to spread the news of a new book or series, and no one does that better than happy readers! Thank you for supporting what we writers love to do!

Peg

Books by Peg Herring (listed in series order)
The Simon & Elizabeth Mysteries *(Tudor Era Historical)*
Her Highness' First Murder
Poison, Your Grace
The Lady Flirts with Death
Her Majesty's Mischief
***

The Loser Mysteries *(Contemporary Mystery/Suspense)*
Killing Silence
Killing Memories
Killing Despair
***

Clan Macbeth Historical Romance (medieval Scotland)
Macbeth's Niece
Double Toil & Trouble
***

Thrillers
Shakespeare's Blood
Charlie Dickens' Documents
***

Standalone Mysteries
Somebody Doesn't Like Sarah Leigh (contemporary cozy mystery)
Not Dead Yet... ('60s-era mystery/suspense)
Her Ex-GI P.I. ('60s-era mystery/suspense)

The Dead Detective Mysteries (paranormal but not scary)
The Dead Detective Agency
Dead for the Money
Dead for the Show
Dead to Get Ready—and Go
***
Caper Novels: Suspense with Humor
Kidnap(.)org
Pharma Con
The Trouble with Dad
***
Women's Fiction
Deceiving Elvera

Writing as Maggie Pill

The Sleuth Sisters Mysteries (cozy Michigan)
If you like lighter mysteries, and if you have sisters, had sisters, or know a little about sisters, you'll love Maggie's series.
The Sleuth Sisters
3 Sleuths, 2 Dogs, 1 Murder
Murder in the Boonies
Sleuthing at Sweet Springs
Eat, Drink, & Be Wary
Peril, Plots, and Puppies
Captured, Escape, Repeat

And if you've ever been in an over-55 vacation park, you'll love Trailer Park Tales (cozy Florida)
Once Upon a Trailer Park
Twice the Crime This Time

The Max and Lucy Mysteries: a private investigator meets a precocious kid, with hilarious and dangerous results.
Cutest Little Killer

Peg's website: http://www.pegherring.com
Maggie's website: http://maggiepill.maggiepillmysteries.com/